WE WROTE IN SYMBOLS

We Wrote
in Symbols

Love and Lust by Arab Women Writers

Edited by

Selma Dabbagh

SAQI

SAQI BOOKS
26 Westbourne Grove
London W2 5RH
www.saqibooks.com

Published 2021 by Saqi Books

ISBN 978 0 86356 397 3
eISBN 978 0 86356 495 6

A full CIP record for this book is available from the British Library.

Printed and bound by CPI Group (UK) Ltd, Croydon CR0 4YY

Contents

CONTENTS

CONTENTS

Introduction

Showcase No. 38 of the National Museum of Damascus contains a tiny figurine identified as Ishtar, the ancient goddess of beauty and love. The catalogue says she was made in the city of Ur in around 2500 BCE. The curvaceous figurine stands naked and wide-eyed, ready to challenge the centuries to come. If anything symbolises the spirit of this book, it is the sight of her tiny, tightly clenched fists.

We Wrote in Symbols is a selection of writing on love and lust over three millennia, that is often, but by no means always, celebratory. Here are over 100 pieces of prose and poetry written in different languages and many styles. All the authors, wholly or partly, may be considered Arab women writers. Some of these women are living and some are long deceased. They are the voices of all ages, and range from highly acclaimed to the emerging. Several writers have never been published before – others are well known in other languages, but appear in English here for the first time. Names and dates can't be attached to some of the oldest works, and some writers chose to use pseudonyms. They are, or were, residents of towns and cities from Andalusia to Baghdad, Beirut to Berlin, Damascus to New York.

As a writer whose parents are English and Palestinian, *We Wrote in Symbols* is an exploration into a part of my heritage. As a teenager in 1980s Kuwait, I grew up, like many teenagers, in opposition to my location, which appeared to me to represent confinement. This collection is the product of a – not untroubled – love affair with the Arab world, which I came to later. As an adult, I lived in and visited other Arab countries (Bahrain, Egypt, Palestine, Lebanon, Syria). Through experiences and the work of writers, historians and translators I discovered a diversity, spirit, warmth and humour that is admired throughout this book.

It feels important that a book like this should exist – to the best of my knowledge there is not another one like it. It was fated to be an eclectic collection. The works range in approach and style, from the assured, sensitive love poems of Naomi Shihab Nye, Nathalie Handal and Samira Negrouche to the explicit thrusts and plastic gloves in Mouna Ouafik's short verse; from the arch, provocative tone in Joumana Haddad's narrator's visit to a swingers' club to the vexed intellectual narrator of Rasha Abbas. The point of view switches from complex male protagonists, to housebound housewives, imperious princesses and indignant witty foul-mouthed slaves. But the intensity of feeling remains.

Many pieces here have been translated. To translate writing about love and lust, in tones often subtle but highly charged, is uniquely challenging. English – imbued as it is with puritanical sensibilities, with an frequently blunt approach to erotic writing – is not an easy landing point. In French and Italian, to say that you have had 'a story' with someone ('*une histoire*' / '*una storia*') clearly denotes that love and lust were involved. The word '*qissa*' in Arabic can in many contexts denote the same. I like the idea of romantic associations being imbued in the word for 'story'. Stories and love affairs form part of our worlds; they are histories which live in our present and inform our futures.

One of the writers in this collection, Salwa Al Neimi, considers the connection between '*sarir*', the Arabic word for bed, and '*sir*', meaning secret. Then she writes: 'In my life, I have been addicted to beds and stories.' For her 'every man is a story and every story is a bed.' And so opens a conversation about a very different kind of 'bedtime story' that can be shied away from by those of us functioning in any language.

Women were writing in Arabic long before the first book known to have been written by a woman in English, *Revelations of Divine Love*, by Julian(a) of Norwich, was produced in the fourteenth century. Readers may be aware of the ancient literary tradition of the erotic in the Arab world among its writers. *We Wrote in Symbols* is distinctive in relying on the women themselves to present this tradition, using a variety of literary forms.

*

In Baghdad, a couple of millennia after the little Ishtar figurine was moulded, but still more than 1,000 years ago, a female poet was allowed entry into an elite literary salon. The poetry of the *Majiun* group focused on the erotic, the bawdy and the lewd. The poet Inan Jariyat an-Natafi (d. 871 CE) become one of its first female members, if not the only woman there. Her talent was the envy of others, including her friend the poet Abu Nawas, whose name has come to be synonymous with wine poetry. Only recently has the work of this group of Abbasid poets (known as the 'Lewd Ones') been given the serious consideration it deserves. Subject matter aside, these witty, humorous poets demonstrated 'unprecedented experimentation with poetic device, form and diction',[1] playing an important role in the modernisation of Arabic poetry.

The intricate art of seduction flourishes at times of prosperity and peace, as well as under societal duress and enslavement. The Abbasid court of Harun al-Rashid of *The Thousand and One Nights* fame, and the worlds of Umayyad and Andalusian palaces, are reminiscent of the complex sexual intrigues found in the Venetian Republic in the eighteenth century. Social mobility for a concubine in the Abbasid court was partly dependent on verbal, sexual and musical skills in the way that soldiering skills were essential for male slaves during the later Mamluk era.

---

1 *The Poetry of Arab Women from the Pre-Islamic Age to Andalusia* by Wessam Elmeligi (Routledge, 2019). Location 2786 of the Kindle Edition.

3

During the Umayyad (661–750 CE) and Abbasid periods (751–1258 CE), economic prosperity and the questioning of socio-religious taboos 'helped create a society bent on enjoying Allah's earthly gifts to full'.[1] In the later Andalusian period (711–1492 CE), the Arabs turned the Iberian peninsula of al-Andalus into a 'paradise on earth'.[2] During these eras there is evidence that it was common for love poems to be transmitted secretly via intermediaries. The recipient's name was often changed, female names being replaced by male ones and vice versa. Lines from poems went back and forth between lovers – not just as missives, but embroidered onto everyday items of all kinds, including sashes, slippers and turbans. These pithy declarations not only voiced desires, but grievances too, and not just to the object of these feelings, but to anyone in the court (or the street) who cared to read them.

It is not known how classical poetry was received or circulated at the time, but there is no doubt that in the subsequent centuries these poems were curtailed, controlled, rewritten or otherwise prevented from being shared. This extended moratorium was caused mainly by more orthodox, proscriptive interpretations of monotheistic religions prevailing, along with high levels of female illiteracy and greater sexual conservatism in general. Of works that have survived, there are few. A couple of centuries after Wallada bint al-Mustakfi (d. 1091) embroidered on her robe 'I walk my walk and boast in pride,' women's writing on love and lust disappeared, almost entirely, corresponding approximately with the 'fall' of Andalusia in 1492, when Muslim and Jewish populations were expelled from the Iberian Peninsula. It was not to revive again for several hundreds of years: an extended blackout of half a millennium.

In the late nineteenth century, a tentative return to addressing

---

1 *Classical Poems by Arab Women: A Bilingual Anthology* edited by Abdullah al-Udhari (Saqi Books, 2017), pp. 19–21.
2 *Ibid*, p. 21.

the subjects of the erotic was made again by 'novelists writing in Arabic, in Egypt and the Ottoman Empire, who challenged the practices of marital courtship and particularly arranged marriages, as against the desires of young people,' according to Professor Marilyn Booth. Although she wasn't the first, Zaynab Fawwaz challenged these norms in both fiction and newspaper essays. Her debut novel (translated here for the first time by Professor Booth) linked love and respect to good political practice. She also wrote an extensive biography of the lives of historic women figures in the Arab world and Europe, to show just how much women were capable of. By the twentieth century, writing by women was picking up momentum again, often in novels, which was a newer form of literature in the Arab world compared to poetry. Arab women returned to writing about love with increasing clarity and self-assurance. The writing grows from this period onwards in literary creativity, style and variety – a trend which has continued to increase into the twenty-first century.

To try to pretend that the Arab world has experienced a sea change in its approach to women's sexuality would be a misrepresentation. But women's writing in the Arab world and beyond has become more daring, experimental and creative in recent years. The exuberant voices and experimentation of the classical periods echo through the centuries.

*

The writers in this anthology are of the three main monotheistic religions, or of none. Some lived before their respective prophets were even born. They include academics, archivists, biographers, doctors, engineers, homemakers, lawyers, mothers, playwrights, performers, professors and novelists, as well as medieval concubines, court singers, princesses and political exiles. Many have public profiles as political actors for change, such as Ahdaf Soueif, Hanan al-Shaykh, Shurooq Amin, Rita

El Khayat, Joumana Haddad, Mouna Ouafik and Leïla Slimani. A large number of the authors have had their works banned in their countries of origin and beyond. Their fearlessness and articulacy have enabled other women to write, act and forge a space for themselves with greater confidence.

The Arab world is largely united by a language whose origins predate the monotheistic religions but is, of course, strongly bound and preserved as the language of the Holy Qur'an. Although the Arab and Islamic worlds are distinct from each other, the influence of the Islamic religion since its birth in the seventh century has prevailed across the Arabic-speaking world. It is worth noting (with a brevity that puts me at risk of distortion) the religion's relevance to this collection, because Islam's approach to female sexuality is distinctive. As the pioneering sociologist Abdelwaheb Bouhdiba puts it, 'the Qur'anic exercise of sexuality assumes an infinite majesty.'[1] Sex does not have to be for procreational purposes, it can also be for its own sake and contraception was permitted. It is a union and an art form to be cherished and respected. The giving and receiving of sensual pleasure, within prescribed relationships, is viewed as enhancing the harmony of marital union and society at large, providing the believer with an insight into the nature of heaven while still on earth.

Throughout history we find writing that juxtaposes mortal sexuality with celebrating love of God and religious festivities. This has always proved uncomfortable to some. The juxtaposition of ecstasy in sex and religion, it must be noted, has also provided ripe subject matter for song lyrics throughout time – contemporary hip hop artistes Missy Elliott and Kelis boast their sexual prowess and praise the divine in the same breath, for example. During the heyday of the Egyptian night-club scene in the 1920–40s, Arab women were centre-stage performers challenging patriarchal ideas of what was, and wasn't,

---

1 *Sexuality in Islam* by Abdelwaheb Bouhdiba (Saqi Books, 2012), p.14.

acceptable for women to say and do in public. Many female singers played a role in composing the lyrics they sung, but little documentation of the song-writing process has survived. Heba Farid, granddaughter of the singer Naima al-Masriyya, provided me with a sample of the types of lyrics her (fairly shy and conservative) grandmother sung at the time: *Com'on, big boy, let's go to the Qanate / Do me a favour, don't be my mood killer.*[1]

In certain eras and places, women's capacity for sexual desire has been accommodated and eulogised. Court records show that there was a time in Abbasid history when women could seek a divorce on the basis that they were not satisfied with their husband's sexual performance. Quality foreplay became a serious matter worthy of scholarly attention. Abbasid scholars would expound on erotology in the same way that they would write on minerology, or astronomy, with the sciences frequently appearing in the same work.

At other points in history, women's capacity for sexual desire has been used as a reason to censor them. Threats made against women for expressing lust in person or in their writing have been made persistently throughout the ages. The pre-Islamic poet Jariyat Humam ibn Murra was killed after reciting the poem in this collection. Prohibitions, even if they are not used as an overt sanction, have a chill factor and set a challenge for writers, who can be shamed by friends, family and community if they write about such liaisons, even in a fictive way, without hiding their identity. Male writers are under far less scrutiny when it comes to the behaviour of their characters. It appears to be a universal trait to associate sexually explicit writing with the behaviour of the writers, in a way that writing about say crime fiction, does not lead to aspersions of criminality in its authors.

However the illicit is hard to police and often adds fuel

---

1 Translation from Arabic by Frédérik Lagrange and Claire Savina. Reproduced with permission of the translators and Hiba Farid of the Na'ima Masriyya project.

to desire, as I discovered at banned teenage parties in Kuwait. Sensuality and liberality do not necessarily go hand in hand. The harem, represented most frequently as a place of dulled imprisonment, could also provide solace, solidarity, intrigue and protection from the public sphere and men; a place of sensuality between women and a place to exchange sex tips and advice. Prohibition also gives rise to rabid hypocrisy, creativity when it comes to subversion, mind-bending wars of nerves, ludicrous situations, hilarity in camaraderie – all wonderful material for the writer's pen.

*

Throughout the centuries, words have connected lovers and divided them. Finding the time, space and privacy for lovers to find the right words in matters of the heart now seems an extravagance of the past; our time-poor modern existence is constantly interrupted, photographed and surveilled. On the other hand, the modern heroines of Malika Moustadraf and Yousra Samir Imran's works are adept with technology, using Messenger and Twitter to flirt with men who have avatars, sending coded messages expressing their desires and allowing them to arrange rendezvous. Technology makes new ways of connecting and disconnecting possible. These virtual communications also allow for the discourteous and devastating 'ghosting' of a lover, a phenomenon explored in one of the stories in this anthology.

For these articulate writers, words are also able to have completely the wrong effect. In Adania Shibli's sensitively observed *Without Rhyme*, word games wrench lovers apart. Rasha Abbas's narrator in *Simon the Matador*, published here for the first time, forms an obsession for a man of renowned promiscuity, only for her to be bluntly turned off when he talks to her. In some pieces, loving couples are at odds with one another when they fail to find the right words to transform love and lust into erotic realisation – the barriers of shame gagging communications between the most committed of partners.

Alongside lovers failing to connect are lovers who have found equilibrium. The elation of this kind of union ranges from teenage fondling on the beach in Randa Jarrar's *A Map of Home*, to moments of realisation in Naomi Shihab Nye's *San Antonio*: 'It was then I knew / like a woman looking backward / I could not leave you / or find anyone I loved more.' Then there is the ecstasy in the poem *Contemplation* by Hiba Moustafa, where a woman watches her naked lover sleeping in the morning, drinking in his beauty and their love. There is much peace in reading these alongside the primal poem written almost a millennium earlier by Nazhun al-Gharnatiyya, 'If you had been there, you'd have seen us locked together under the chaperone's sleepful eyes like the sun in the arms of the moon, or a panting gazelle in the clasp of a lion.'

This kind of equilibrium is rare and sacred. Many of the relationships described show an imbalance in the power dynamic and disconnection in the lust and communication felt by a couple for one other. The question, 'What if a couple are suited to each other in all respects except when it comes to lust and the erotic?' generates a central tragedy and anguish in several of these prose pieces. This is painfully captured in Ahdaf Soueif's excerpt from in *The Eye of the Sun*, which describes the impasse that can develop in marriage where communication about the physical fails. It bewilders a committed wife in Hanan al-Shaykh's story *Cupid Complaining to Venus*, which describes her attempts, encouraged by her friend, to excite her unimpressed husband with a Japanese film. In both these and other pieces, shame and notions of chastity imprison husbands and wives in the privacy of their own bedrooms.

*

The love of women by women has been described in both coded and celebratory terms throughout history. Ulayya bint al-Mahdi, the sister of Hurun al-Rashid, loved men, women and a court eunuch, to whom the poem *We Wrote in Symbols*, is addressed, according to Dr Marlé Hammond. To put these works into context it should be noted that, during early periods of Islam and pre-Islam in the Arab world, sexuality did not have the heteronormative assumptions that existed elsewhere at the time. It was not until the Western imperial legacy, including the works of Sigmund Freud, crossed the Mediterranean into the Arabic language, that categorisations began 'erasing the more extensive and flexible medieval Arabic model of sexuality, declaring it "deviant" [imposing] instead a binary view of sexuality onto the Arab world'.[1]

In most Arab countries today, same-sex relations are banned by law, and sexual minorities live and love under threat from persecution. Regardless of what Arab women writers may do or say in the real world, even to write fictively of these relationships is a risk. There is great vulnerability here.

Eloquent veneration of other women can be found throughout this collection, including in Mariam Bazeed's triumphant poem *the most expensive mushroom*, where a girlfriend finds her lover to be some 'Provence purple / postcard / lavender running all along my snatch'. The elation and despair of such love is also prevalent, for example in lisa luxx's *Arachnophobia*, where flirtation is carried out over a pint of cider, and in khulud khamis's short story *At Last*, where whisky is drunk, art is discussed and records are played. A high-stakes woman-on-woman crush takes place in a Dubai airport lounge for the crime writer Fadwa Al Taweel.

Male beauty and vulnerability is also venerated and explored. One of the great liberations of fictive writing is the fluid, ageless

---

1 'Medieval Arab Lesbians and Lesbian-Like Women' by Sahar Amer, published in the *Journal of the History of Sexuality* Volume 18, Number 2 (University of Texas Press, May 2009) p. 244.

androgyny its narrators are permitted to assume. Several writers here are freed up by adopting the male points of view.

Some of the classical writers explore polygamous practices, a hotbed for both jealousy and hypocrisy. Nuzhun al-Gharnatiyya reassures her jealous lover, 'Abu Bakr you landed in a place / Just for you and I denied the rest / Who but my lover would have my breast? / If I have more than one lover / Those who are fair know / Abu Bakr's love comes first.' But she also points out that he had 'a thousand intimate ones' – asking therefore, why shouldn't she have others? 'Enjoy this girl,' Qabiha Jariyat al-Mutawakkil magnanimously states, while encouraging her man to return to her afterwards. The concubine musician Zad-Mihr is less dignified in her approach when her master banishes her to Basra so that he can enjoy lovers of different sexes in Baghdad.

*

Many contemporary writers have chosen to set their work in another place or era. In *A Free Girl's Tale*, Saeida Rouass travels back in time to rewrite the classic myth of Psyche and Cupid. Her young heroine is a character from *The Golden Ass* by Apuleius (124–170 CE), which is the oldest surviving novel in Latin, and which contains the first version of the myth of Psyche and Cupid. Noor Mohanna's story *Tangled Roots* is based on the story of a Bedouin's encounter with a naked female djinn at the turn of the last century. Isabella Hammad's novel *The Parisian* opens in 1914, and the extract included here from Samia Issa's novel *Fig Milk* is set after the Palestinian expulsion (the 'nakba' / catastrophe) of 1948. Here, Issa manages to write scenes of sexual longing, sensuality and beauty against a backdrop of dire poverty where the protagonists, confined to a watchful, cramped Palestinian refugee camp, simultaneously masturbate in the latrines, surrounded by excrement. Place and time are suspended altogether in Colette Fellous's bewitching story

Mahdia, where the sense of the loss of a lover is intertwined with the loss of a land and a home. An association between returning to a homeland and love-making is one that occurs more than once in these works.

The pieces in *We Wrote in Symbols* also move geographically. Not all of them are set in the Arab world – far from it. Love and lust know no borders. Farah Barqawi's narrator in *Four Days to Fall In and Out of Love* can only find the freedom she craves by travelling to Europe, reversing the voyages of nineteenth-century writers like Gustave Flaubert who fled bourgeoise provincialism to seek sensuality in the East. Abbas's heroine is in an unnamed European city. Salomé's is set in a field in the West Country of England.

The reader is encouraged to find connections between the works and the times in which these women wrote, for the human heart never grows up, nor have the body's desires changed through the ages. Recurring themes include the idea of innocence, as symbolised by virginity in the extract from *The Almond* by the pseudonymous Nedjma, as well as in the poetry of Shurooq Amin and in Rita El Khayat's *Skin.* For Amin and Nedjma, sex and love, 're-virginises' them, to paraphrase a line of Amin's poem *Hymen Secrets: Girl with a Box.* Hand in hand with virginity comes the idea of the wedding night, the focus of the excerpt from Isabella Hammad's *The Parisian,* where politeness both separates and bonds the newlyweds, and Suad Amiry's *Yummy as Kibbeh,* where the bride does not share the taste, or experience, of her relatives when it comes to the joys of sex, which has been sold to her in culinary terms. It is rewarding to look for patterns in theme, content, language, voice and approach in these texts from across the centuries. Much has changed. Much has not.

Some of the most explicit sexual writing in this volume is also the most romantic. The graphic – rather grotesque – backdrop to Joumana Haddad's *Lovers Should Only Wear Moccasins* serves to reveal the deep connection between the headstrong narrator and her casual lover. In this and other pieces, female characters strive to surmount a sense of shame and awkwardness in navigating sexual situations when intoxicated. The outcome of this is mixed. Earlier poets, such as Umm al-Ala bint Yusuf, counsel against combining drinking and sex: too much wine prevents her from making love or singing in the way she'd like.

Given the restrictions on the women writers and the lives of the characters they depict, it is not surprising that 'judgement' is also a theme that runs through much of the work contained in this volume. It takes the form of outrage at the condemnation by a lover, a family member or society. Ulayya bint al-Mahdi's cry, 'Lord it's not a Crime!' echoes through the centuries with as much resonance as it surely carried when it was first written. Those who defy judgement, such as the woman in Rita El Khayat's poem *Messalina Unbound* (where the 'whore' trope appears, inspired by an infamous wife of a Roman Emperor), do not just transgress societal expectations but are also able to disconnect emotional engagement and sexual pleasure. This is surprisingly rare in this collection, where even narrators who work in the sex trade are at risk of falling in love. This includes the narrator Tali in *TALI: one day when I worked at the bakery* by Sabrina Mahfouz, along with the voices of many of the classical poets.

*

Many of the women whose writing is contained here are bold and forthright. They write against the grain of what society deems 'acceptable', and their psychological insight and confidence is palpable. Wisdom and self-knowledge come through in the voice in Zeina B. Ghandour's *You Cunt,* where the speaker reclaims her body from transposed values, desires and rhapsodies of the male gaze. Her self-assured manner is similar to that of

Aisha al-Qurtubiyya's defiant assertion of independence over 500 years previously, when she declared, 'I am a lioness: never will I let / my being be the break / in another's journey.'

Most of the prose pieces are funny, such as Malika Moustadraf's *Housefly*, where the narrator imagines the man she's flirting with on the internet to be wearing 'orange knee-length underwear full of holes'. In the midst of the Lebanese civil war, Najwa Barakat's narrator Luqman watches the devoted Salaam, and tries to find her attractive: 'Salaam was cleaning the dishes, and her butt was talking vigorously. Luqman was sweating. His partner stood straight up to reply to Salaam's butt.' The tenor of Abbas's lover is heightened, hyper-vigilant. Shibli's tender and torn. Haddad's overblown and mock-heroic. The writers have fun getting their characters into fixes and sharing their asides with the reader.

For all the variety in this collection, the pieces here share a belief, which can most eloquently be expressed by the words of Goliarda Sapienza, a writer from an island between East and West, in the midst of the Mediterranean. 'But isn't sex, love? Love and sex are two sides of the same coin. What is love without sex? The veneration of a statue, of a Madonna. What is sex without love? Nothing more than a clash of genital organs.'[1]

The voices of these writers show how the words of lust and the erotic can remove the barriers between sex and love and illustrate how respect is as essential a component of love, as shamelessness can be to sex. These writings provide an eloquent vocabulary to cross from the known to the unknown, exploring infinite possibilities in the way people forge intimate connections, both physically and mentally. If the erotic is partly a mind game, then these writers invite the reader to experience it with some of the most sophisticated of players – living, dead or completely imaginary.

---

1 *The Art of Joy* by Goliarda Sapienza (Penguin Modern Classics, 1976) p. 229.

We Wrote
in Symbols

Hafsa bint al–Hajj Arrakuniyya

Shall I Call?

Shall I call on you or will you come to me?
I'm always yours whenever you want me.
When you break at noon you'll need a drink and you'll find my
    mouth a bubbling spring and my hair a refugeeshade.
So be quick with your reply, as it's not nice of Jamil to keep
    Buthaina waiting.

Translated from Arabic by Abdullah al-Udhari

Mouna Ouafik

Eloquent Tongue

But
No

He
Does
Not lick
His tongue
Over your
Thighs

He

Fishes for
The fishes
Small
Caught there between
The waves
And shore

Translated from Arabic by Robin Moger

Saieda Rouass

A Free Girl's Tale

As I look back on my life's trajectory, I see it as nothing more than the articulation of love as shown to us by the gods, in both its beauty and most sullied form.

Each unique form of love has revealed itself through my life.

The gods have taken hold of my body and very being and made of it an eternal story.

I am a woman possessed by the divine immortal in my fate.

My love is a manifestation of all loves, my life nothing but an agent of the heavens. There to demonstrate to the people the violence that comes with passion.

I could be bitter like the citrus that grows in these parts. Love can often leave a woman bitter. But I am not.

My life has not been my own. I am merely a reflection of you, a myth to be deconstructed for the instruction of man. For I am not seen as being real, not made from flesh that quivers from a touch, blood that rushes from a kiss or bones that open and fold in the convulsions of passion.

And now I sit here eternal, a testimony to former selves. A statue to be marvelled at. Placed in a museum for others to view from intrusive angles. A tale to be pondered and retold. Lessons of caution that cross time and space. A painting to be enjoyed. My moment of love and loss immortalised in its detail.

A didactic metaphor.

I am not and never have been, myself.

I was the third girl from an insignificant communion. My

childhood no less or more remarkable than any girl of my station. I was not born with a mark that foretold my fate. But as I transformed into womanhood my beauty rose with me. News of my beauty travelled through our Numidian kingdom, at first like a whisper that bounces on the wind and then like a sandstorm that enters into every crevice, leaving invisible but annoying traces in its wake. I first became aware of it when I walked through the market one day with my sisters.

Traders stopped their demands and clients stopped their haggling.

Ripe melons sat on stalls un-prodded.

Tomatoes burst their red juice from the pressure of being squeezed by hands in shock.

My later strolls through the city's gardens and markets caused pandemonium. The citizens acted peculiarly. Florists waited every morning at our door for my appearance to throw their most precious flowers before me. As I crushed petals beneath my feet, they would release a collective sigh of desire. Women would thrust their new-born daughters into my arms, begging I plant a blessing on their foreheads, and men would stand back with their mouths gaping and their hands travelling towards their groin, rubbing and pulling and doing such things that beggar belief. It was as though I had become a mist that casts a spell over everything it passed. As I wondered in my naivety, I had no inclination that my simple existence shook the very foundations of power. News of my beauty reached the Queen herself. Known as a vain woman, she saw me as competitor and usurper of the people's love. I had, through no action of my own, angered the powerful.

My father, aware of the trouble that followed me, confined me to our home insisting I was not to leave. He locked himself away with his oracle. After three nights he emerged, announcing that my beauty was a heavenly curse that would only be lifted if I were to wed a beast. The only solution was to surrender me to the evil of others. I was to be sacrificed because the beauty I held revealed the ugliness they carried. They made me the cause of the monsters within them.

And so it came to pass. I was led in the most macabre of wedding processions, myself a walking corpse to the edge of a mountain crag and abandoned.

As I sat in the darkness of the forest, I understood; there is a love that is temporary, born out of novelty. It is a love of aesthetics, of whom we imagine the beloved to be. It is love for the virgin. It burns from a desire to possess and destroy, rooted in entitlement and fear. I was worshipped by all and loved by no one, looked at and yet not truly seen. Their love was predicated on a lifeless and static version of me that I myself did not recognise. And when it went unfulfilled that love was turned on me as a punishment. I became the object they could not have.

I waited, broken by the betrayal of my father, too grief stricken to see that there were more menacing enemies surrounding me. My crime, to be young, beautiful and female, yet still standing at the precipice of my mortal destiny, with the inherent capacity to direct it, was unforgivable to others. It was not enough for them that I be broken once. I must be broken into a thousand pieces, in a way that only a merciful god could reassemble.

Lost in my melancholy in the woods, a whisper reached me and lured me in a daze to a palace built by angels. I stood at the gates shivering from the cold, mesmerised. As they opened before me, the whisperer guided me through desolate hallways into a warm chamber with a bed that could sleep a dozen. My gilded cell.

Platters of the most exquisite foods appeared on the table, enticing me with scents and colours. Once I had my fill, invisible hands lifted me removed my ruined clothes and placed me in a luxurious bath. I was scrubbed and rubbed, my hair washed and combed. I was placed in the expansive bed, the silk sheets layered over my tired and naked frame.

Night descended and shadows moved in the corner of the room. A light breeze entered through the window, fluttering the curtains in a liquid dance. My mind wondered into its own realm. I closed my tired eyes and succumbed to the night's serenity.

A voice, with no bodily form, entered into my dreams. Between sweet words of seduction, it whispered warnings of danger. My new husband would soon make his presence known and when he did I was to not cast a glance at him, not even a fleeting one. To do so would render me ruined. I succumbed, stretching and opening my body to its tune, desperate for the passion it promised, trying to construe the foreboding in my stomach for anticipation.

'You are my wife and I am your husband.' My husband instructed, his voice holding out authority, yet teasing me with it too. His scent as he lent into me, was that of citrus leaves and the light sweat of youth on summer days. My eyes flickered. Placing a kiss on each of them he warned me once more to keep them closed. I nodded my agreement. Impatient for our union. That first night exists in my memory like a blind vision.

I awoke in the morning and he was gone. I looked at my naked form and speculated that it had all been my imagination. Perhaps I had been alone all night imagining the stirring of my body. I touched the parts of my body that had been roused, retracing where a hand caressed, where a tongue licked and teeth had bitten wondering if I had done all this to myself. The evidence was there to be seen; yet I was alone. Red marks where flesh had been grasped. My nipples were sore and a pulsing heat lay between my legs. I spent the day longing to know the truth, yearning for it to happen again. I wondered around my chamber lost in desire, unable to eat or consider the peculiarity of my new situation.

I attempted to recreate the pleasure of the night before. My hands went to places they had never thought to go before. And yet I felt nothing except perhaps mild reverberations, like vague memories of a past moment that left me frustrated rather than certain. As the sun began to set, I climbed into bed and waited.

At first, a tickling breath behind my ear so soft I doubted it was real. And then the deep whispers, the panting and lips caressing mine. I lay naked ready to experience it again, my earlier frustrations dissipating under a touch whose origin I could not locate. We began what would become our nightly ritual. Our bodies danced like shadows against the wall. When he climbed on top of me my legs opened to welcome him and then wrapped themselves around him to lock him in place. As he held my wrists down, I raised my mouth to meet his. As he entered me, I arched my lower back to guide his direction. Our bodies moved in unison, dipping and rising in intensity and time, measured by our laboured breath.

And so the ritual was born. He joined me in my room on a nightly basis repeating that our union was only possible if I never saw him. So enraptured by pleasure I readily accepted his conditions. At night, it was how I felt with him that mattered most.

But by day, my mind was consumed with dark thoughts. These were quickly forgotten as the sun began to set and I readied myself. Was my nightly companion the monster I had been destined to marry? I could not imagine this husband of mine to be a monster. How could he be when he was so generous with his words and touch? He had not just awoken my body but had also awoken me to it. My body until that point had been a vessel to carry my soul, a benign necessity. To discover within it lay secret pleasures that no other human experience could induce was a revelation. I looked at myself differently, gazed at my form with a newfound respect. Suddenly, it became prized to me; a source of pleasure that I would not trade for anything. And yet I desperately wanted to see him.

At first, I found freedom and strength in my blindness. Our love was something felt between us. It was transferred through touch and the giving and receiving of pleasure. It stood in contrast to the demands of the people that was imposed on me through their gaze. But then the days turned to weeks and the weeks to months and my nights were spent wrapped in a love I knew but could not qualify. I yearned for my sisters and the times we had shared, I thought of days spent basking in sunlight with my feet dangling in the river, of those evenings watching the sun set over our home. My entire being had been channelled towards one source of pleasure. Every emotion I was capable of and every thought was to be consumed by my husband. My happiness was bound to him and yet I was expected to not see it in its entirety. My feeling of empowerment turned to one of vulnerability.

I thought of my sisters more and more. I knew what their counsel would be if they could visit. 'It is not fair,' they would say. 'What harm would come from seeing him?' they would ask. 'It is your right to see him as he sees you,' they would argue.

Resentment began to boil. Days lost waiting for my faceless lover and his refusal to let me feast on him with my eyes. Was it not an act of cruelty to let me know him in all ways except one? What purpose did he hope to achieve by denying me a vision of him?

There is a love that is illicit and hidden from view. It is not for public consumption. Entering into such a union is only possible if you agree to not share it with others, to not speak it. It requires silence and is cloaked in a shame of its own making. I longed to see my lover's face because his face was denied to me. While he feasted on me through all his senses I was not allowed to. I had been run out of my city because of the hungry eyes of its people and was now being denied my own sight. The injustice of it would not fade. I believed a more equal companionship was possible, where neither was denied what the other claimed as their right. So, I resolved to equalise our love, convinced that whatever punishment lay in wait could not be worse than the continued injustice. I would rather see him and face my fate then continue to love in the darkness.

One night as my lover slept beside me, his presence felt only by the subtle movement of the air, I raised a candle to make him visible. I expected to see a monster that I could somehow still love. His form seemed not of this earth, perhaps born in heaven. His hair darker than a moonless night dropped in curls around his strong jaw. His lips – so full – were red from where I had bitten them night after night. The light from the candle revealed the contours of his body, casting parts in shadow and others in glory. I watched his chest softly rise and fall, and in that moment, he seemed to me to be the embodiment of life itself, all its joys and pleasures, its quiet wisdoms and persistence. He was the most beautiful of creatures. My eyes had confirmed what my hands already knew. What lay before me was no monster.

Now that I had seen him my love was whole and complete and my sense of justice restored. I went to snuff out the candle but a drop of wax fell on his bare chest and he awoke with a start. He took flight, angry at my betrayal, and I grabbed his leg hoping to pull him down back into our bed so that we could return to our pleasures. Instead he carried me away up over this palace that had been a sort of prison, and dropped me beside the river. Perched in a tree he looked down at me for the destitute woman I had quickly become, his eyes full of rage.

'I gave you everything and asked only that you comply with my one condition. But your curiosity would not let you. You have made your choice and the punishment for your betrayal is my absence,' he stated. And abruptly, he left.

At first, I sat in shock, unable to comprehend my new lot. I chastised myself for my own undoing. Was it really that important that I see him? What had seeing him achieved except that I had driven him away? The price for my sight was the loss of his touch. I would no longer feel his hands pressed into my hips as he rocked back and forth or hear his breath in my ear as he panted his pleasure, the sound growing deeper and more desperate as the night went on.

I looked out at the river and considered throwing myself in. Standing, I went to its edge and looked into its murky waters. A woman I did not recognise looked back. She was older, but no less beautiful.

I moved away from the river and sat on a rock. Ants collected at my feet and I watched as they organised themselves in neat lines. I observed them for a while distracted by their perfect coordination and harmony. The wind blew reeds across my path, which curled and combined into each other in infinite formations.

I could go in search of him. Convince him that our union could overcome this small disruption and swear to never betray him again. If that failed, I could seek out others and plead they intercede on my behalf. I could prove my love by undergoing whatever trial fate deemed appropriate. In doing so I could bring a new love into existence by making him understand that my desire to see him was not so rebellious, that pleasure built on more equal ground would be greater than what we already had.

A lone eagle hovered above me. It swooped down landing in a tree by the river. It watched me with curiosity and confidence. I felt it glide over me, and as I stood to approach it, it took flight and soared over the river and up above the treetops.

Was it really love? He had been granted the right to love me through all his senses and I had been denied that same right for no obvious reason. Is that what love is, and is that what is required of me? I had failed in my love with him because the rules of love were designed that way. Love in this world, that I had no part in making, was rooted in injustice. To seek it inevitably meant to accept my own subjugation.

There is a love not yet created, still waiting to be birthed. It is a love that comes with no conditions and no judgements, rooted instead in mutual acceptance. It does not seek to assert itself over others or confine them by invisible chains. It is a love not tied to the pursuit of power and does not act from insecurity. It wants for nothing but itself.

I turned in search of a different world and a love of my own making.

This story is inspired by the original tale of Psyche and Cupid as it appeared in The Golden Ass, *said to be the oldest extant novel in Latin. Its author, Lucius Apuleius Madaurensis (c. 124–170 CE), was a Numidian from a region of North Africa that is now part of modern-day Algeria. The 'Free People,' or the Amazigh, is the term used by the indigenous inhabitants of this area, sometimes referred to as 'Berber' by outsiders.*

Wallada bint al-Mustakfi

I Walk My Walk

By God I am fit for the highest of peaks
And I walk my walk and boast in pride.
I enable my lover to have my cheeks.
And if someone craves a kiss, I provide.

Translated from Arabic by Wessam Elmeligii

Aisha al-Qurtubiyya

On Being Proposed to by a Male Poet

I am a lioness: never will I let
my being be the break
on another's journey.

But if that were my choice
I would not answer
to a dog, for to O!
how many lions
am I deaf.

Translated from Arabic by Yasmine Seale

Malika Moustadraf

Housefly

He was wearing a shirt with a big, checked pattern, black and white. It looked like a chess board. Only the top half of his body was showing on her computer screen; she guessed he might perhaps be wearing yellow pants, and tall winter boots, green socks and threadbare orange knee-length underwear. She clamped her lips shut but an audible snort of laughter escaped through her nose.

Boughattat[1] 70 wrote to her:

—Your neck in the picture looks as tasty as a stick of *jabaan kul obaan*.[2]

She laughed and wrote to him:

Eat and see, such sweeties!
Clucking squawking kiddies!
We give holy guarantees,
Candy blessed by Sufis
Sweeties, who eats sees!

---

1 A legendary Being of the Night, a scary ghoul who preys on the sleeping. Nightmares are said to be caused by him strangling the dreamer.
2 A brightly-coloured candy pole sold to children outside schools and in fair grounds; the lyrics she quotes in her retort are from a popular old derija salesmen's jingle sung by the sellers.

He replied:

—And I bet your tongue is as sweet as that *faneed al-makana*[1] we all used to grind away on with our molars, back when we were kids.

—I don't like *faneed al-makana*. When I was a little girl, we travelled to a shrine to celebrate the *mawsim* festival there. It was for the *marabout* Sidi Rahal, actually. I bought some *fareed al-makana*. I stuck my head into that plastic bag and didn't pull it back out till I had snaffled the very last piece. I didn't sleep at all that night: my bum was teeming with too many little worms.[2] When I got sick of scratching that itch, I shouted out. My mother threatened to put hot chilli pepper on it or tie me up in the shrine. After that I didn't shout anymore.

—Tell me about yourself.
—I don't feel like talking about myself.
—Are you a ghost?
—I'm a ghost, and you're Boughattat.

*

Her child cries so she breastfeeds him, and gurgles gentle sounds to soothe him. 'There, there, gah gah gah, booboo baby'. His fingers are tiny and pink. One day she's going to bite them off, or hug him so hard he expires. She wipes his bottom with Johnson's baby lotion, puts nappies on him, and doesn't hug him so that he won't die. When her husband comes home she'll serve him his dinner: tripe with turnip and red olives. He loves tripe. That's why she cooks it up in such big quantities then puts

---

1 Tiny rock-hard multi-coloured children's candy beads threaded on elastic or string.
2 In Moroccan slang, someone 'having worms' means they are feeling horny.

it in the freezer to reheat when the need arises. In the freezer there's also enough bread to last a week, washed vegetables, and . . . all that stuff.

Jupiter 1960 is now online.

She writes to him:

—I just this minute performed the '*tagunja*' rain ritual.
—The rain is so late coming, and the land thirsts.

She licks her lips. Here comes her rain, it's gushing torrential.

Jupiter1960 writes:

—When I come to Casa, are you spending the night with me?
—Dream on! You're out of your mind.
—But let us dream, for a life without dreams, my friend, is loathsome. I'll bring a bottle of gin with me; it tastes good when it's blended with Schweppes tonic. Our encounter's going to be as hot as 'summer in the southern cites,' in the words of the poet.
—And what else?
—When we meet, don't strangle your breasts in a bra . . . Let your hair hang free onto your shoulders, like in the photo. I want to fill my eyes with the kohl of you: I'm a Bedouin, and my eyes are as big as my desire.[1]

(Her husband says: *a woman's hair is shameful.* His head is like an old piece of ivory, his beard is like a broom. Someday she's going to grab him by his beard, swill him around in the air three times

---

[1] Big eyes are associated with insatiable sexual appetite; Bedouin men are thought of as not having much exposure to women. The combination suggests immense passion.

then throw him into the toilet and slosh the pail of water out over him. She'll be shouting at him as she does it: *your beard is shameful, your bald spot is shameful, your arse is shameful!*).

Jupiter1960 writes:

—Do you want to make love?

(Her husband doesn't ask. She grants him his desire however he wants, whenever he wants, wherever he wants. Even if it's during the daytime in Ramadan. Ibn Qayyim al-Jawziyya says *he who fears his testicles will burst, for him coitus is permitted during Ramadan.* And she obeys her husband and obeys Ibn Qayyim, so that her husband's testicles don't burst open and she isn't barred from entering heaven.)

She grabs the keyboard and hammers out:
—Does love taste different when it's made over the internet?
—Of course it does. And it's as delicious as our mothers' couscous.

(She licks her lips. On Friday she's going to her mother's place to eat couscous made with *gueddid.*[1] Her husband will go with her of course, and she'll wear her black clothes, as usual, looking like some mobile tent – her siblings call her 'the Ninja'. The tent stifles her, her husband stifles her, and Jupiter1960 is writing to her now: *a woman isn't just a body*).

She writes to him:
—When we meet we'll go to the sea. We'll watch the sea gulls alighting and we'll eat ice cream . . .
—I'll read Juwaida's *Poem of the Seagulls* to you.
—I'll gift the sea my body, and I'll tell it *Come to me!*[2]

---

1 Dried, cured meat similar to jerky, made from ribs and tripe.
2 From the Qur'an, Surah Yusuf / Joseph, 23: 'The woman in whose house

—Gift your body to *me*, and say that to me, and you'll see that I won't be like Yusuf and shun you.

—You're crazy.

—When we sneak into my friend's room, I'll read you a poem by Rimbaud. We'll smoke a couple of roll-ups and drink a glass or two of gin. I'll fan the flames of you until your fires roar; I'll awaken those timeless volcanoes slumbering deep within you. I'm a Zoroastrian lover: I worship fire.

(She recalls Rimbaud, Nass el Ghiwane, University… she was pushing forty before she got married).

—Why am I buying a cow when there is plenty of milk already?

The clock on the wall strikes eight. In half an hour her husband will be home. Her heart will shrink, as always, back into the gloom that eight-thirty heralds. She shuts down Messenger and puts everything back in its place. When her husband arrives he'll wolf down his plate of tripe, pray the evening prayer, shut his office door and be alone with his computer.

A housefly buzzes near her ear. It hovers over her child's face. He wakes … *shhhh* … she swats the fly. Her child goes back to sleep. Her husband always repeats: 'If I found out that the fly entering my house was male, I'd kill it.'

Translated from Arabic by Alice Guthrie

---

he dwelt sought to seduce him and shut firm the doors upon them. She said: "Come to me!" He said: "God forbid!"' *The Qur'an: A New Translation* by Tarif Khalidi (Penguin Classics, London, 2008). In this Surah, there are potent tales of seduction, attraction, restraint and rejection. Having resisted seduction in this ayah, later Surah Yusuf's beauty is so overwhelming that the women who see him are overcome by desire and begin to self-harm with knives.

Zainab bint Farwa al–Mariyya

You Who Are Riding

You who are riding your mount early,
Come here that I might tell you what I find:
People have not had passions that enwrapped them,
That were not exceeded by my passion.
Suffice it for me that he would be content,
And, for his pleasure and good company,
I would labour for the last of days.

Translated from Arabic by Wessam Elmeligi

Khadija bint al–Ma'mun

That Buck

By God tell that buck with the heavy buttocks
And a waist so small,
He is sweetest when he is ready,
And, when in ecstasy,
He is the most gorgeous of all.
He built a pigeon house,
And released a dove in the loft.
I wish I were one of his pigeons,
Or a falcon,
So he could do to me what he would love.
If he wore white linen,
The fabric would hurt or scratch him
Because he is so soft.

Translated from Arabic by Wessam Elmeligi

Samia Issa

Fig Milk: An Excerpt

He was still holding his member when he heard her moan. The mix of pain and pleasure made Rakaad pause to listen. Moans rose and faded, then rose and faded again, until a scream, and then silence.

Rakaad had not imagined, before that night, that someone, somewhere in the camp, let alone in its sordid public toilets, would dare to drop the mask of the Nakba. This mask suffocated Rakaad and he was often thinking of ways to liberate himself from it; yet, instead of doing so, he would let it harden the features of his face, harshen his voice and make him grow crueller.

Cruelty shall be matched with cruelty ... for us to survive?

This is the way Rakaad had been talking to himself, ever since he had been dragged outside his home one night, barefoot. A hand had caught him. He did not know whether it was his mother's or his older sister's hand, as, he could hardly tell the two apart at the time. He was the youngest of ten siblings born in al-Ghabsiyya, in the Galilee. He had lived at the camp ever since that fateful night, when everything around him had changed.

But now, on the other side of the wall, a voice was tearing off Rakaad's Nakba mask and piercing through his harsh disguise. His spirit was breaking from his body, drawn to the holes in the wall that stood between him and the woman.

Holes!

As his spirit responded to the sound of the woman through the holes, it occurred to Rakaad to look for her through the holes in the wall, too. How had he not noticed these holes before, even though they pit the faces of all the camp walls? As he approached the largest hole, Rakaad heard the toilet door open on the other side with a slight squeak. He shuddered at the thought of a real woman materialising there and finding him listening.

Better not go out now – she might realise that I heard her moan. Think!

No, it's fine, she can't have suspected anything, or she would have stopped.

How do I know when she will do this again? I have to find out who she is. I have to follow her.

In the end he didn't find out who the woman was. Not because she had gone and he had missed her, but because he was scared.

Scared? Of what?

Who knows.

He punched the wall with his fist: 'dumbass, stupid, idiot! What are you so scared of?'

He got out of the toilet. The fear dragged around his knees and he almost stumbled into the open sewer that flowed through the alleyway. That was close. 'Stop being such a baby!' Rakaad mumbled to himself like someone possessed.

Outside the toilet, Rakaad met a group of young people from the camp loitering about. So as to hide his unease and inner turmoil he yelled at them:

'What the hell are you doing at this hour? Everybody go home!'

The three boys rushed to a nearby alley, scurrying out of Rakaad's sight without understanding the rudeness they had come to expect from him. Rakaad had to preserve his importance as 'Head of the People's Committee'. But in that moment he wanted to move the heaviness inside himself, so he breathed out deeply: 'Ah!' The 'Ah' emerged from his chest, blending with the scents of the alleys and the daily lives of those who lived there.

Ducking and weaving between the open sewers, Rakaad made his way home as if he had just woken up from a long coma. It was half past midnight. He was not worried that his wife, Halima, would notice. He thought she'd be asleep by now. He began to open the door, which squeaked, faintly. He shuddered suddenly and his heart beat audibly. He heard a crying child, far away. He listened harder, putting his hands behind his ears to determine where the sound was coming from. He couldn't work it out, and deciding it was nothing to worry about, he sat on the edge of the bed, tucked himself under the quilt, and lay down to warm himself up against Halima's body. He suddenly remembered the stormy nights that kept people up, that first winter after the Nakba. He recalled how he used to tuck himself in between the bodies of his two sisters inside a tent that was in danger of being blown away. He used to crawl in between them, to get warm and would then fall asleep. As soon as he crawled in next to Halima, the crying of the child began to fade away little by little, and Rakaad gradually began to fall asleep, slowly, slowly ... and, as he was losing consciousness, his member ejaculating the hot fluid slowly, slowly, *s.l.o.w.l.y.*

Fatima too came back in a daze from the toilet that night. She slipped into the bed next to her two grandsons and started to fall asleep. She was feeling light. She embraced this feeling of lightness and enjoyed a peaceful sleep.

The next morning, as the darkness of the night began to fade and the rays of the sun penetrated the thin walls of her house, a single ray of light shone through the crack right into her eye, as if urging her to wake up. She decided to lie down in the opposite direction next time. *God!* She remembered the previous night and felt a strange and perplexing sensation that she could neither understand nor ignore. Fantasies of a body shedding its heaviness and taking on a lightness came to her. Her soul moved downwards and felt goosebumps across her skin. She smiled bashfully even though no one could possibly have seen or known it was her. Recalling the details of the night, she shivered. It was as if her quivering fingers, adventurous and eager, had again slipped away in search of secret territories that were waiting to be trodden upon. As if her body, that night, had stopped being a mere heap of flesh and bones.

All that remained of the previous night was a fantasy whose reel unwound from Fatima's fingers, groping its way over the terrain of her unexplored body. Arousal took hold of her. Her fingers, desirous and curious, sought for the fleeting pleasures that had been so recently woken in the corners of her body.

A flood of images came back to her and Fatima began to talk to herself:

I didn't mean to do it! Of course not! If I didn't feel so suffocated and cramped, I would never have unbuttoned my dress.

Throughout the day, she tried unsuccessfully to find excuses for what had happened. She could not comprehend it. She did not know where the waves that swept through her body were coming from; the waves that made her face flush with heat and moans burst from her body. Moan after moan, muted and delicate. It wasn't the first time she had looked at or touched her own body. Today, she was torn between giving into the unexpectedly overwhelming pleasure of the moment, wanting to find it again later, and feeling guilty about what she had felt. Fatima struggled alone with her inner conflict. The one thing that she was certain of was that she would not talk about what had happened to *anyone*. Her eagerness to conceal the sensations she had felt was as strong as her body's irresistible yearning to give in again to the heights of pleasure and arousal.

The night before, Fatima did not know that on the other side of the wall was a man who could hear her moaning. She didn't even know that she *was* moaning. She moaned, not knowing what moaning was. How could she be careful? She tried to keep herself quiet by grasping at her throat, as if trying to grab something suffocating her. Her other hand fell onto her chest. Inside the darkness of the toilet Fatima's two sagging breasts were revealed, white as the moon. She gasped at the sight of them, as if seeing them for the very first time. It was as if she was looking at another body. No sooner had she recovered from the brilliance of her two white moons than she felt a spasm coursing through her body where she stood leaning against the wall, bent over the opening of the latrine. Bewitched, she started searching for her breasts in the darkness. Still with one hand on her neck, her other hand circled her chest and made its way towards her breasts. Her fingers accidentally touched one of her nipples and she suddenly felt lighter, as something had opened between her thighs.

Since that night, Fatima's world started to expand every time she went to relieve herself.

She repeated the attempt. She let her fingers approach her nipple, this time deliberately. She sighed faintly, 'Ah.' Her breathing accelerated, her head began to shake, her voice rose, her moaning grew deeper, her body trembled violently under the weight of arousal. At that moment, Rakaad heard her and became erect. He had tried to get closer to the wall and peer through the holes, but his foot had hit a metal bowl. Fatima had heard the sound and stopped. For a while, she had remained motionless. She peered through a hole in the wall, but seeing nothing in the darkness, and feeling nothing but the lust that drove her, she continued.

Fatima found herself kneading her breasts with both hands, while her fingers greedily worked her nipples. She became a child again, desperate to explore and discover new things. She wanted to go all the way, not knowing what she would find. She was scared, yet she loved what was happening to her, and caressed herself for a whole hour. Resting from time to time, she tried different positions, oscillating between pleasure and fear, when it finally occurred to her that someone else might try to come into the toilet and surprise her almost naked. Fear paralyzed her, and she stopped.

Shame on me!

She decided she'd come back, at the same time, the next evening.

Fatima did not *come* that night, for the very reason that she was not aware that there could be a final destination to get to. Instead, she hastily buttoned her dress and opened the door.

The next day, as soon as evening fell, Fatima hastened to return to the exercise of the previous evening. Her desire to recapture the sensations she had felt had become unbearable. Fatima did not know yet that, this time, the experience would take her further than she could imagine. She did not know that she would discover a secret life that she did not live. And she did not know that along with this great discovery she would find a new flavour of the Nakba, colourful and alive.

That evening, Fatima, eager to come, *came.*

It was a strange night. She climaxed without realising what climaxing was, or how it occurred. She then longed to ease into the darkness of ecstasy. But the toilet was narrow, and the floor was covered with shit. When she opened her eyes, it was as if she was seeing its squalor anew. The smell, which she hadn't noticed the previous evening, hit her. She fixed herself and ran off quickly before Rakaad knew she had left.

He moaned, faintly.

Two months passed and Rakaad never failed to be waiting in position in the next-door toilet just before Fatima entered. Each evening, on the other side of the wall, Rakaad would begin his exploration at the same time as Fatima. Each of them would get to know themselves, without ever meeting, or knowing who the other was. He was not ready to take the risk of following her or arriving late for the rendez-vous with her moaning. He wanted to make sure that no one else would hear her and steal that voice which, when she started moaning, overturned the earth itself, and allowed him to explode in unison with his warm, stickiness exploding to her abundant cries.

Her and him and the wall. Each of them on their own side: they lit up together. They messed around together. They arrived and parted over and over again. In and out of time. When they would come, they'd come together – but apart and alone.

One night, Rakaad had arrived early as usual, only to find his preferred toilet occupied. He waited for a while. He realised that he was going to be late and started to bang at the door, to rush the unwelcome visitor out. A voice answered from inside, 'It's a big one. A big one. You're gonna have to wait a bit.'

As if he hadn't heard, Rakaad banged the door harder and harder, with a violence that made his heart beat faster. Eventually, the man came out of the dark toilet. When the man saw Rakaad, Head of the People's Committee, standing there in the dark outside the toilet, he was furious. 'It's you? What's wrong with you to bang like this? Are you waiting to shit or to fuck?'

On hearing these words, Rakaad was so embarrassed it was as though he had been caught red-handed. He knew the man, Abu Ali. Abu Ali was so startled by Rakaad's red face that he thought Rakaad was actually constipated. It was Rakaad's habit to appear calm in front of people. He would say to himself, *the centre imposes the mask on me, and I must know how to play my part. I'm in charge. The people should fear and respect me.* But that night, Rakaad felt his mask fall. Paranoid, he wondered: *Why did he mention 'fucking'? Does he know?*

Paranoia chased the questions around his head, one after the other, his heart beating under a turmoil of doubts, when he stepped right into a pile of shit. It was fresh and its smell was overpowering. He shouted, 'Come on, Abu Ali. Do you only eat beans?' He shouted it loud and clear, so that Abu Ali would hear him and be so embarrassed by the shit he had left behind that he'd forget about the banging. Rakaad switched on the tap to wash his feet before the owner of the ethereal voice arrive, but the water was not running that night. Before Rakaad could think of a solution, the door to the women's cubicle opened and closed behind the one he was waiting for. He forgot the shit, the water, and Abu Ali, and listened closely.

But after their encounter that night, Abu Ali did not forget about Rakaad. He began to wonder what it was that could have brought Rakaad to the toilets of Ouzou camp. Because Rakaad, with his elevated station as Head of the People's Committee, lived in 'Ain al-Helweh camp in a two-storey house, where they had a toilet on each floor. Abu Ali's curiosity was so strong that he began to keep an eye on Rakaad whenever he saw him entering Ouzou. Abu Ali realised the strangest thing: that Rakaad would not set foot in Ouzou camp except to relieve himself. Abu Ali's first conclusions were that he was suffering from some kind of psychological complex, but his attention turned to the repeated synchronisation between Rakaad's presence in the toilet, and Fatima's – Khalil's widow. In the beginning, he had not noticed the relationship between the two attendees' presence. Then he assumed it was just a coincidence. But now he was certain it was not.

Abu Ali was too kind-hearted to suspect anything untoward, especially from Fatima, who was a woman so good natured, she appeared almost simple. Two weeks after his first meeting outside the toilet with Rakaad, Abu Ali inadvertently passed by the camp's public toilet one evening, unaware that both of them were already inside their respective cubicles. As he leaned against the toilet wall, edging along the side of the alley to avoid falling into the open sewer, he heard a woman moan. Initially, he thought that the moan sounded like someone was suffering from stomach pain. But before he'd finished negotiating his way around the sewer, the moans had risen to such a crescendo that they reminded Abu Ali of the sounds his ex-wife Amahl had made when she was high in lust. Amahl's overwhelming desire had led him to divorce her, as he no longer felt that he could satisfy her. Fearing that his spunk was no longer enough for her, he had got scared that Amahl's lust might lead her to betray him, and so he had divorced her. Whenever he had felt that it was time to pleasure Amahl, the ghost of another man appeared to him, like a phantom lover in their bed.

But this sound is coming from the toilet!

Abu Ali waited to see if a man would come out before or after the woman, but none did. Fatima was alone when she came out, and he could not distinguish who she was in the dark. When she was out of his sight, he was surprised to see Rakaad emerge from the other side of the public toilet, his face even more flush in the full moonlight than the last time that they had met there.

How? How is that possible? But Abu Ali didn't dwell on the situation. His imagination was running wild after he, a divorcee who had not slept with a woman for over a year, had been aroused by the moans.

Abu Ali decided to return the following night and to occupy the toilet before Rakaad got there. He arrived fifteen minutes before the estimated time of Rakaad and Fatima's 'date'. As expected, someone knocked on the toilet door shortly after. He did not respond, did not say a word. The knocking on the door intensified to a violent banging, and Rakaad's voice, rising louder and louder, shouted at him to get out. Abu Ali startled with fear at each and every bang on the door. It occurred to him that Rakaad might break down the door. But after only about five minutes, he heard Rakaad's steps rushing away, as other footsteps, soft and heavy, shuffled towards the cubicle that shared the back wall with his own, on the side of the women's toilets. Within minutes, Fatima's murmurs began to grow and fade, turning into moans that found their way through the holes in the wall, igniting the flames of lust in Abu Ali's body.

Abu Ali held his breath.

On the other side of the wall, Fatima had fully undressed and was groping her body with the eager hands of the hungry reaching for food. She had already visited her toilet once that day. Early in the morning she had brought some basic tools with her and had hammered a nail into the wall where she could hang her clothes. In the hustle and bustle of morning, no one had heard her. Fatima had decided to spend the night there, masturbating until morning.

She was prepared. She had brought a candle with her, which she lit with a matchstick, so that she could properly see her white moons and those nether regions that, as soon as she touched them, turned to feathers of pleasure and abandon. Fatima was around forty-five years old, yet the curves of her body remained firm and her clear skin shimmered in the candlelight. She explored her contours. Belly, thighs, waist, arms and breasts. Despite the damage of the years and five pregnancies, her body felt like a virgin body, still untouched by a man's hand. Her hands began to explore her rounded abdomen at the circumference of her navel, and she contemplated her luscious folds of skin and ample curves. Relaxed, she looked for a surface to lean on. She chose the wall that separated her from Abu Ali. And kept going.

Her thighs, under the caresses of her fingertips, went up to her waist, stomach, arms, breasts. She went wild: it was as if she was both rising and falling, when something between her thighs contracted and widened to contract again and pull her fingers inside, a little bit deeper. The liquid gushed out between her thighs and she could feel its source. She groaned, her voice betraying the extent of her desire and anticipation.

What now? She wondered. *How far to go? Was there more to come?*

Fatima didn't know how her fingers had learned to play like that. Her breath began to work in fits and gasps, her body arched with pleasure, her trembling accelerated and took her to another place. When she came, she could not suppress her scream. Better: her scream surprised her. It had come from nowhere, from the borderline between life and death. It was as if she was dying and being born at the same time. Past, present, and future ceased to exist, as she departed from her body.

Abu Ali ejaculated at the sound of Fatima's scream, and he put his fist in his mouth to silence his own cry. Lightheaded, he leaned against the wall and saw directly through one of the holes in it. There he saw Fatima's face caught in the raptures of ecstasy. All sign of sadness had left her features, now soft as a baby's. Her eyes had closed gently in astonishment. There was now a soft smile on her lips, and her round cheeks were rosy. He wished he could break through the wall, penetrate her, hold her in his arms and fall asleep.

Abu Ali remained there and kept observing her, enjoying the childish, flamboyant face, until the face awoke, and the body stood up, reluctantly. She looked drunk, almost.

Fatima! Unbelievable! Abu Ali whispered, sceptical. *And I thought she was so innocent!*

Translated from Arabic by Claire Savina

Laura Hanna

Communion

I didn't expect to see you praying,
kneeling on the same floor
with parted lips and hands that had so skilfully
opened and closed me
the night before on this same, carpeted floor.
your brother's furniture store.
A first for anyone, for no-one but you;
converted at first sight, the slice of skin between your shirt and
    jeans
that mad-hot day in Opera Square.

Hovering helplessly over one another, like fruit flies,
parked up under balconies in paternal shadow,
no space between to slip a shared ice-cream spoon.
The fuse lit, a sudden ambush of teenager tremors at 30,
that thirst that lives in the skin and prickles, tickles as it perspires.

I felt like such a fool
simmering in my seat, devoted fingers resting on your neck,
waiting for that dirty smile
and dazed by the dangers of road check points and hotel-room
    check-ins.

You surprised me when you said no.
Pressed together with sweat and caught in the current, mid-flow,
safe in our store-fronted sanctuary,

set free from fabric restraints that had waited for removal with
    saintly patience,
beyond parked-car climaxes.

So stepping from the shower, wet like the newly baptised,
I was surprised to see you sitting there on your knees,
delicate creation craving attention,
amused, embarrassed to stand
dripping on the carpet.

Unconsciously fulfilling some grand plan, I pressed
the palm of my hand on your hair, your lips
to my thigh, anointing them like those of the worshipful.

And you smiled.

Anonymous

You Don't Satisfy

You don't satisfy a girl with presents and flirting, unless knees
bang against knees and his locks into hers with a flushing thrust.

Translated from Arabic by Abdullah al-Udhari

Zad-Mihr

Letters of Zad-Mihr, Slave Girl of Abu Ali ibn Jumhur

He would say, 'This Zad-Mihr, the slave girl of Abu Ali ibn Jumhur, was beautiful in the extreme, with a sweet voice, and the queen of the female companions. Her owner was one of the stupidest rudest people around, full of nagging, bickering, spoiledness, and tedium. Once Abu l-Hasan al-Dawraqi[1] visited him and demanded that she sing, so he wrote to her, during a time when she was somewhat peeved with him,

> Dear Mistress of her Master,
> Today I have a friend over, Abu l-Hasan, who came only to hear you. So I'd like you to favour me and come, and no joking around, for the man is not a joker.

She wrote in response

> He's the one I see with his moustache cut short! A shit-well, that's what he is. And I, by God, am unable to open my eyes from this headache, and my throat is clogged up from the eggplant I ate yesterday!

He wrote to her

> I have, by God, conveyed to him your apologies, but he isn't satisfied. He said, 'come today with the charitable

---

1 Not identified; apparently someone born in, or from a family deriving from, Dawraq, a town in Khuzistan (S.W. Iran), not far from Basra.

donation of your song!

She wrote on the back of this note,

> Damn your eyes! If this our lord Abu l-Hasan, God bless
> him! suggested further and demanded a lay, and said,
> 'Make it a charitable donation of your cunt this year!' Tell
> him, if you please, that by God I can't open my eyes! How
> many times do I have to say it, damn it, leave me alone!
> Rid me, O God, rid me of you!

And one day he said to her,

> O mistress of her master, take some of these peeled
> almonds and make of them some fragrant incense, for
> indeed the *mahleb* of the market is not well scented. And
> cast ground rice in the potash, and Khorasani clay, and a
> little frankincense.

And she replied to him,

> May God heat your eyes, you braggart, you blowhard, I've
> never seen someone who eats barley and farts white bread
> before!

This Abu Ali had floppy lips, a wide mouth, and a fat tongue,
whereas that poor woman had a petite mouth. One night he
said to her, 'By my life, put my tongue in your mouth.'

She replied, 'And why not? Perhaps the end of the world has
come, so that the camel can pass through the eye of a needle?'

When he slept with her, he would pull out, and she got
angry one night and threw him off of her, and said, 'Does a
toothless mouth really need a toothpick?'[1]

---

1 cf. al-Tawhidi, *Basair*, i, 230, al-Abi, *Nathr al-durr*, iv, 253 (about the *jariyah* of

One day one of the Baghdadi guttersnipes came into his house in the winter with no overcoat, in a thin robe. He was obliged to hear her singing through to the end, and they had already finished eating, so they only offered him some food in passing. He refused to eat, affecting elegance, although he was nearly dying of hunger, for he was keeping up appearances for the slave girl. He started drinking sweet date wine and quickly became drunk, and the world with all its lights became dark in his eyes, so that he walked up to some roses in the party and began eating them eagerly. The slave girl noticed him and realised what was the matter, so she said to her master, to the side of her tambourine, 'By God, call for something for that one to eat, or he's going to be shitting honeyed rose jelly!'

When the young man's drunkenness reached its limit, and the night grew cold, he began trembling, his teeth clattering, as all he was wearing was a diaphanous robe. He approached the slavegirl, all the while undergoing this torment, and said, 'I long to embrace you!' And she said to him, 'Wretch! You had better embrace an overcoat than embrace me, if you had any sense!' The young man went away, the slave girl still burning in his mind, and in courting her he began a correspondence, writing letters, but the slave girl, being a Baghdadi, knew nothing but the real world and hard cash. He began to describe to her in little notes his passion, and his foolishness, and his sleeplessness at night, his tossing and turning as if lying on a frying pan, his inability to eat or drink, and other similarly inane sentiments, with no point to them and no benefit. When he grew tired of this, and despaired of winning her affection, he wrote to her in a note, 'If you refuse to visit me, or let me visit you, then, by God, at least send me your phantom image in a dream, and cool the fever of my heart!'

Direct me to your image so I may

Ahmad ibn Yusuf al-Katib).

demand a rendezvous . . .[1]

Another:

Your absence was pointed,
point your image to me now . . .

So she said to his messenger, 'Damn you! Tell this idiot, "Loser,
I'll do you better than send my image in a dream. Give me two
dinars in an envelope and I'll come myself, and we can be done
with it!"'

This man, Abu Ali Ibn Jumhur, was actually one of the prominent
merchants, and He had granted him (He who blesses bountifully
when He grants), Sir, a load of wealth that would slow down
a donkey[2] or wear out a good horse. Indeed, God had made
him the master of more flocks and property than He granted
to most others. Zad-Mihr was his slave girl, and he also had a
wife, the daughter of his uncle, and between the two of them
he was between two fires, one burning him with her fire, the
other branding him with her blaze. He was in a real dilemma,
so he took his slavegirl to Basra, and his wife to Wasit, and he
went to Baghdad.

Baghdad was the paradise of the prosperous, and hell to the
poor, and he took it upon himself to devote himself to 'higher
things': the sizzling of frying pans, breaking open the wine jugs,
listening to singing girls, seeking pleasure, meeting full moons
of beauty, between myrtle and oxeyes, and goblets and wine, and
the sounds of lute strings and the wail of the reed-pipe, with a
'give-me-a-full-cup!' and a 'take-the-empty-one!'. He left them

---

1 Attributed to Ali ibn Yahya al-Munajjim in al-Raghib al-Isbahani, *Muhadarat*,
ii, 72.
2 *Himar al-shawk*, 'a donkey carrying thorns', cf. al-Tanukhi, *Faraj*, ii, 152. The
syntax of the Arabic sentence is incomplete (cf. De Goeje, Review, 732).

both and did as he liked with himself, until Zad–Mihr got fed up in Basra, and wrote him letters which are too many to quote in full, among them the following:[1]

I am writing to you from Basra, where I am in good health, in spite of your Qatuli nose,[2] which is like the nose of an Aquli goat.[3] I have written you numerous letters, none of which have received a reply. Is this evidence of your intelligence and taste, or of the vileness of your soul? Tell me with whom you left me in your damned house in Basra? You dumped me on your wasteland estate or with your stupid house managers!? By God, this house resembles nothing so much as the [insane asylum] of the Monastery of Ezekiel,[4] and I am imprisoned within like one of the madmen! I get nothing in return except by renting out your buildings, thirty-five dirhams a month, worth about a glass shard, or some chicken scratch. It wouldn't pay for a cheap beer or cover the cost of lime to wax with! Or perhaps you want me to leave it with its feathers on, unplucked, so that you can come back to it, and put your hand on it, and know that no one has touched it except you (an arrow in your heart!)? Or do you want me to grow its hair out long? A lance in your liver! I have to clean it up, especially since I need it now, and have been forced to rely on it, since I go out singing, and end up screwing. If I make any money off it,

1 cf. al-Abi, *Nathr al-durr*, iv, 264.
2 After al-Qatul, a canal off the Tigris at Samarra, dug by the 6th-century pre-Islamic Sasanid ruler Khusraw Anushirwan. Its connection with noses is obscure.
3 Probably after al-Dayr al-Aquli a monastery on the Tigris some 90 km downstream from Baghdad.
4 Dayr Hizqil, a corruption of Dayr Hizqil (the monastery of Ezekiel), see Yaqut, *Buldan*, Di'bil, *Diwan*, 182, al-Jahiz *Bayan*, ii, 243 (al-Farazdaq meets a madman in Dayr Hizqil). See Dols, *Majnun*, 203, 360, 391.

I'll save it for you! By your eyeshadow, it won't be but a few months until a baby comes, swaddled and lotioned: I'll put saffron on his hands. I'll now send this letter, God's blessing on your pen, and on my inkwell! And in the ass of the one who comes up short, a stick!

She also wrote to him,

O Ibn Jumhur, send me something to tide me over, and please me with clothing. Otherwise, by God, I'll go out and sing, and put my body up, and ten others with me. And you know that if a slave girl goes out a-singing, someone soon gets in her panties! I've warned you, and you know it full well! If you want all mankind to fuck me, I won't get in the way of your plans. I'll fulfil all your desires! You've got your own whores who suit you, and seven of them for the price of a slap in the face. If you get up off of one of them, you get off of her with twenty farts in your sleeve. But still they brag about you, saying 'We were with Abu Ali the Sultan's merchant, the great and magnificent!' Yes, it suits you, the likes of that stupid female donkey in your house! You can crack a walnut on her head and she won't dare say a word to you, because she thinks you're Vizier Ibn al-Zayyat or Ibrahim Ibn al-Mudabbir.[1] As for Zad-Mihr, who pounds you like bulgur wheat and grinds you down like flax, well she's not something from your spice rack!

By God, this house of yours in Basra is nothing so much like the monastery of Ezekiel, and I am one of

---

[1] Muhammad ibn Abd al-Malik ibn al-Zayyat, vizier under the caliphs al-Mutasim and al-Mutawakkil, known for his cruelty and his poetry, executed 233/847. Ibrahim ibn Muhammad ibn Abd Allah ibn al-Mudabbir (d. 279/893), state secretary, poet, and literary critic, boon companion of caliph al-Mutawakkil.

the madmen locked inside! May the Lord spare me from my sins as he spared me from the sight of you, for I have become the happiest of people due to your long absence. But from suffering these financial tribulations I am wearing out my body and losing my youth, waiting on you. And all the while you forget about me, fooling around with your loser buddies in Baghdad, while I am in Basra sitting on straw mats and rags![1]

Damn you Ibn Jumhur, burn your eyes! You've become a sodomite, friend of slave boys with downy beards![2] God protect me from your wantonness! When the weaver's belly's full, he thinks his daughter a princess. By your life, I'm going out to sing and get fucked in Basra, while your boys in Baghdad rent out their wares, and you can be in the middle, Ibn Hamdun,[3] with a happy spirit. I'm not going to judge your actions, even if you're sometimes friends with boys, and sometimes women! By the life of your crooked nose, your eyeliner and your hair-do, I can compete with you, blow by blow! If you get into boys, I'll take lovers, if you get into girls, I'll do some tribbing. But I'll do you one better, because you're never wanted unless you pay gold, while I am desired and paid gold for doing it! And in the ass of the one who comes up short, a stick!

May God not bless you in what you've chosen for yourself, and by the life of your dainty hair-do, and your combed love-locks, and the elegance of the makeup on

1 The word *al-k.r.n.d* (as in al-Shalji) or *al-k.z.n.d* could be connected with Persian *gaznand*, 'A sack filled with straw' (Steingass, *Persian-English Dictionary*, where one also finds *kazindah*, 'A teasel ; a meshy sack').

2 The growth of the beard marked adolescent boys as being too old to attract the sexual attention of grown men. A similar theme is found in the literature of ancient Greece.

3 Possibly a sarcastic allusion, but the meaning is unclear. Ibn Hamdun is the name of several drinking companions of ninth-century caliphs. Al-Shalji silently changes the manuscript's *Ibn Hamdun* to *Ibn Jumhur*.

your eyes, and your roomy slippers and shoes.[1] I expected nothing less from someone like you, that you would lose interest in me. Well I have lost interest in you, so if you fall in love, I will fall in love with someone better than you, and if you get married, I will marry someone more elegant than you. Damn you, it's like you're always flying off the handle. You forgot me, got distracted from me! Send your dear lady some money,[2] and bring her to you from Wasit, before she starts to get angry. And by my life, give me a lute to use with a teak border and ivory inlay and gold embroidery, so that I can go singing with it.

Fie on you, O Ibn Jumhur! How quickly you forgot what you used to say to me: 'No sleep can satisfy me until I hold it in my hand, then I fall asleep.' Or perhaps you found one greater than it, softer, hotter, and tighter, and that is what has distracted you? Damn you! By my life, tell me the truth about it, even if the truth is something alien to you!

Translated from Arabic by Emily Selove and Geert Jan van Gelder

---

1 For *bawaik*, 'mocassins', see Dozy, *Supplément*. *Tamshak* (here in the dual) is a kind of shoe, variant of *shamshak*, from Persian *chamshak*. See the long poem by Abu l-Hakam al-Maghribi on a badly made pair in Ibn Abi Usaybiah, *Uyun*, ii, 165–66.

2 This must refer to his wife, who is in Wasit (see above).

Qabiha Jariyat al-Mutawakkil

Enjoy This Girl

You have spilled the cattle's blood seeking better health,
May God bring with it strength and health for you.
Drink, my master, this goblet
And with it enjoy this girl.
But keep some for the one who gifted her to you,
To enjoy the night that follows.

Translated from Arabic by Wessam Elmeligi

Farah Barqawi

Four Days to Fall In and Out of Love

She opened her eyes, abruptly, waking up from poor sleep, as if she were preparing for a difficult mathematics exam. She despises curtains and all kinds of veils, and with these curtains drawn, she jumps out of bed to check if the morning light has arrived. There's no light to be found yet, but she can hear a cock crowing in the distance. She resists looking at the mobile screen until 4:33 in the morning, when she surrenders. This is the second night in a row that she has awoken here, effortlessly, with no sense of fatigue. Outside the walls of her city, outside her bed, and outside her intimate circles.

On the bed next to her is a sleeping body she does not know well. A body she only just began exploring, two nights ago. A body like her body, with a length close to her length, with stretched and enchanting legs, with hair more rebellious than hers, carefully stylized features, silky lips, ears so tiny you want to eat them, a nose moulded as though one has never moulded so finely, and eyes she cannot describe.

The breasts are large and wide, crowned with two solid nipples. She used to mock the metaphor equating nipples with cherries until she saw these two literal cherries that disappear when it's night and warm, and they cling to urgency when craving and cold.

4.33 am, the body that she does not know well is in a deep sleep. She gets up, sneaks into the bathroom, sits on the toilet and expels out of her everything from last night. Venturing outside the walls of her city helps her bowels to flush out the unnecessary more quickly: body shit, and soul shit as well.

In the window of the small hall, the morning is slowly making its way towards the sky. The windows here are high. The other body once mocked that these windows were made for white women *and not for us*. Does anyone see her, walking half-naked, in front of this window? She sits on the sofa opposite to it, raises her bare legs and a slight tremor of cold strikes her. Her nipples too are soft, but they do not resemble cherries at all. Her nipples are like the heads of two rich pomegranates.

After two months of pull and push, she finally met up with her. They chose a neutral ground, a home that would not be affected by memories, a place with pure energy. They chose to encounter and engage with the unknown face to face. The woman had been waiting for her arrival at the airport with a mutual friend, hugged her warmly, put her mouth on her neck as if she had found her, lost after a long absence; then finally left her to greet their bystander friend.

The body is still in a deep sleep. The head rests on the left palm above the pillow, as if softly listening to words that could only be said in bed. The eyes retract for seconds, you see, what can she see in her sleep? The soft lips closed and fluffed, as if sleep had a bitter taste. As she returns and lies in the bed still warm, the body turns to surround her with a burning arm, finding its way around the abdomen and ribs.

On their second night, in the evening, she kissed her in front of her friends. It was not their first kiss, but it was the first kiss in front of others. Within two days she had travelled to her, secretly kissed her, soaked in the foreign body, and ultimately kissed her in public. She kissed her without feeling embarrassed. Her lover, with such piercing eyes, leaned slowly over her, just like that, and her lips curled as they would when she has a sip of red wine.

How had the kiss become so easy, natural, automatic, devoid of any confusion? On the plane she had thought of the first kiss:

How would it be and how would it be afterwards??

How was the kiss and where did it come from? Men, she knows them well, she knows the sensation of their big lips on hers, she knows she is a good kisser, and even takes pride in her kissing. But how to kiss these two smooth riverbanks?

It is all quite simple. Have two or three glasses of wine. Sit on the sofa in the small room and make sure to share interesting news and exciting funny stories. Then reach your hand towards her hair. Comment on the white spread in it. She will also make a comment on the silver that has started visiting your hair. Move away from her a little further to maintain the distance of doubt, the distance of an absence. After two more stories, and another glass, put your head on her shoulder. It will slide to her wide chest, where divine pillows wait for you, raise your head with a smile in search of her face, find her lips falling on your lips, falling without calculating, without warning, without asking for permission, and without fearing rejection. Two lips against two lips, two eyes against two eyes, curly hair against curly hair, pulpy breasts against pulpy breasts, and sequences of lightning and thunder of kisses longed for, for two months.

And kisses do not come alone for those who have missed each other, for those who are longing. Kisses come with wetness, lust and strong pinches on the skin. These kisses do not like clothes, they do not like to see something covering a body they desire. They do not like to see a single piece of fabric left on a body they crave. These kisses love the nakedness of the body and to strip the soul of all the knots, old stories, sticking stuff, and of any remaining confusion.

The body, ranging from sleep and arousal, clings to her as though they were alone in a sanctuary. Sleepy eyelids open her captive eyes, two eyes who know what they want, and know what to look at. The soft lips split open to say, 'Good morning, *'omri*, my life. Have you been up a while?' Cuddling grows deeper, a head slips over softened breasts and settles down to receive a swift round of kisses.

The both of them will spend the morning, noon and afternoon under the white sheets. They will talk about everything. Repeatedly, she will be determined to get up but won't succeed; they will smoke together; they will starve; they will thirst; will remain sunken in and beyond love until the phone rings letting a friendly voice come into idle day. She will kiss her before she gets up, 'For real' this time, and tell her: 'Tonight, we try my favourite move.'

The evening will come, and she will kiss her again in front of friends, then the night will get darker and they will fall asleep in orgasm; then the morning will rise after three successive orgasms and she will tell her: 'This is the life I want, if, in orgasm, I fall asleep and, in orgasm, I wake up.'

On that day the sky became bluer, embellished for them, so that they could walk together, wander in the market together, and talk about their fathers' annoying habits, eat as fast as starving women and listen to music. When the evening came, they returned to their temporary home, their little cloud. In the kitchen they had dinner and prepared for a farewell the next day, exchanging hugs, kisses and pinches. Rai music is playing in the background: 'sh'hal nhebbek enti ya bniah, ya bniah, ya bniah', 'O girl, how much do I love you.'

They opened the last bottle of wine and swallowed it down, insatiable, to intoxication. Tomorrow she will buy two bottles of the same wine before boarding and she will search for the scent of 'omri's perfume in the duty-free shops and she won't find it, so she will try not to take it as a sign that the scent will disappear. She will walk slowly as if every step was taking her further away from her sanctuary; she walks slowly. How can she walk at all, now that she has lost her balance?

On the plane back to her daily life, she sits by the window and remembers everything she had left four days ago to dive into her lover – all the reports, deliveries and calls. She thinks about her friends who are waiting on the other side, and replays the last evening with friends, relaxing in her lap without fear of being seen, the spontaneous kisses between two comforting lovers, the loneliness again, the love, the tears at the end of the night, the self-pity for her loss, the inebriation, the confessions, the long hugs, more confessions again, the last morning, the last moaning, and *I want to live with you. I wish I would come back to you at the end of a very long day. I wish that we'd meet your friends together, and laugh, and chat, and fuck. I wish you'd complain to your friends about me, and I about mine about you, you'd forgive me and I you … and ultimately we'd go home together to cuddle and immerse in our beloved passion.*

Translated from Arabic by Claire Savina

Nayla Elamin

boy, dancing

The sole of his foot touched the tile, white,
what? how does it feel?
cold would be the obvious answer but
no no no
it is a step on my hearts of hearts
Cold?
no no no
it will leave salt marks around your ankles, bracelets of salt
Red?
no no no
it will dance on your membranes
sharp elemental pain when you lift your eyes
naked feet on white tiles
boy's feet
no no no

Salomé

A Wedding Night for Zen

Breakfast the morning after the wedding was in the largest house in the row that ran along the side of the hill. Coffee had been set up in the conservatory, where moss grew around the *kilim*, and crayons were stamped into the floorboards like sealing wax. Zen had left her new husband alone in their tent and entered the house with a book in her pocket, in search of a bathroom and a place where she could sit and read and wouldn't be expected to introduce herself all over again. Only the newlyweds had slept in a hotel – the rest of the guests had camped on a sloping field with the smell of cow dung, joints and burnt sausages.

Zen and her husband had taken a day off to make a mini break of their weekend away for the Friday evening wedding. Zen had insisted on a trip to an exhibition of Japanese erotic art on the Friday morning, before they drove down. In the car, her husband, who had been unswervingly antipathic towards the exhibition, made conversation in the form of sharing gossip about the other wedding guests. There were two brothers and a woman she should look out for in particular, he told her. The woman had been married to the younger brother before she divorced him and married his older brother. The wedding was the first time the brothers were to meet since. Zen could see the scandal in that, but could not find it in herself, not for all the tea in China, or dual carriageways in Britain, to ask her husband why the exhibition had been such a source of annoyance to him.

The wedding invitation came from Zen's husband's

university friends. The weekend of the wedding, a group of them had, he told her, bought weed from a mature student who grew it under a leaded roof in a west country valley. The roofing was apparently impermeable to the police helicopters' heat monitoring equipment and preserved the integrity of these essential hydroponic skunk farms. On the first night, the Friday, there had been a lot of talk about how to confound, thwart and get around policing among the guests. Zen watched the wife of the two brothers glide around the party; her beauty hoisted high on her cheekbones.

Zen and her new husband were the only guests who lived in the city, though the wedding crowd came from no one place, for the groom was from Isfahan, and the bride was a descendant of Suffolk clergy. The hosts had also welcomed gypsies from the valley who'd arrived with their instruments, silver teeth and wide-brimmed hats. With the exception of the gypsies, who seemed to already know Zen better than she knew herself, the guests had been intrusively friendly and by midnight, Zen hadn't another engaging word to offer them. She had given herself up to alcohol and weed supplied by her husband's friends who had, by then, become less inquisitive. After the July sun that had engorged the marquee with a vast horizontal light sunk away into the valley, they'd been left with the light of torches stabbed into the ground by the tent pegs. The lighting had contorted the guests into eerie shapes with ethereal eyes.

Zen had not expected to recognise anyone in the morning.

For Saturday night, the day after the wedding, the bride and groom had a follow-up party planned. But first, breakfast in the conservatory was to be followed by a tour of the local burial grounds, which lay like nodes across the countryside's ley lines pulsating positive vibes into the local inhabitants, according to more than one of the guests Zen had been embraced by the previous evening.

Zen's chosen book, which she held in front of her face to

avoid making contact with the other campers who were now shuffling in for bread and eggs, was Franz Fanon's *The Wretched of the Earth*. She found herself reading the same sentence over and over again, getting no closer to realising the author's meaning and unable to make her own interpretation of what was written. The book had the desired effect on those guests who had heard of the author. There were nods of recognition, but the title was daunting enough, thankfully, to prevent anyone from engaging further with her on its content.

The younger brother, whose wife had left him with the style and treachery befitting a Greek goddess for his older sibling, had brought a new girlfriend with him for the wedding. The night before, Zen's husband had shown unusual interest in her and her dress, which clung to her body like fish scales and winked confused, solitary signals from dusk onwards. *Sexy*, he'd told the younger brother, who stooped over a tankard and let his hair touch at the high bump in his nose. His older brother had small, bite-sized tattoos running along his inner arms and walked with his legs placed apart, as though preparing to lift an object of some weight. When Zen's husband said s*exy*, the younger brother had looked at his girlfriend, who seemed to Zen more of a formula for a girlfriend than a person with any individual characteristics or atypical behaviours of her own. The girlfriend's body could not have been more different from Zen's; she flattened where Zen swelled, and grew to heights that Zen would never know. *Really sexy*, Zen's husband had said with approval, chuckling as though Zen wasn't there. The girlfriend emptied the space around her when she moved on the dance floor and Zen couldn't tell whether this was because she made the other dancers feel dumpy, or out of embarrassment, because she moved like her limbs were held onto her body by pins.

'Appearances are only one part of it,' the younger brother replied, avoiding the beckoning motions of his girlfriend to come join her on the dancefloor.

'I'm sure,' Zen's husband said. *The connoisseur*, thought Zen.

'Rarely up for it,' the younger brother looked towards the yurts on the edge of the forest before settling back on Zen's husband, who took it as an opportunity to flaunt his stuff.

'Oh, she's always up for it, my wife,' Zen's husband said, now remembering introductions. 'Zen, have you met?'

'Cool name,' said the younger brother.

'Short for Zenobia, not the Buddhists' Zen. Zenobia was the Queen of Palmyra–' Zen started, trying to inject new emotion into an old line, but she was thrown by the eyes behind the younger brother's fringe; they had the stare of refugee children, who can tell you with one look that you will never know what they have known. The younger brother cut her off by examining her neckline, causing Zen to lift her glass to her mouth, her eyes picking up his, before he looked away at the dance floor, now also empty of his girlfriend.

Zen returned to their tent before her husband on that first night. He'd blundered his way back later, stoned, telling her about the opium the uncles had smuggled through customs. Zen watched him zip a sleeping bag around his fully-clothed body, complaining about the thinness of the ground mattress and the pains in his stomach. He'd removed an arm only to tap Zen's arse to tell her they were getting him on stage with a microphone the next night, if she would believe that, before he passed out. Zen had turned off her torch and lay still, her body trying to settle into the English country earth, listening out for the Biblical lowing of cattle in the valley. A light had come on in the neighbouring tent and she could make out the movement of the older brother and his gliding wife in their tent next-door, streaks of limbs silhouetted against the thin fabric, entwined shadows reaching up to the stars. Zen heard their supressed laughter; their orgasmic pulses rocking the earth. Even the movement of nylon sleeping bags under bare bodies could be made out, a grunt followed by a sharp, distinctive gasp, the groan of male satisfaction, the murmurs of praise followed by the cooing congratulations of love. Zen couldn't believe how it was that a woman could come so fast, for it had sounded immediate, but genuine. Not for the first time she wondered whether there was an anatomical glitch in her body's wiring.

To make herself sleep, Zen put her hand between her legs and thought of the Japanese Shungo painting of the young wife being awoken by a man with a penis that, like all Shungo penises, was as thick as the trunk of a birch tree and headed by a slit concave cap. The elderly husband with his neat moustache sleeps on his back as the young wife opens her legs to this engorged limb, protruding from the groin of the young male intruder. In that moment the dimensions of the Shungo penis no longer felt like a joke, but an absolute necessity to Zen.

As the breakfast crowd continued to file into the conservatory, Zen curled up on her seat in the porch, trying to absorb wisdom from the printed page. An unhealthy-sounding car pulled up by the house, and footprints crunched across the gravel. Zen looked up as the door opened and the younger brother entered, his face and jacket shining with drizzle, his hair hanging in straight, wet bands down his face. Zen didn't smile. Neither did he. If it were anyone else, she would have assumed that they didn't remember who she was, but it wasn't that kind of look. He disappeared next door, into the room with the fire, which the uncles had come in to from their yurts to congregate around, build, and feed from. The younger brother had been taken in by the uncles the day before. Along with a couple of the other guests, he was in the yurt-rental business and had helped the uncles construct theirs. From her seat, Zen heard the uncles clapping their leathered arms around the younger brother's leathered body, asking him where he'd been. Zen heard him say 'station' and the name of the girlfriend. Still staring at the page, she recalled the sound of fractious voices and tears from the girlfriend of the younger brother late in the night; extracting words from the dreamworld of the night before to piece together a narrative of rupture. *Better,* said one of the uncles who gave a purr with the front of his tongue at the end of his words. *She was too, too* – and then a discussion for the right word amongst themselves – *stiff for you. Better, you will find another.*

The rest of the day – the walk to the ancient stones, the walk back, vegan hotdogs, cold tea – happened to Zen, but the memories of all that was flat, like photographs someone else has shown her. But even years later, Zen was acutely aware of how she'd felt later that day, in her body as well as her mind, when she was getting ready for the party, her hand shaking as she held the mascara brush to her lashes, whilst trying to stop misting the mirror propped against her bag. She recalled leaving their tent, drinking whisky from a silver flask passed to her by a man with a red cotton string tied around his neck, dancing with the same man, his leg catching between hers, his arm around her like a crowbar. Her hair, wettened by the summer showers, her head in a frenzy, the man pulling her in all directions across the dancefloor.

Then looking for her husband, trying to ensure that her dance partner did not take her for the wrong kind of amusement, Zen had wandered off and found a yurt perched above a clearing. Half of its flaps were rolled up, leaving those inside free to gaze out over the split hills. The uncles sat in a semi-circle around a stove. Zen later imagined the men wearing black eyeliner and red leather slippers, although she knew this was not the case, it was the way she wanted to remember the evening. They watched her as she entered and asked the stooped figure of the man who had not yet looked up about Zen. *Zenobia* the younger brother said. *She's named after a queen.* The uncles liked this. They passed a small bong between them. One inhaled, and looked at Zen with inflated eyeballs, nodding his head. When he let out a breath, he indicated a cushion, 'for the queen'.

The uncles watched her like a potential sister, wife, whore.

They wanted more information. 'Mo' the younger brother said, using the abbreviation of his name that Zen's husband liked to use among this crowd, 'She's Mo's wife.' The eyebrows rose, the eyes slid, the mouths paused. They didn't seem willing to accept this. The younger brother gave the name of the state boundaries that Zen and Mo's parents came from, which appeased the men to a degree. Then a joke that was not in a language Zen understood, but she had to look down anyway, for she was sure that they were laughing at what even strangers could see about her and her husband at a glance. The younger brother passed Zen the flask and she pulled at its smoke.

There was a scratching from outside. A microphone was being set up on a stage. Then the voice of the host announcing the band, talking about Mo – a good time kind of a guy. Zen excused herself from the yurt and its men. Outside she found the evening strangely bright; the sun setting in the valley caused stark flames of dying light to tear at the darkness, as though a fire was coming from the belly of Zoroaster himself.

She waited as minutes passed with Mo and the band still mucking around on the stage. The crowd was getting restless. They were a bunch who knew what to expect from musicians. Leaning against an outer tent post, Zen knew she did not want to be there watching her husband and she also knew that he wouldn't really care whether she did or not. She was trying to decide which realisation was sadder, when, instead of retreating back to her tent, a hand took hers and led her away from the lights, down a path towards a semi-lit yurt at the far edge of the field.

The yurt has a door. The younger brother steps out of his unlaced boots and Zen too, without a glance or a word, takes off her sandals, now pasted with blades of grass. He ushers her into a space where a fire in a bulbous pot casts shadows and throws heat onto the sides of the tent and across the sheepskin-covered floors. He allows her time to take in the domed space, but not enough to reflect on why they're there. She doesn't want to think, either. He pulls up her skirt with his hands, spreads them wide to cover her buttocks with his palms, and tugs off her panties. Having only washed herself in a basin she flinches at the thought of her odour, but his head is already bent beneath her. She catches her balance against a post of the low bed, her dress is now unbuttoned, her breasts pulled out of the bra cups encasing them. The bottom of her skirt is around her waist and he's sucking her into him through his mouth, breathing the sweat around her crevices and her armpits, squeezing her nipples between his fingers.

An opiated blur has invaded Zen's body. Her head is disconnected, her nipples are raw nerve endings and feel as though they've been turned inside out. Her pulse lies firmly between her legs. The sight of the younger brother's profile angled against her breasts makes her widen her legs under him, she watches him stand as she pulls at his belt and undoes the buckle with quick fingers. He puts his hands in her hair and thrusts himself towards her face. Her dress is ruched around her middle, pulled down from her chest. Zen later remembers crawling to get high enough to take him in her mouth. She only just tastes him when he indicates that he doesn't want more of that. He gets her to lean forward on the bed, his hands moving up and down her, his fingers pushing her cheeks apart, plunging into the source of her. She pulls a cushion under her raising herself to him as she hears from afar the opening bars of a guitar with lines sung too close to the mic. A cheer from the audience and she's so scared that the younger brother will stop, that he won't enter her, that she begs him to go on and he laughs a bit at her determination as he nudges against her untouched lips, before he enters, waiting for the drummer to crash on, so that the band's noise will hide their own.

Zenobia and Mahmoud leave early the next day to avoid Sunday traffic. At the slip road onto the motorway, she reflects on the second time when she came on top and he took her breasts in his hands, before pulling her down so he could bite them. She is certain that fragments of the explosion that came out of her are still lodged in her innards. The couple listen to the news on the radio as they move into the fast lane. Mahmoud gives commentary which she mainly agrees with, but he concedes on one point that she argues on the basis of a recent article she's read. On the Oxford bypass she thinks of the younger brother's mouth buried in her.

Zen wonders whether by the middle of the week the throbbing will stop. That doesn't happen, but both Zenobia and Mahmoud do go on to be most successful in their respective professions and good companions throughout the rest of their lives.

Umra bint al-Hamaris

Rock and Shake

Who would tell a single man about the unmarried
Daughter of al-Hamaris, the short old man with thick haunches,
The girl whose legs are shapely and knees are round,
And who would rock and shake when a phallus is found?

Translated from Arabic by Wessam Elmeligi

Qasmuna bint Ismail

The Unnamable Remains

It is said that Qasmuna's father, Ismail, enjoyed improvising verse with her. One day he said: 'Finish this poem'.

I had a friend whose rare delight,
Though it rewarded care with spite,
Itself exonerated.

Qasmuna thought for a moment and replied:

So the sun, to which for all its light
The moon is obliged, is still by it
Obliterated.

One day she looked in the mirror and considered that she was beautiful and had not married. She said:

There I see a garden ripe
For reaping, but not one
Palm spread for picking.
With what pains tender
Days are wasted. Only
The unnamable remains.

Her father heard this and began to think of her marriage. On seeing a passing doe, she said:
Doe, forever grazing

On meadows, we are sisters
In wildness, in the contrast
Between eye-white and iris.
Alone, companionless,
We bear the fate
Set down for us.

Translated from Arabic by Yasmine Seale

lisa luxx

to write the wrongs of centuries,
we must brew our own tools

no physician predicted this
between major & minor notes
an itch   of a bird song
        & you, my dawn

            grinding saffron

year ٢١٠
pestle & mortar

bury   in me   your sigh
as our soil carries dead
            in airless secrets

        i hold your breath

        centuries persist
        men dumb & ink

my saffron grind   crushes
                            beard & bible
                                to dust

all of this, embroidered in waistbands

ya zarrifa   *how I dress you up*

    petrified   in gold thread
                  sewn by mist

                we survive the long hush

                i hold your breath

drench   tonight's bedsheets in sweat

wet, tip, & reaching
we open   lips

    exhale   saffron ink
    your cupped hand, gathering

    they call this *lesbian*

       I kiss your knee   call you *comrade*
       we laugh & the sound is a language that
               hasn't been written yet

Anonymous

What is its Name?

In a Baghdad market, a beautiful woman (referred to only as 'the buyer' in the text) engages the services of a porter, who carries all her shopping home and discovers that she lives with her two sisters – 'the keeper' and 'the owner'. Amazed by what he glimpses of their life of pleasure without men, he persuades them to let him stay for dinner. Wine is served.

'Drink,' said the buyer, 'and be well. The wine will bring you health, banish the pain and quicken the cure.'

And they drank, draining and filling and draining their cups, until the porter, full of wine, fell to singing bawdy songs, began to dance, and set upon them with his teeth and fingers, pinching, prodding, and one of them fought back with food, the other with words, the third with flowers, but he was in the fold of pleasure.

They went on like this until the wine played in their heads, and when drink had outdone them, the keeper rose and stepped out of her clothes, loosed her hair and let it screen her, and threw herself naked into the pool.

Surfacing, she danced in the spray and dipped her head duckwise, filled her mouth with water and shot it at the porter, and washed her breasts and navel and between her thighs.

Then she rushed out of the pool into the porter's lap, pointed to her heat and said, 'My lord, my love, what's this?'

'Your womb,' he said.

'Whoa! You have no shame,' she said, and cuffed him on the neck.

'Your mound,' he said.

And one sister shouted, 'Ugly word!' and nipped him.

'Your cunt,' he said.

And the other hammered at his chest to cries of 'Shame!' and knocked him back.

'Your sting,' he said.

And the naked woman smacked him and said, 'No.'

'Your dip,' he said, 'your dingle, your disclosure.'

'No no no.'

And every word he said won him a slap and the same question, 'What is this?' as this girl hammered, that one pinched, the other prodded him until at last, he said, 'What is its name?'

'Basil of bridges,' she said.

'Basil of bridges! You could have told me sooner – ow!'

The cup was passed around.

Then the buyer rose, stripped as her sister had done, and threw herself naked into the pool, dipped her head duckwise, and washed her belly and around her breasts, between the thighs. Then she rushed out of the pool into the porter's lap and said, 'Heart of my heart, what's this?'

'Your mound,' he said.

She gave him a blow to shake the room and said, 'You have no shame.'

'Your womb,' he said.

And one sister shouted 'Ugly!', with a slap.

'Your sting,' he said.

And the other sister cuffed him and said, 'Whoa! No shame at all.'

They went on like this: one pricked, another swatted, that one elbowed him as he kept trying (cunt, womb, dip) and they said, 'No no no.'

'Basil of bridges!' he cried at last and all three women laughed until they fell, then came down on his neck with blows harder than ever and said, 'No.'

'What is its name?' he said.

'The sesame seed, we call it.'

'Hallelujah! The sesame seed!'

Then the girl put on her clothes and they sat back to drink, the porter moaning at the pain in his shoulders and his neck. Then the owner, the most beautiful, removed her clothes in turn as the porter rubbed his neck and pleaded, 'For the love of God, my neck, my shoulders . . .'

The woman dived and disappeared into the pool, and the porter's eyes settled on her naked form, which was like a slice of moon, and on her face, which was both full moon and yellow dawn, and took in her full length, her breasts and heavy dancing hips, bare as her Lord had made her, and he let out a long 'Oh', and said these lines:

> If I compare your figure to the tender
> Green bough, the lie oppresses me
> For boughs all robed in leaf are lovelier
> But you unrobed are loveliest to see.

The girl, at these words, rushed out of the pool into the porter's lap, pointed to her heat and said, 'Light of my eyes, my little liver, what is this?'

'Basil of bridges,' he said.

'Bah!'

'Sesame seed,' he said.

'Uff!'

'Your womb,' he said.

'Yoh! So little shame,' she said, and came down on his neck.

To make the story short, my King, it went like this: the porter said, 'Its name is so-and-so,' and she said, 'No no no,' and when he had his fill of bites and blows, when his neck was bruised and swollen he said, 'Well, what is its name?'

'Hotel happiness,' she said.

'Hotel happiness!'

She rose and dressed, and they passed the cup between them for a while. At last the porter stood, took off his clothes (a dangling thing between his thighs) and leapt into the pool … But morning gained on Shahrazad and cut her speaking short.

Excerpt from 'The Porter and the Three Women of Baghdad',
The Thousand and One Nights

Translated from Arabic by Yasmine Seale

Ulayya bint al–Mahdi

Love Thrives

Love thrives on playing hard to get, or else it wears off.
A bit of unmixed love is better than a cocktail

Translated from Arabic by Abdullah al-Udhari

Fadwa Al Taweel

Sky Lounge Dubai

The roof terrace glowed blue like a sapphire. Couches were scattered around artfully, facing out over the dark water. Someone was glancing stealthily at me between cigarettes and sips of their drink. I got up and walked towards her, the wind toying with strands of my hair. The pounding in her chest must have felt as loud as the click of my high heels, but she lifted her chin like a hero and crushed her cigarette in the ashtray, ready for me. I sat down on the edge of her table, poised like some tableau from a renaissance painting. My dress rode halfway up my thighs. Leaning towards her, I lit her a fresh cigarette, and, just for a second, her gaze rose to admire the line of my breasts before she leant back in her seat, and looked away indifferently.

I smiled, and like a warm knife through fat, I went straight to the subject:

'I hear you've been making false accusations.'

A brief inhalation conveyed her disdain. 'False accusations?' She replied. 'Twisting the facts, making things look like something other than what they are – isn't that what you're good at?'

'So people seem to think. But do you really think I'm a murderer?'

Slowly, she blew a long stream of smoke into my face. I inhaled it greedily.

'You tell me: are you a murderer?'

'You saw the police report. Death by natural causes.'

'That's what the police concluded based on the evidence as

it appeared to them. But what things look like, and what they are, are often two very different things."

I was clicking my fingers along to the beat of the background music playing in the lounge. As the song came to an end, I let my red lacquered nails of my right hand come to rest on her shirt collar.

'There aren't any loose buttons here, are there?'

She narrowed her eyes and smiled grudgingly.

'I'm not wearing a hidden mic, if that's what you're looking for.'

I bit my lip.

'Or something else,' I said casually, and slid my hand into the inside pockets of her jacket.

She sighed, then calmly moved my hand away from her body. 'Stop it.'

'Why? Planes don't stop mid-air. They can't go backwards. It's takeoff, enjoy the ride, or land.'

She looked at me, her eyes bright, unreadable. 'We're not on a flight right now. I'm investigating a string of murders, and you're the prime suspect.'

I nodded, impressed. She was tough.

'Okay,' I said. I took one of her cigarettes from the open case on the table and toyed with the idea of lighting one for myself. 'Let's agree on one thing, then I promise I'll tell you the truth.'

'And what's that?'

'We go to the bathroom together. You take off everything you're wearing, and prove to me you're not wearing a microphone. Then I'll talk.'

She laughed throatily, her legs apart.

'You just can't control yourself, can you? That's what this is all about. You kill your husbands when they begin to disgust you in bed. You're desperate for it. Nobody's lived up to your wild fantasy yet, and you can't put up with their sweaty smell, their ugly, rasping, voices. Their vapid oriental masculinity. Killing them is the only way out. You get rid of one partner in the hope the next one might be able to satisfy your sex drive.'

I got up from the table and waved to the waitress.

'Two more glasses please.'

I held out a hand.

'Shall we go?'

She took my hand firmly and pulled me behind her, leading the way to the bathroom. We went into one of the cubicles, which was only just big enough for the two of us. She emptied her pockets – wallet, keys, mobile phone – into the sink then, without hesitating, took off her clothes, one item at a time. When only her bra and black trousers were left, she stopped and looked me in the eye.

'Is this enough for you?'

I leant against the wall.

'Your trousers,' I said, savouring the word like a red lollipop.

With a half-smile, like she'd known it was coming, she undid the top button and then the zip. It cut straight through the muffled quiet of the public bathroom. She was wearing white underwear that reflected the clear, wheatlike colour of her skin. She didn't blink once: our eyes were locked, like the simultaneous orgasm of a newly-married couple on their third night alone together. Without giving her any warning, I tugged her trousers down with both hands and let them drop to the floor; nothing concealed fell out. I picked up her clothes and tossed them over the dry washbasin, and said, 'I'll wait for you outside.' I was about to slip out, when she pushed me up against the wall so the smooth tile pressed on my cheek, and her body pressed on mine.

'You'll wait right here,' she whispered. 'Is that clear?'

Suddenly there were several sharp knocks on the door outside.

'Your drinks are at your table,' the waitress called. The message was clear enough: you're being watched, enough messing around, get out of there right now. The detective dressed quickly, her eyes wary; she still thought I'd run for it and break our agreement.

We returned to the table and sat down in the same places as before. She took a sip from the drink, wetting her lower lip.

'Sitting on the table like that – is it meant to give you the upper hand?'

'No,' I said. 'I just like to sit where the breeze can touch my skin instead of hiding it under the table.'

'Drink,' she said, pushing the other glass toward me. 'It's time to confess.'

I took three sips: one for each dead husband.

'Sure, I killed them.'

She straightened in her seat, like she'd nearly reached the finishing line but not yet broken the tape.

'Why?'

I got up from the table and shouldered my bag.

'Our agreement said I'd tell the truth, not prove it. That's your job, not mine. See you around, detective.'

I walked away, but she caught me up instantly. She was too good; she left me powerless.

'Let me walk you to your room.'

'No need, it's on the same floor as the lobby.'

'Even easier.'

She followed me to my room, where she graciously took the keycard from me and opened the door, then handed it back. We were separated now by the contrasting patterns of the carpet in the room and the carpet in the corridor. Seeing myself on her tongue like a piece of soft candy, I couldn't resist lashing out.

'By the way, I don't love women. I don't have any particular interest in them. What you said before – that I killed my husbands for sexual reasons – it's true. But unfortunately, it's not like a woman would be able to stop me killing again. So I wish you luck with the case. And with arresting me. Good night, detective.'

Her eyes glinted like a key had turned in its lock.

'I've just closed the case,' she replied. 'I'm not wearing a hidden mic, but you should have checked the room before you let your tongue run away with you. Good night. Maybe this time it will be a woman that stops you.'

Translated from Arabic by Katharine Halls

Sahib Jariyat ibn Tarkhan An-Nakhas

Your Cool Lips

I saw in my dreams,
That you let me taste your cool lips,
As if your hands were in mine,
And we spent the night in the same bed.

She responded,

You dreamt well,
and all that you envisioned
You shall get, in spite of those who envy us.
I hope you embrace me,

And stay on my top of breasts upright,
And we remain the most blessed lovers at night
And have a conversation with no one watching us.

Translated from Arabic by Wessam Elmeligi

Nayla Elamin

Drink Me, Smash Me

the long fingers are resting.
one hand on the small of my back
the other around my neck

pressing and pulling
caressing and hurting

the pale long midriff fits perfectly
roundly, between my thighs
like a cup on a saucer

drink me smash me
I want to feel your thumbs pressing my orbits
diaphragm deflated by the weight of your knee
your hipbone blooming bruises on my shank

my arms are flaying the darkest air
I gasp like fish on the shore
my head in your hands, turned the other way
as you leave for the wilderness, again and again

Randa Jarrar

A Map of Home (An Excerpt)

The cool thing about Baba being gone was I could do whatever I wanted. One night I lied and told Mama I was sleeping over at Jiji's and I indulged myself and took a taxi, orange and rickety, its leather and driver scented with fumes, out to Montazah. I had fears, fantasies, of the driver swerving into the wood in the pitch dark and raping me beneath the sky. He didn't, and I forgot to tip him. I walked to the fence by the private beach and skipped it, then tiptoed around onto the sand. It was closing time and no one was in the water.

I slipped off my shirt and shorts, balled them up into my high tops, and left them in the sand. The grains were cold and soft, like semolina, and I got into the water slowly. It swallowed me in its darkness and I floated in to honour it, closed my eyes and listened to its familiar sound. Under the water. Under the water, a few miles out, lay ancient ruins, and I pretended to swim down to them, to those sunken subkingdoms and cities of Heracleion and Canopus where I touched the statues' eyes, watched their dead-awake faces. I saw pink granite gods, and a sphinx of Cleopatra's baba, Ptolemy XII. I saw silverware: I saw pots and pans, bottles and plates, weapons from Napoleon's sunken 1798 fleet, and a green statue that held something huge in its hand. I couldn't tell what it was until I swam closer; it was a pen. I opened my eyes again. I was just a few yards from the shore, and I saw Fakhr sitting in the sand, his shirtless torso facing the street, waiting for me. I waved, then decided to wade out and get him; he saw me before I was out all the way and came after me.

I swam away from him and he swam faster toward me. I didn't say hello, he didn't either, and I stopped stroking the waves when I could no longer reach. I turned around and watched him watch me until he stood in front of me; he could still reach the sandy floor bottom, and I wrapped my legs around his waist. He cupped me in his hands and I kissed his salty mouth, salty with sweat and salt water, and he grew against my bathing suit bottom. I rubbed myself against him then and the waves gently rose and fell, and he bit and licked my neck as I found out again how used to water I was and the wetness inside me rivalled the wetness that surrounded me.

Laura Hanna

Pole Play

Eyes open
it starts
lit like a wick and white hot,
a firework fuse.
Trace the liquid chalk line and feel the burn.

See me
sea creature, all jellied and spiked,
a surging current with a steal spine
winding tighter with each electric tide,
rising higher with each climb.

Watch me
brave flesh breaking free in blushes
from undercover living, cuffed in quiet crimes,
flushed with blood and bruised with incarnadine kisses.
The criminal softness of bronze.

Feel me
strength in my grip to lift you up
and squeeze out stillness
a shudder, submission to the heel-clack crack of a whip,
loud as Lucifer's hooves,
scoring my dominion in the scorched earth
I'll lay my damsel down.

Eyes open.

Keep watching, follow me now.

The dance isn't over if you can still hear the sound.

Eyes open

the dance isn't over until I touch the ground.

Eyes open

the dance isn't over.

I'timad Arrumaikiyya

I Urge You To Come

I urge you to come faster than the wind to mount my breast and firmly dig and plough my body, and don't let go until you've flushed me thrice.

Translated from Arabic by Abdullah al-Udhari

Salwa Al Neimi

Seventh Gate: On the Ecstasies of the Body

I opened myself to him with all my senses. I gazed at him.
Savoured his smell. Hung on his every word. He would talk and
I loved his words, words that ignited my desire. He mixed the
poetry he recited and the words of his own pleasure in his cries.
When I drew close to the abyss, he would control the rhythm
of my movements. This is torture! I would cry in protest. Later
I would understand and learn in turn how to hold back my
quest for the final shudder, the shudder that left me breathless,
smeared with honey and semen; I would learn how to hug my
freshly picked pleasure like a heartbeat between my legs.

The first time I saw him. We were with a group of friends,
men and women, at a dinner party. Mezzé and Lebanese arak and
chatter and political discussions and risqué jokes and laughter.
He was doing the rounds, saying goodbye to everyone. It was
still early. When he got to me, he gave me a polite, distant kiss,
and suddenly the smell of his body reached me: the smell of
desire. I breathed it in and realized that we would meet again
and that this smell would fill my lungs and the pores of my skin.

'Whence springs love?' asks Ibn Arabi.

'I love what fills me with light and increases the darkness
deep within me,' answers René Char.

Between the question and the intimidation of the reply, I
moved ever closer to the Thinker, becoming more aware of the
dangerous game that was defining itself in the space between us.

Ever since I met the Thinker; even after all these years, not
a single day has gone by without my thinking of him. I cannot

desire a man without thinking of him. I cannot read a newspaper without thinking of him. Every day, something reminds me of him.

What? What reminds me of him?

Every day of my life is linked to him. With him I learnt to swim slowly, to sink beneath my own undertow, toward the bottom, calmly, confident that he was with me, and that when I opened my eyes I would find him there.

Open my eyes? I didn't really close them. I tried to remain wakeful, alert. To see him, and be seen by him.

The first time I saw him. I was in the metro. I was reading a satirical newspaper. I raised my eyes and saw him staring at me. He was sitting opposite me, talking with friends. I went back to my reading, but I was distracted. There was something in him that called to me; something in his look that called to me. Our eyes met again, and that stubborn, exploratory look was trained on me. We got off at the same station. We each went our own way with a last, lingering look. But I didn't have enough time to register that look so that I might recall it and try to decipher it.

The first time I saw him. He was sitting in front of me at the political conference I had come to attend. He was with a group of people that I knew. A mutual friend introduced us and from that point on he did not leave me. He stayed by my side, and I felt good. For two days we did not leave one another; we parted only in the evening, each returning to our respective life.

He gestured to his throat. 'It grabs me here,' he said at the end of the second day, for my ears only. Had I heard him correctly? When he repeated these words, I knew that I had been waiting for them. I almost gave that half serious, half mocking laugh that I use to avoid the issue. But then I didn't dare. I didn't dare play with him the game that I play with others. His presence was so complete that it obliged me to answer him. I felt dizzy. How did

I know that I had to make my decision at that instant, or lose him?

I didn't want to lose him.

The first time I saw him. I was with the Palestinian film director. He was in Paris for just a few days and we had agreed that we'd meet at a café in the Quartier Latin known for its Arab clientele. He was with two other men at the next table. I heard something in Arabic about the situation in Lebanon. I could see his face; the two others had their backs to me. He was opposite me, talking somewhat angrily, and his eyes never left mine. As one of his friends stood to leave he recognized the Palestinian film maker. Greetings and congratulations all round, and they put the two tables together. He sat next to me, and from that point on, never left my side. He talked and laughed, as though a sudden happiness had taken him unawares. His bare arm brushed against mine. How many times did his bare arm brush against mine? 'I'm sorry. I don't usually behave like that, but something stronger than me made me move closer to you.' He told me later, when I was in his arms.

He was forever reciting poetry. Whole poems that he'd learnt by heart. He'd read them to me and I'd imagine he was writing them over again, for me alone.

Was poetry one of the keys to my body?

Poetry was there between us. He loved me through the poems of others. When he was travelling, he would phone me to give me the name of a collection and a poem. I would look for the poet, read the words, and know that he was with me.

Pessoa, Cavafy, Char, Michaux; others I didn't know. I became like him. I would learn the Arabic poems that I loved by heart and recite them for him, and only him.

Was poetry always there between us?

With him, I started writing my short poems once again and it became an opening ritual for each of our encounters. He'd ask me about my words. In silence, I would offer him the poem and he would read as though discovering the dark side I concealed with frivolity and laughter. He would discover things that I didn't dare reveal even to myself. In silence, he would fold the paper carefully and put it in his pocket.

Was my body one of the keys to poetry?

The first time I saw him. I was at a Book Fair in an Arab capital. I was filling in for a colleague who'd fallen ill at the last moment; the director had chosen her to represent the library. I went in her place, somewhat grudgingly. When a representative of the fair came to welcome the five people arriving from Paris, he was next to me. His questions gave off a magnetic force, under the mask of a legitimate curiosity. A form of conversation without end. He opened up to me, and I to him. He told me how he'd seen me at the airport, and how he'd watched me from his seat on the plane. It was as though he knew me. I told him the same story: it was as though I knew him. Our encounters do not end, and the body is always the preamble. The body was the basis of our story.

Every morning, the Thinker accompanies my nudity. It's enough for me to look at myself naked in the mirror to remember his words about my body. About my breasts, my ass, my sex, my skin, my smell, my colour.

I recall his words and I shudder, but I want to forget, to get on with my life.

The Thinker used to ask me, 'Do you know what it is I love about you?'

I would give him a knowing look and I laughed.

'No, it's not what you think, even though *I do love your dirty mind.*'

Laughing, he repeated the well-known English phrase.

'I wasn't thinking anything. I was just waiting for the answer.'

'I love two things about you. Your free spirit and your Arabness.'

'Never in my life would it have occurred to me that a free spirit and Arabness could be the height of sex appeal,' I replied, with a light-heartedness that tried to hide the pain racking my consciousness, as the words penetrated deep within, to re-emerge later on, letter by letter.

Now I recall his words and I shudder. Now I recall his words, his touch, his gaze and I shiver.

I recall them now and I do not want to forget.

I want to remember.

I want to write.

Multiple scenarios; identical first encounters. The sudden discovery of the other, the looks exchanged, the words repeated, the nervous laughter, the unintentional touches, the anguish of the moment of declaration. How is it that we re-create all these details differently each time?

Which of these first times was the Thinker's? All, or none of them? The minor details differ, but the story remains the same. I love details, in any story; their colour gives a new meaning to each story.

Every new man is a new story. Which of these stories is the Thinker's?

The Distant One sent me an email, in English, with a stupid joke called 'The Woman and the Bed.':

When she's eight, you take her to bed to tell her a story.

When she's eighteen, you tell her a story to take her to bed.

When she's twenty-eight, you don't need to tell her a story to take her to bed.

When she's thirty-eight, she tells you a story to take her to bed.

When she's forty-eight, she tells you a story to avoid having to go to bed.

When she's fifty-eight, you go to bed to avoid her story.

When she's sixty-eight, if you take her to bed, then that's the story.

When she's seventy-eight, what bed; what story? What devil of a man are you?

A stupid joke of the sort men tell one another in an attempt to forget the trap they've fallen into. What I found interesting were the two alternating motifs – the bed and the story.

In my life, one has led to the other, and vice versa. In my life, they have been intimately linked, and I oscillate between the two.

In my life, I have been addicted to beds and stories. Every man is a story and every story is a bed. I don't want to lose the bed. I don't want to lose the story.

On the bed of stories I sway and strut.

I touch the sky with my fingers

And dig valleys in the desert of my soul.

'I would use *firash* for bed,' the Distant One wrote to me after I'd emailed back to him the translation into Arabic of his joke. 'Why do you use *sarir*?'

I replied, 'The *firash* for me, is for sleeping and sickness, childbirth and death. The *sarir* is for pleasure. The *sarir* is for pleasure. *Sarir* is from sirr, or 'secret'. Two words which have the same root. Desire is secret. Pleasure is secret. Sex is secret. Sex is the secret of secrets. That is why in my mind it remains linked to the *sarir*, even if I do it in a lift.'

'Have you done it in a lift?' asked the Distant One in his reply.

I pictured his thick eyebrows raised in avid curiosity.

'Not even on the beach!' I replied, shortly.

I love secrets. These stories that no one knows by me. These stories give my life meaning. An entire life that belongs to me alone, that I share with no one. It's enough for me to close my eyes to taste the honeyed juice of pleasure, as it is called in the Hadith, the sayings of the Prophet. It's enough for me to close my eyes and the image rises before me, the sound, sight, smell, touch, and taste. It's enough.

Could I go on living without them? Could I wake up every morning and find the strength to begin a new day without them? The answer comes clear and sharp as the blade of the sword, and I am not afraid.

In the long spans between stories, I live off memories, confident that the coming days will bring me my new story.

I could not merely wait, because I don't know how to wait. Nor could I principate them. And then? I often asked myself this question, without ever really looking for an answer. The answers, like the stories, came of their own accord, in their own time, as ripe fruit falls from the tree.

An Excerpt from The Proof of the Honey
translated from Arabic by Carol Perkins

Shurooq Amin

Hymen Secrets: Girl with a Box

Seed-rich box carry my secret pulp scraped
virginity pressed
    like a new flower
between old pages
cloudy blue   behind me   moon glowing
shaft cut scandal-stained   cretaceous white
carry my hymen's secret   oh scabrous secret
of   one   more   protean   woman
r   e   –   v   i   r   g   i   n   i   s   e   d.

Ulayya bint al-Mahdi

Give My Greetings

Give my greetings to this buck,
Swaying in beautiful dalliance.
Give him my greetings and say,
'You are the lock of the hearts of men.
You left my body exposed in the morning sun,
While you resided in the shade with doves.
You have reached a place within me
That I cannot handle.'

Translated from Arabic by Wessam Elmeligi

Nedjma

The Almond (An Excerpt)

Driss got me settled in his living room, gave me strawberries and blueberries. Then he ran a bath, carried me at arm's length and sat me fully dressed in the bathtub, its water fragrant with orange blossoms. Chopin whirled between the walls of the house, and through the collar of Driss's shirt I glimpsed his dense black hair.

He took my shoes off, caressed my toes and the bottoms of my feet. I was frozen. His mouth and breath burned my neck, ran down the full length of my legs. My breasts engorged and the wet fabric that was clinging to my skin made the nipples stand out, making me even more naked under his watchful eye. He squeezed and nibbled on them, and they doubled in size between his teeth. I was trembling, terrified, like a bird caught in a tornado, my womb aching with desire, my belly contracted with terror. What was he going to do to me? What had I come looking for?

He undressed me slowly, delicately, the way you loosen the fragile skin from a green almond. In the steam of the bathroom, I could barely distinguish his features. Only his eyes, which bored into me, drilling my heart and my vagina, masters of my fate. I told myself I was a whore. But I knew that I was not. Unless it was like the pagan goddesses of Imchouk, who were uninhibited femmes fatales, stark raving mad.

He soaped my upper and lower back, covered my pubis with foam. Its hair concealed my privacy from his look, but his fingers quickly slid beneath my panties and opened the lips, finding my clitoris, hard as a chickpea, then pressed down with a delicate and meditative gesture. I moaned, tried to take down my panties, but he wouldn't let me. He turned me over, embraced my thighs, and made me arch my back. There you are I said to myself. You are his plaything. His object. He can do anything now, rip out your tongue, tear open your heart, or make you the Queen of Sheba.

Lowering my panties, he put his cheek on my buttocks, spreading the crack with his fingers and making room for his nose. I was wet. Then he took a small flask from one of the shelves, removed a drop of oil, and perfumed my anus with it, massaging it for a long time, to the point that I forgot my trepidation and my muscles began to relax as his knowledgeable hands became more focused. I had no idea what he wanted to do to me but was wishing that he would just do it and certainly not stop the circular motion that was driving me wild, opening me up for him, as my vagina discharged its joy in long translucent strands.

He found the spot, reaped my wetness, and daubed my buttocks with it before sinking his teeth in. No bite has ever been dearer to me. I could hear my belly laugh, weep, then bubble over with excitement. I begged, 'Enough…enough,' praying all the while that he wouldn't stop.

Then he carried me, dripping wet and moaning, to the bed. As soon as he bent over to lay me down, I pulled him by the collar, put my mouth on his, sucking his tongue, making the buttons on his shirt pop open, and bit his torso. He was laughing, beaming, squeezing my breasts with both hands, drawing their incandescent tips into his mouth, one finger roaming the edge of my soaking entry. My patience exhausted, I managed to inhale the dawdling visitor. My orgasm threw me up against him, panting and deeply embarrassed.

He didn't give me any time to catch my breath, guided my hands towards his fly and watched me open it. Incredulous, I discovered a sex organ that was stronger and larger than those I had seen before. It was brown and ripe, its skin silky and its glans impressive. I put my lips on it, improvising a caress until then unknown to me. He let me do it and watched me almost faint. I had him in my mouth and the magic of that touch alone made my belly convulse. I had no idea what animal was churning around inside there, nor why this cock provided me with so much pleasure as it came and went between my lips, rubbing my palate, gently tapping my teeth as it moved by. Driss remained upright, eyes closed, his flat belly filling me with the amber smell of his sweat and skin.

He left my mouth, raised my legs. The head of his penis knocked against my vagina. I pushed to help and let him in, but a hideous burning bowled me over. He took up the charge again, tried to interfere, ran into an unforeseen tightness, withdrew, and wanted to force the passage. I was moaning but not with pleasure anymore, now with pain, still wet but incapable of letting him enter. He took my face in his hands, licked my lips, then said smitten and laughing:

'My word, you're a virgin!'

'I don't know what's happening to me.'

'What's happening to you is what happens to any woman when she neglects her body for too long.'

He realised that I was in pain, caressed my back, licking and nibbling, sucking at my labia for a long time. He never lost his hardness for a moment; his cock feverishly striking against my belly, my buttocks, and my legs.

It was only when he supported my back with a pillow, placed his sex at the entrance of my rosebud, insisting on slipping in a few millimetres at a time, that he was finally able to fill me up, dilating my dripping wet walls, massaging my womb, pounding me with long slow movements, his sweat dripping on my breasts. He managed to open me, possess me, widen me until I was breathless, smoothing my lungs and the tiny fibres of my belly. His sperm gushed out in long streams and, like rain, flowed against my exposed wetness, purifying its earlier debasement.

He remained snuggled against me for a long time, and it was only when he was groping for his packet of cigarettes that I saw his tears.

He didn't want me to get dressed again or put my wet panties on; he just smiled when he saw me hide my private parts with my hands. I sensed his bafflement, caused as much by my modesty as by my awkwardness. Eyes half closed, he muttered, 'Ah, if only you could see yourself!' I was afraid he might dislike some detail of my body. He guessed that, held my arms behind my back, drank from my mouth, then put his head between my legs. I shrank back, bruised with pleasure and pain. My second deflowering had made me unable to tolerate any further caress.

'Don't go home tonight, Badra, my wounded kitten,' he asked.

'Aunt Selma won't sleep a wink all night.'

'I'll deal with her tomorrow. In the meantime, look what I have for you.'

He took a midnight blue box from the inside pocket of his jacket. Two diamonds lay sleeping inside it. Two limpid drops of water. I gave him back the opened box.

'What are you doing?'

I kept silent, tormented by too many contradictory feelings.

'They've been waiting or you for a month. I didn't know how to give them to you without offending you.'

He took my hands in his, as he had done the first evening, and skimmed across them with a kiss.

'I've been waiting for you for so long, Badra.'

I looked at him, dying to believe him, but mistrusting the man after being showered with the male of him.

'You're a *houri*, you know? Only houris recover their virginity after every coitus.'

I answered in cold and almost sarcastic anger.

'You're like all the others! You want to be the first!'

'But I am the first! And I don't give a damn about the others and what they want. I want you, you, my almond, my butterfly!'

He attached the water drops to my ears, caressing the lobe of each with the tip of his tongue. As if in a flash of lightning, I became aware that he was completely naked and that his cock had not grown slack. Worse, I discovered that I was still hungry and thirsty for his kisses and his sperm.

Desire is contagious, and Driss was very astute. He forced my legs open, smoothed my crumpled flesh, and applied a balm to soothe my irritated spots. Then he slipped his sex between my breasts and pressed them together, half serious, half playful.

'Every particle of your skin is a bed of love and a source of ecstasy,' he said.

I blushed, remembering the power he had used to explore my every nook and cranny. But I couldn't feel guilty, disparaged, or outraged. His cock came and went between my breasts, gently bumping against my mouth at the end of each motion. When he flooded my chest with his milk, I sighed, sated. He delicately spread his liquid on my throat, put a finger to my lips to have me taste it. Driss was sweet and salty.

I shivered when he whispered in my ear:

'You'll see, one day you'll drink me! When you feel completely confident.'

I felt like answering him, 'Never,' but remembered the pleasure he had just given me. The taste of eternity. The world had suddenly become a caress. The world had become a kiss. And I was nothing but a floating lotus flower.

The following day it was not only I who was in love with Driss. My genitals, too, revered him.

Happiness? Happiness is making love because of love. It's when the heart threatens to explode because it's beating, when an incomparable look lingers on your mouth, when a hand leaves a bit of sweat in the hollow of your left knee. It's the saliva of the beloved that flows down your throat, sweet as sugar and transparent. It's your neck stretching out, letting go of its knots and fatigue, becoming endless because a tongue is running up and down its full length. It's your earlobe pulsating like your lower belly. It's your back becoming delirious and inventing sounds and shivers to say I love you. It's the raised leg, consenting, the panties falling down like a leaf, useless and bothersome. It's a hand penetrating the forest of hair, awakening the roots of the head and generously watering them with its tenderness. It's the terror of having to open up and the incredible power of giving yourself when everything in the world is a reason to weep. Happiness is Driss, hard inside me for the first time, his tears dripping into the hollow of my shoulder. Happiness was he. Happiness was I.

Translated from Arabic by C. Jane Hunter

Nayla Elamin

Djinn

Last night someone was in my room (the yellow one)

    I heard him move towards my bed
with sweaty hands I tried to turn
on
   the light,
he moved so fast I could not see the features of his face,
he flipped me over, face in my pillow

   he stretched on top of me,
his cheek on my cheek,
collar bone cutting into my shoulder blades,
belly in my lumbar curve,
penis pointing left on my sacrum,
knees painful and bony in my lower thigh,
his toenails scratching my ankles

    he smelled of burnt incense and his breath was shallow and
  r a s p i n g

    my right eye could see the tip of his nose and the curve of
his wing

   seed and knowledge filling every corner
of my heart

Ulayya bint al-Mahdi

Lord, It's Not a Crime

Lord, it's not a crime to long for Raid who stokes my heart with love and makes me cry.

Lord of the Unknown, I have hidden the name I desire in a poem like a treasure in a pocket.

Translated from Arabic by Abdullah al-Udhari

Isabella Hammad

The Parisian (An Excerpt)

By evening Fatima considered herself the victor. She did not feel particularly cheerful about it, however. Midhat had not touched her all day, nor made any reference to the night before. They continued to speak in the same genial, sidelong manner, but with none of the behaviour one might expect between a husband and wife in private. Fatima kept thinking about the laughing woman in the hammam. They knew how it was supposed to be. This marriage really belonged to them, those naked figures gossiping in the steam, loitering in the corner of her mind. As afternoon progressed, she found she had used up all her self-possession in making those vine leaf parcels. She took a moment to cry weakly at the kitchen window. In retrospect, the terror of last night seemed easier than this footless unknowing of the waking day, now that the light was turned off the positions of a woman's body in one part of a room and a man's in another, and onto the vaguer profile of future uncertainties, in which time and space far exceeded what one girl's mind could map, and dwarfed by thousands her fear of a few inches, a few moments, the sound of his breath. Even standing there at the window, she did not know what to do with her hands. She ended by clasping them so tightly together the fingers blotched pink and white. She tried to concentrate on the hours ahead, but her unruly mind kept expanding to the panorama of years, years of this same unknowing, to which an end was swaddled in mist.

As night fell, Midhat read in the salon while she played the oud. This was taken for a virtue, a woman who play the oud.

She tried to play as though for her own pleasure, as if she barely knew he was there, and she even half sang the words, as though pratising for another event. But there was no danger of him looking up, and this left her free to examine him. He looked tired, she thought. He was pale and his lids hung low. She quite liked the sights of his arms under his rolled-up shirtsleeves. After abandoning the halfway point of a few melodies, she rested the instrument on her legs, and touched the tuning pegs.

'What are you reading?' she said.

'Hm?'

That was the same look he gave her earlier, when she asked him what he was thinking about. His face was quite demonstrative. An appealing quality, but perhaps, also one that spoke of a kind of carelessness. He lifted the spine of his book to show her. It was written in a European language. The woven cover was red, and black silk bookmark dangled from the binding, heavily frayed.

'Flaubert,' he said. 'You speak French?'

'No. Some English. I know three words in German.'

'What are these three words?'

'Abendessen. Mittagessen. Heisse. There were some others, I forgot.'

He frowned, head to the side, lips parted. She answered:

'After the Turks left, we had Germans.'

'Oh- yes, I remember this. My father told me that.'

He lingered on her, then returned to the page. She wondered if the story was sad. He looked up again, apparently on the point of speech. For a second he held the position; she waited, unhappily, until he shook it off. She set the round back of the oud against the wall.

'Where are you going?' he said.

'The kitchen.'

There was nothing to do in the kitchen. She ran a damp cloth along the edge of the table, where a little ridge might gather dirt. The cloth was clear; she had done the same thing earlier.

She made sure to precede Midhat to the bedroom, undressed before the mirror, and donned a nightgown. When he knocked and entered, he was already wearing a two-piece pyjama suit, blue with black piping. Last night, this was an image that might have terrified her. Now, she giggled: it meant he had anticipated her, and collected his pyjamas earlier. The shirt, not buttoned to the top, flapped open slightly beyond the lapel as he climbed into the bed. She slid in beside him. The sheets were heavy. They lay for a while in silence on their backs. Then Midhat said:

'Did you see the Nebi Musa procession in Jerusalem?'

Her breath stopped. 'Yes.'

'I saw you there.'

Danger shot through Fatima's mind. Husbands were like parents, conscious of a woman's shame. She waited, frozen.

'Did you go alone?'

'Yes,' she whispered. She felt a powerful urge to weep.

'Don't be afraid.'

But all those words did was bring to mind the night before, which seemed no longer distant but rather very present, and her heart thumped hard. She longed for the darkness, she wanted to cover the heat rising to her neck and face, and she glanced, helpless, at the lamp beyond him. She felt exactly as exposed as she had before she climbed onto the cupboard.

'Why are you afraid?'

The sheet shifted. He was turning towards her. She could see his white eyeballs.

'I can feel you; you are afraid. I don't mind that you went to Nebi Musa. I was asking because … I wondered if you had seen anything. Anything terrible.'

'I saw nothing. I was hardly there, I came, I left …'

'It was odd, though, didn't you think?' he said. 'That crowd, all those angry people.'

She inhaled too loudly. 'They are uneducated. Ya'ni, poor people. Poor people are angry. That's why we have *zakat*.'

Midhat turned onto his back. He switched off the lamp. Fatimas's blush began to fade, and she listened to the soothing murmur of a draught. When she was calm, she addressed him in a quiet voice.

'Will you tell me about Paris?'

'Paris?'

'I want to know.'

He began, with slow, formal phrases. 'I lived in Paris during the war. There were only a few men. Except for old ones. And, in addition, there were some Arabs.'

Although at first he seemed reluctant, he soon relaxed into a monologue. His words drew pictures, and Fatima saw balconies and terraced cafés, heard voices and the sounds of glass and crockery as she walked down deserted streets and theatre aisles full of women in glitter pining for men at battle. Set free by the dark, she came closer to the vibrations of this voice, low in his throat, to the heat coming from his half-bared chest. She felt it on her shoulder as he turned over, surprised by how near his body was to hers. She was sensitive enough to realise that in this speech he was revealing some part of his inner life, and that it was a struggle to hold onto and translate it for her. It moved her to be taken into his confidence. With fresh temerity she put her hand on his chest, and under the silk of his pyjama shirt she felt his heart come to meet it.

'Might we one day go there?'

He pressed the back of her fingers. 'We might.'

He said something else she didn't hear. She had found his mouth and kissed it. Their foreheads touched awkwardly. There was some perspiration on his shaven lip. She immediately reached to touch him between the legs, amazed and shocked by her own courage. She was even more amazed at the weird shape of his anatomy that reared under the fabric, and snatched her hand away.

'Don't look at me,' she said.

'I can't see you. It's completely dark.'

That was clearly a lie, because she could still see him. She closed her eyes, boiling with shyness, and his fingers began, very gently, to wrinkle the nightgown over her legs. When it was necessary, she raised her hips off the mattress, and then lifted her arms to help it over her head. Though her skin was flushed she was also pimpled over with cold, and when his hand met her hip she winced. Then she saw his shadow hesitate, and grasping him by the neck pulled him over her.

The pain was incredible. Whatever shame was left over, it evaporated at once in that unbearably specific heat. His arms trembled under his own weight, and his hair, flopping from his head, brushed her brow. Only when his eyes met hers and he said, 'Are you all right?' did she realise how heavily he was breathing.

She smiled. 'Yes. Thank you for asking.'

Rita El Khayat

Skin

On your skin's silk
I see blue veins swollen
by the work of love.
Your flushed cock a flourish
admonishing
but I want this

You see,
the blueish sheen of your brown skin
is what fuses me to you,
in fear of your violence, even
unholy thing
men so adore

Love is crisis.
My body contorts beneath yours
I'm dying of desire
when my breath you crushed out
rushes back:
air reborn through pleasure

To me your body
is all surface, pure pallor
in candle-light.
The skin I stroke
shy, enthralled,

is you, entirely mine

With each replete embrace
I await your entering,
my virgin anticipation
ready, rapt.
This is what I love most:
melting into you, animal, mythical

The kinks of your skin
are my refuge.
You fill me with pleasure,
growing with the scent of your hair
haloed by my desire;
you approach and you swaddle me in velvet

And now I burn to a climax, to an eclipse –
your back the canvas where my hands come to rest.

Translated from French by Sophie Lewis

Zahra al-Kilabiyya

I Keep My Passion

I keep my passion for Juml to myself.

It's burning me up like a sick man's dream of getting well, or a mother stricken by the death of her only son or a refugee watching a gathering of friends.

Translated from Arabic by Abdullah al-Udhari

Mouna Ouafik

Orgasm

Quick as that, the tissues of my clitoris fill up with blood.
Each time I see white plastic gloves
I get turned on.

Translated from Arabic by Robin Moger

Joumana Haddad

Lovers Should Only Wear Moccasins

The woman had not had an easy day: her dalliance in Paris was coming to an end, now she had far too many errands to run and as many places to dash between, a few people to see briefly, last-minute, a lunch with the man in the ardent hat, and then, cherry on the cake: a troubling, salt-edged goodbye with him that lingered for a long while, catching in her throat all day, and she would not at any cost let that rise to affect her eyes. No. Not she.

Our woman who had not had an easy day went home to prepare for her evening. She had already decided what she wanted from the few hours she had left in this city. She would give herself a 'first time', the kind of present she usually kept for moments of deep distress. She washed her long black hair, stroked it under the stream of water, and thought: 'Mary Magdalene is indulging in her old tricks again, but this time she'll take care not to repent.' She stepped out and a few drops fell to her shoulders, the kind of drops not to be wiped away, that only a tongue thirsty for stars should desire, should gather and drink. She outlined her mouth, applied her fragrance, selected the skirt that came to hand (even as the kind who leaves nothing to chance), and accidentally on-purpose forgot to add any knickers. The woman who, accidentally on-purpose, forgot to wear knickers went to dine with a couple of friends, G & Y, at a restaurant where artificial gaiety was the rule. Two hours and three bottles of wine later, the trio landed in a swingers' club in a basement garage on the rue du Cherche-Midi.

A man with a mouthful of dodgy teeth was guarding the entrance. My immediate reaction was to turn on the angelic expression I used to adopt at school, when the good sisters wanted to scold me for a misdemeanour I had well and truly committed but was fervently determined to deny. *We are good people, Mon Frère; allow us to come in.* Then I realised my mistake and adopted the opposite expression: *We are wicked people, Monsieur. You'll not regret it, believe me.* I cast a few furtive glances at the promised land behind its highly muscled ramparts. So much lay beyond that hair's-breadth-open door, I thought! Hidden things revealed only to those who 'deserve' them. A consideration following which my expression grew all the more depraved on facing the abyss, pouring all the debauchery of which I have been, am and will be capable into a single conclusive look.

This door, then, will it open or won't it? That is the question.

The guy, G, who'd come with us had conscientiously repeated over dinner that I was their passport, and I secretly dreaded the responsibilities such an 'honour' would entail, but he was right. For an inspection from toe to top of my worthy person seemed to be enough (the man with the dodgy teeth did not stand even as tall as my eyes, so needlessly composed – or rather topped up with wantonness – for the circumstances). An infra-red once-over, then, and our Anti-Saint Peter magnanimously waved us in.

We gingerly tripped down the steps, gingerly crossed the last metres of our uncertainty, tore the hymen (which was, by the way, ever more elastic; at least mine was) of our upbringings, and here we were inside. I could feel your disapproving gaze following my every step and ordering me to turn back. But wasn't it you who wrote after our first encounter: '*I so enjoyed the disconcerting freedom that you have, this superb sense of daring*'?

Then let me go all the way, to the very end...

It was very dark in the room, but the three friends could clearly make out that the hostess who greeted them had a neckline cut very low, to her navel. She propelled her breasts majestically forward, hastening to take their coats and bags. The woman who wanted to go all the way removed her jacket, sweater, beret and scarf one by one, docile as a Japanese tourist with that absolute confidence in her guide, and kept only her cigar (and the remainder of her clothes, of course, which was no small statement considering the extravagant nudity on show all around).

It was like entering Ali Baba's cave, except there was no treasure in this one: just empty coffers, disenchanted and disenchanting bodies without any sparkle, worthless rocks, wedding bands and broken bonds, chains of first-water fears, bracelets of costume joys, cut-glass solitaires lost in the twists and turns of their solitude. A wave of disappointment swept over the good sisters' pupil. The more she observed, the worse she felt, sitting in her red velvet armchair, for she could see the parade of clammy frustrations that had played out here over the years. Filthy. Everything looked filthy and she took care that her skin did not touch the fabric.

What would you like to drink? Wine, I told the waitress without hesitation. You know, since I met you, I've been drinking too much wine, for I feel that with each sip, it's you flowing into me. It's not really wine any more. It's your lips and your smell and your sap and tongue and the memory of you... No. Not your memory. Talk of memories will condemn you to a shackled past, and the past means nothing to me unless it be also, above all, a hand freely reaching for a fruit set to ripen. I see myself, then, wantonly lying on your bed, between a bottle of Bordeaux and a dream, my body reaching for your glass like a tipsy longbow that aspires only to let fly, rain of desires that wants nothing but to be poured out.

For it's the vine that ripens the sun; you must have known this for some time.

The red arrives, and you with it. I drink it with delectation drinking you. At the same time, I continue my navigation in these louche waters, in this tightly packed, barren space, overlaid with hang-ups and filled with desolation and reclusive extroverts: it's something like stealing forbidden fruit through a giant keyhole. I should say that despite all the bravado I exude I am a fish out of water in this place. Even the men looking me up and down convey a mix of wolfish desire and 'what's a woman like this doing here?'

I was beginning to be a little bored. I crossed and uncrossed my legs nervously, then remembered with a jolt that I'd no knickers on, my memory revived by the ecstatic expression of the octogenarian with shirt undone and shaggy hair sitting opposite. *Did he really wink at me? Does he think he's Michael Douglas confronting a brunette Sharon Stone in some x-rated version of Basic Instinct?* I peered at G, the guy who had come with me, getting his vital stats down by eye, then did a couple of quick comparison sums and realised that despite his flaws, I was not inclined to exchange him for this faded Casanova. *Is he actually coming our way? No, I must be dreaming; quick, how to get out of here.* I decided to take a look around the corners of the dark main room. So, in a show of confidence and to my friend Y's great surprise, I got to my feet; she seemed scared even to take a breath and was swallowing great gulps of whisky, almost without stopping. My non-exchangeable bodyguard rose too, but I indicated he should sit back where he was. He obeyed.

The woman who ripened the sun now went up to the bar. A good-looking dark-haired man sitting at an angle to it was whispering into the ear of a curly-haired blonde whose bra hung open. Without pausing his whispered monologue, he noticed our woman, motioned her to stop and smiled. She did not return his smile, but stared back. Then she went on with her inspection of the premises and, a few metres further on, came to a row of cubicles apparently intended for group fornication. She stepped into one: a fully-dressed man, just his fly open, in the act of anal sex with a woman who was sucking a man who was kneading the breasts of a woman who was masturbating a man and so on… An endless loop, an ouroboros of sex.

Despite all her reservations and her blasé attitude of youthful depravity, the woman notes that live sex is really quite exciting. Were the forbidden and the freakish not the two clitoral zones of the mind? She watches more closely and shivers a little when they increase the air conditioning. She shivers too because she wants to. Her areolas prickle, call out for, demand a mouth, a tongue, teeth. There are tyrannical appetites that a woman cannot appease alone.

Luckily.

I move closer still. I have never seen men engaged in sex so close up – except when having sex with me, of course, but that's not the same thing, at least I hope it isn't. I feel like a scientist observing lab rats. Although there is nothing to discover here, only an established truth to confirm: the guaranteed obscenity of desire condemned to drain away at the instant of its satisfaction.

The lips of the one sucking and being fucked wander, slide down, work their way up. With sorcery they make the magic wand of their desires disappear and reappear and disappear again. I clench my fists. My nails score my palms as if clutching the back of a lover. Each gash a shriek of desire and pleasure: the way the lioness in me marks her territory. The man fucking and the one being sucked summon me warmly to join their party, but I feel no desire for them.

It's you I want, you I am conjuring. You who will not appear. I step out of the cubicle resolved to return to my seat, when someone tugs me by the elbow. It's the dark-haired guy who was whispering into the blonde woman's ear. I take him onto the dancefloor. *What's your name where are you from your eyes slice right through me I'm Michel I'm a teacher (indeed!) what do you do you must be a model* (typical flirtation, ineffective). Even I, novice that I am, can't see the point, in such a place, of getting to know each other in any depth (had he been after something shallow, I would at least have understood). This man, Michel, is short on professionalism for a swinger. Worse, he keeps saying 'cooooooool' every 5½ seconds (I time him): the mental equivalent of a shower of icy water. I get a crazy urge to defy, to surprise myself, to vault yet another of my own boundaries. So I pull off my black top, leaving only my bra. I am astonished by this move, as with every time I am opaque even to myself. I have never done this in public before, and I take care to preserve an off-hand air. The other women are much more 'exposed' but I feel like the least dressed of them all. Besides, I've always been more the voyeur type than the showgirl. I'm sure I can hear people muttering: *Lebanese, she's Lebanese, she has Lebanese parents, Lebanese legs, she's drunk Lebanese milk, studied in a Lebanese school, she lives in a Lebanese apartment and the body moisturiser she uses is Lebanese! Arab blood runs in her veins – who would have thought?* But with one last push I sweep away all the difficulty of my identity, and quite simply enjoy the moment. Carpe diem, sing the beauty spots scattered like a thousand indecent invitations over my chest.

Are you scandalised? I'll admit at first I was a bit too, but nudity is an easily acquired taste. As for the teacher, he was in seventh heaven, imagining my bold move a direct consequence of the 'Michel effect' (equivalent for my libido to the fridge effect, thanks to the man in question's small stock of grey matter). How I miss you, my scandalometer! I miss it all: our complicity, our fits of laughter, the poetry we make together, my passionate restraint, your restrained passion, my heat under your hands and your ardent hat on my head... I know, we are bookends to each other. My impatience for you must be resigned to this frustration wrought by time. But not right now. Later, later...

The music was pulsing through her. The woman with the Lebanese legs opened her body to the rhythm, completely and deliciously abandoned herself to the pleasure of allowing this violent wave to penetrate and sweep her away. She forgot everything: war, wars, big and little, around and inside her, loneliness, self-sabotage, fears, masks, blows, regrets, vulnerability, secrets, incomprehension, shame, betrayal, guilt, lies... As many wounds (given and received, but what's the difference?) as experiences in her life. She forgot the mistakes she'd made and those she was still to make and began to really dance.

I dance thinking of you: eyes closed, mind open, fantasy flowing in waves. I sway slowly and call you with my hips, my hair, my lips. With all my lips. I plunder us, invent possible and impossible dream versions of us, and I burn. I adore the burning so rooted in me, I nurture and sustain it, I feed it in the hope that you will feed it too, knowing that too much dreaming damps a fire, and that now and then it must have real fuel to keep it white-hot. Alas, my lumberjack, it has to be now that Michel's Franco-Spanish lips alight on my fragile Lebanese neck, and I'm swiftly awoken from your absence to put him in his place.

The valiant teacher bounces back with a change of tack, now determined to show his prowess at disco. He is very limber, almost impressive in his suppleness (although you might imagine that 'stiffness' could have been preferable in this context). Eventually he gets down and dirty on his knees (Michel will not stop taking to his knees à propos of nothing) and I take advantage of the improved field of vision to look over at the infamous red armchair where I left my friends half an hour before. And realise that Y, who normally drinks nothing but Diet

Coke, has imbibed at least 22 gulps of whisky too many, for she too has removed her blouse, doubtless encouraged by the edifying example of my deliberate amnesia, and she is flirting with G with all the support her lilac Wonderbra can muster.

But dammit, here is Travolta up and back to his ear-chewing habits again. *You're so beautiful I spotted you straight away you're classy I want you let's go for a wander round the back, hm, don't you want to?* Now Michel has outwhispered his welcome, I return him to the ear of his blonde and head back to save Y from the abysmal remorse of the morning after, but they've vanished. So I head for the cubicles, and dip into another. The very moment I step through the door, a woman is pulling her thong aside and lowering herself astride a man. She has him penetrate her slowly and begins her moaning right away. They are the polished moans of a frigid woman but I envy her anyway. I love the first penetration. If I had to choose the moment I enjoy most in making love, that's what I'd choose every time: the moment a man parts my lips, the first endless moment when he penetrates me, with a shiver of pain too for I never open up altogether until I feel the touch of his sex. All the possible preludes, luscious as they may be, can't bring me that. And nothing in the world can match that sensation, that entering, that violent and tender flood of all we have into one.

The woman–river begins to flow. Slowly but urgently, a hand surfaces from the dreaming and runs over her skin. It isn't her hand. It is turn by turn the hand of each of the men who have desired her. The hand of each or of them all at once. The ideal plural singular. Firm, strong, brazen, insatiable yet gentle: a hand that knows. A hand, above all, that does not wait but takes. Her brain flares, delirious. She is venturing where so much that is unspoken, undone and unexpected lies waiting to be exploded. The honey of his eyes admires and praises her. His fingers are breathless, they slow, dive, abscond at the temple doors. They feint and tease, hover and return.

The woman spreads her standing thighs wider to receive her own fingers, then slaps them closed again. Her hand tickles the vertical smile, dips in, titillates, persists then escapes. Now she is working at it, now merely prompting. The wellspring gushes, wine courses. A tongue, thirst, now!

I come back from you. On my right, the thong has returned to its place between the simulatrix's flat bottom cheeks. On my left, as well as above and below me, my tormented yet outrageously well-fed conscience floats like a gluttonous cat. Out of nowhere, a sticky palm lands on my neck and forces me to move on a little early for the tastes of the party. It is my shaggy octogenarian, his shirt open even lower than before. *You got going without me, my chickadee? Never mind, we shall catch up.* No panic. I've a glare specially perfected for situations like this: I turn it upon his face and Mr Douglas's long-lost twin snatches back his paw as if it were burnt.

No 'as if' about it, really.

I get out of there and go back to my hunt for my companions G and Y. Carving a path through the waves of sweat and whimpering, I feel like a trained swimmer coming to rescue a couple of shipwreck survivors, for G and Y certainly make the swiftest and worst matched couple in history (Arthur Miller and Marilyn Monroe included). An elegant dark-skinned guy mid-flirtation with his great-great-grandmother's childhood friend spots my disorientated air and feels the need to console me over the heartache he's sure is at source: *life is beautiful enjoy it don't be sad you are young you are delicious blah blah blah let me snatch all those bitter thoughts out of your head.* (Should I tell him it is mostly the word 'snatch' that I'm struggling to get over, in this unfortunate head of mine?) He kisses me softly on the inside of my wrist. My pulse appreciates his lips' touch. *Let's go now relax I know what you need to be happy…* With this I admit he has at last caught my whole attention. It's a modern marvel! This man, an amateur wizard perhaps, in his spare time, *knows*, by some intuition beyond my ken, what I need to be happy! And what do I need? I ask him eagerly, awaiting some life-changing philosophical insight. The reply comes, more staggering even than anything I could have predicted:

'You need a Caribbean boy!'

In fact what I need is a few seconds' space to absorb the full impact of his wit, before I can shoot back:

'Ah, of course! Why didn't I think of it before? And where might you be from?'

'Martinique.'

Of course.

Our greedy feline drops Philippe, philosopher of the Caribbean – she also lets go of the inconvenient preference for happiness – and goes on with her exploration while still hoping to find her friends. One after another she looks into each room and sees how the people inside are alike. They look pathetically indistinguishable: half-dressed girls (these days their kind can be seen in the street at midday), men with desiccated smiles and an awkward nonchalance, women in corsets and stocking suspenders, looking most like the dusty old aunt you visit twice a year.

A pretty brunette with heavy breasts was dancing sensuously in front of a little group, and I heard someone say she was Algerian. So I smiled to her out of Arab solidarity (ah – that famous Arab solidarity!), she drew me closer out of female solidarity, we danced together in artistic solidarity, I even reached a hand towards her breasts in aesthetic solidarity! But our beautiful love story shattered when a man with 343 gold chains around his neck, unquestionably her guy, approached with a highly improper proposal involving three people, a couch and an advanced condition of physical solidarity to which I couldn't personally subscribe.

On my way to the bathroom I noticed a large platter of mints on a buffet to my right. Sitting next to the sweets, a man sandwiched between two Lolitas was loosening the reluctance of one and the sang-froid of the other, all the while struggling with his own slacks and shoes, which he couldn't seem to untie. I just managed not to burst out laughing, remembering your words only a few days earlier: 'Lovers should only ever wear moccasins.'

The bathroom was intriguingly clean and well ordered. Who would have guessed the existence of this haven of hygiene and harmony in the midst of such a chaos? Our woman opened the front flap of her skirt and looked tenderly at her curly mop. The man without moccasins had asked her to let the hair grow for their next encounter.

She gazed at herself, imagining him well planted in this passionate garden that called for him, and said to herself: 'Next time, as soon as he's here, I'll not let him come out again. Here he'll stay for the rest of his life, a brand new column erected in my eternal temple, the first sexual refugee in history, slowly roasted and endlessly savoured, tenderly wrapped in the clay of my desires, getting drunk and writing stories that no one has ever dared or known how to write.'

Coming out of the bathroom I was surprised to see Y, who was jiggling around on the platform and cosying up to the chrome pole in the middle of it. She must have had this in her genes somewhere, for she was dancing incredibly well, as if it were her vocation. Amazing! Could this budding striptease star be the same girl who so often put me through interminable ear-bashings about the 'bastards-who-just-want-to-get-us-into-bed? I vowed to let her forget this scene by the morning; she'd never forgive me for leading her to this climax of abandon. And proudly I considered that innocence, if it does exist, occasionally has its uses: it offers us the luxury of corrupting it. A luxury I like to over-indulge.

A few similar episodes later and my outsider feeling was gone, the attraction of anonymity likewise. The experience achieved, I was overcome by a vast weariness. It was already 4.30am and I wanted to go and pack my suitcases; I was desperate for a bath. I located my two friends, visibly run out of steam for experimentation, so we took off. Beside the cloakroom, another philosopher (truly, these places seem fertile ground for them) takes my exhaustion and listlessness for timidity (me?) and says: *are you shocked, my dear? Was it your first time? It's all about fucking here, not love, but you are too young to know the difference* (me?).

In the taxi taking them to Charles de Gaulle airport a few hours later, the woman who knows the difference only too well regrets that the 22 gulps of whisky drunk by her friend the evening before were not 222. For, having crossed the gulf between amateur dissolution and repentant sobriety, Y won't stop lamenting for the entire journey: Oh what have we done? Oh my God! Resigned to her shamelessness, the Shameless One listens to her friend serenely and sighs: 'She could still do with learning when the time is ripe to open up and when to shut up shop.'

Airport check-in achieved, the woman who does know when to open and when to be closed for business lets herself sink onto a bench, lets her eyelids fall shut and feels her heart ache a little. Who knows, she thinks, wryly, perhaps I really could do with a Caribbean boy ...

The man in the ardent hat smiles to her from afar.

Translated from French by Sophie Lewis

Shurooq Amin

Another Kind of Love

When one squints, the other
dims the moonlight for her,
such is friendship, or so
your parents think, heedless
of limbs that tangle like
limp honeysuckle petals
in the early evening,
before the sky darkens much,
before the muezzin cries
the day's last call for prayer,
before your mother uncovers
the shallow depressions in
your mattress made by not one,
but two daughters of Muslims.

Ulayya bint al-Mahdi

We Wrote in Symbols

My passion, Tull, for you
Can no longer wait,
I am visiting you now in haste,
Treading barefoot to my doom.

We wrote in symbols amid those who were present,
Insinuations implied with no lines,
But eyes recounting their suffering
With imaginary hands on the parchments of hearts.

A wine addict becomes sober after stupor.
But the one in love goes through time while drunk.
I have become drunk with no wine
Since I remembered him, and I have never forgotten this human
  being.

Translated from Arabic by Wessam Elmeligi

Samira Negrouche

Between Scrawls and Sketches

To be swallowed up in you
in half-light
to profane the walls of the national theatre
make your curves moan in the Square
Port Saïd

*

Algiers, men seek each other out on unaesthetic terraces that
smell of sweat and fried potatoes. Their breath crosses, their eyes
not quite.

*

descending
it's your corridors, their blue
horizon gaze
departures anticipated and frightened
descending
it's fear in the belly, the genitals
tetanizing

*

Poets land in the public squares like timid phantoms and

disappear on silent soles
sometimes a trembling hand sketches a few feverish words

*

to meet you
in a luminous sheaf
made   of the inaccessible beach
and of you   inconsolable always

boats remember, let themselves be snatched up by the white hill

*

my sight
this endless ruin
of disappeared faces
and others
inexpressive, awkward

a muffled humming inhabits and penetrates me

we live on saying nothing
closing our eyes
walking around backstage
of a deserted
casbah

*

to roam in you so some tenderness will bud dreaming from far
    off of your
sunlit port walking your streets in the wrong direction and
    finding you the next day   under a tree that was spared at a

building's entrance on a winter evening when we still
persisted between scrawls and sketches.

Translated from French by Marilyn Hacker

Mouna Ouafik

Candy Crush

Your ears were my favourite sweets

More than once I meant
To leave my tongue articulate
At your damp ear

Your body which would tremble
To my sticky tongue
Would turn
Into a canting bough
On which would perch
The songbirds which would fly below
My armpit
And my navel's dip.

Translated from French by Robin Moger

Hiba Moustafa

Contemplation

I wake up early every morning
To gaze at you
It is my favourite thing to do.
I put my head on my arm
And watch you
The strands of hair
Which you have let grow
Are falling over your generous forehead
The forehead I kiss
And lick its gathering mist
Drunk
When we climb towards ecstasy.
Brows like two burnished swords
Lashes kissing your cheeks in slumber
Make me jealous
A proud Greek nose
A pair of greedy lips
Shamelessly
Light a fire in my body when they wake
A beard tickles and burns
I pretend to be asleep
It stirs, stands erect and moves
Full of naked confidence
I count the moles on your shoulders and back
Drawing lines from their constellation and make a star.
All this is for me to kiss

Touch
Hug
Smell
Whenever I desire
Wherever I wish
But I love to steal looks even more.

Translated from Arabic by Wen-chin Ouyang

khulud khamis

At Last

It is another Friday evening, and I climb the four storeys of Noor's building with its small, rectangular windows that let in only thin slivers of brownish yellow light. The lightbulbs on the third and fourth landings are burned out, so I make my way in almost complete darkness by counting the stairs.

At first, there was something exhilarating about the secrecy.

A part of my life that belonged only to me. A small slice of myself I didn't have to share with Tareq, my mother, my sister, my friends.

Now the novelty of it has faded, and the secret – well, it's not quite a secret anymore.

A few of Noor's friends know. On the rare occasions we venture out of her apartment to a café, or even just a walk on the beach together, I'm constantly on edge, jumpy whenever Noor touches me, afraid someone I know will see the intimacy in our gestures.

I carry this secret with me everywhere; a kettlebell, pulling me down.

By the time I reach the fourth floor, my breath comes in shallow gulps, my heartbeat a small hammer in my neck, and heat has spread in my stomach. I knock on the door and wait a few seconds before unlocking it with the key Noor had given me only a few weeks after we started seeing each other.

That was almost four years ago.

'You know you don't have to knock before you unlock the door. That's the whole point of having your own key,' Noor is sitting at her easel next to the window, wearing just a tank top and her paint-splattered jean shorts, the harsh white light accentuating the cellulite on her thighs, the tiny varicose veins running down the insides of her calves. Her hair, with its few silver strands, is in a messy bun held by a brush at the top of her head. When she turns around and reaches for a hug, I see the painting she's working on. Two female figures, again.

'Whiskey?' Noor holds her half-empty glass to me. I kick off my high heels, take a long sip of the whiskey, and kiss her bare shoulder. 'Hmm, smooth.' She grins at me. 'The whiskey, not your shoulder.'

The painting is of the same two female figures she has been painting, obsessively, for some time now – each time with variations of composition, background, and the positioning of the figures. But this time, something is slightly off. I can identify one of the figures as Noor, not from her features, as the figures are more abstract than realistic, but rather from the carefree, open way she carries herself. But what stops me is the second figure, the one I imagine is me. Or is she? We never discussed the identity of these women. She is usually a bit further in, a little blurred, or blending into the background, and always wearing high heels. Something in the mood around her in this painting is a bit off character, and then there is the way her right foot is in mid-air: fast strokes of the paintbrush, to give the effect of movement. She's wearing only one sandal, on the foot that is grounded.

And then I see it. Or the absence of it. There are no high heels in the painting. The sandal on her left foot is flat.

I am too embarrassed to ask about this change, so I remain silent.

I wait for the inevitable subject to come up – asking if I have told my family yet about us – but she doesn't say anything. The last time we had this same argument, we were both a bit drunk. Later, she apologised for accusing me of being ashamed of who

I was, of living in the shadows, a hypocrisy. I don't know if her silence since then means defeat, that she has accepted this as a fact, or if she's being passive-aggressive.

Two glasses of whiskey later we are in the bedroom, laying naked on the narrow bed, facing each other. Noor runs her fingers up and down my thigh, stopping just for a moment at my cellulite marks. I stroke her small, bare breasts, gently circling her nipples.

Our lovemaking is a slow dance; we take turns leading, gently, our bodies moving in synchronicity. It is as if part of me has crawled inside her and knows exactly what she is feeling at every given moment.

Words become obsolete.

Her touch is a soothing familiarity but at the same time there is always something new, a small surprise, and my body trembles with expectation of the unknown.

I have no need for light, though Noor desires it. Tonight, our bodies are illuminated a dark yellow from several lit candles, scattered on the floor around the room.

Noor takes my body to places I have never known. I had my first orgasm with her, at the age of forty-four. I didn't know such sublime pleasure existed in the world.

Our song is on repeat. Etta James' 'At Last'.

Her hand now travels up my breasts, first the left one, then the right. She squeezes my nipple, at first gently, then gradually harder. I moan into her mouth. The slight, exquisite pain sends a shock of electricity down my body. Noor pulls away. 'Oh, you like it and you want more,' and she squeezes my nipple harder and at the same time pulls on it, all the while watching me. I struggle to remain composed. 'Let go,' she whispers into my ear. 'Let go, Nadia habibti. Yes, like that. Take pleasure in your body.'

I close my eyes and let go, giving up my body to her.

While she keeps pulling at my nipple, her other hand journeys down my stomach, encircles my bellybutton, then starts circling my clitoris, slowly. My orgasm is lava that builds up on the inside, bubbling, boiling, until it bursts out in short, violent waves. I count four before collapsing. Before Noor, I didn't know my body was capable of such intensities.

I lay on my back, spent. Noor doesn't expect me to pleasure her just now, which I still find surprising. She takes the vibrator out of the nightstand drawer, turns it on, and presses it down hard on her clitoris, making fast, tiny circular movements. I watch her with fascination. When she begins moaning, I come and suckle at her breast, my fingers at her other nipple, kneading, pulling. Her orgasm comes in abrupt, short staccato trembles of her whole body.

It is well after midnight when I wake up, disoriented. Then I remember that I never went home.

Home. But where is my home?

I have finally found genuine joy in my life, and yet I have managed to confine it to a few hours once a week on Friday nights.

I cuddle up to Noor from behind, my face close to her neck, and breathe in the familiar sweet-sour scent of her sweat. I run my hand lightly over her naked back, from her lovely slender neck all the way to her tailbone and back up. Her back slightly arches in response to my touch. She turns around to face me. 'You're still here,' she smiles, her voice hoarse from sleep, her breath whiskey. 'Hey,' I whisper, kissing her on the nose. I touch the tiny vertical wrinkles that have been quietly forming above her mouth. She heaves one naked leg over me, trapping my body underneath. I know I should get back home; I keep my eyes open, waiting for Noor to fall back asleep so I can silently slip out of bed and go home, out of sheer habit. Then I remember that Tareq is away for the weekend. For the first time in our relationship, I stay with Noor until late morning.

Monday morning, and I am sitting at my office desk, staring

at the organisational budget excel sheet. Amjad the accountant has been snappy with me all week, impatient about getting him the quarterly financial report. I'm already one week late. I've been staring at the numbers for the last two hours, unable to make sense of them. My mind keeps wandering back to Saturday morning, that feeling of comfort – of home – waking up next to Noor. I want to be that woman with her foot mid-air, stepping out of the shadows and into truth.

The realisation is so sudden I gasp aloud. Suddenly, everything is crystal clear in my head. I know I want to wake up next to this lovely, beautiful woman every day. I want to be that free woman in her paintings.

I am forty-eight years old, and still afraid to live my life without fear of what will people say. It's ridiculous. Tareq is finally moving out of the house next month. My sister will understand; she's been suspecting it for a while anyway, dropping hints at every occasion. When I take a minute to truly think about it, I realise I don't really care whether my friends will accept it. It is not their life I am living. It has no bearing on them. And my mother, well, she won't have a choice but to accept it. I am forty-eight years old. It's about time I start living my own truth. Not this hypocrisy, this pretend life.

I am giddy with this new and sudden joy, imagining Noor's elation at the news.

At last.

Unable to wait until Friday night to tell her, I grab my bag and rush out of the office. On my way, I send a quick message to Amjad: sorry, family emergency. Your report will have to wait until tomorrow.

I climb the four floors as fast as I can in these damn heels, precariously balancing my weight on the balls of my feet, the heels suspended in air at the end of each step. My feet are aching from the walk, but oh, the small, painful sacrifices we make for appearances. At the door, I stop for a few moments to recover.

As I wait for my heartbeat and breathing to slow down, I hear laughter from inside. Then voices. Just before turning the key in, I hear an unfamiliar female voice, 'so when will you tell Nadia?' I freeze at the mention of my name. I stare at the ugly dark brown of the door, which I am noticing for the first time. But then I've only ever been here at night. 'Why should I tell her? I don't owe her anything. She isn't fully committed, so I don't have to be either.' What is she talking about? I can't make out what they say next, as their voices are now lower. Then, Noor's voice again: 'I do love her, but I can't do this once-a-week thing anymore. I need a real relationship. She promised me she'd tell her son and mother months ago, but so far, nothing. She thinks she can live this double life forever. But I can't do this. I can't do secrets like she does.'

Then, the voice of Etta James comes on.

Our song, 'At Last'.

I pull the key slowly out of the keyhole, my fingers clammy from the humidity. My heartbeat again a small hammer in my neck. I take off my high heels, leaning on the wall, and walk down the four stories of the building barefoot, my legs trembling with each step.

Outside, I stand in the scorching sun, beads of sweat a tiny pool between my breasts. A few couples are sitting at the outside tables of the café on the street corner, going on about their daily lives. I take my phone out of my bag and send a message to Amjad: 'You'll have your report by the end of the day.'

I put my high heels on for the last time and head back to the office.

Ulayya bint al-Mahdi

Epigram

To love two people is to have it
coming: body nailed to beams,
dismemberment.
But loving one is like observing
religion.
I held out until fever
broke me.
How long can grass
brave fire?
If I did not have hope
that my heart's master's
heart might bend to mine,
I would be stranded, no
closer to gate than home.

Translated from Arabic by Yasmine Seale

Mouna Ouafik

Regret is a Belated Conceit

The hot girls whom
You blow upon
Before you sip them
Off the spoon

Remind you of
The one
Who burned
Your tongue
Forever.

Translated from Arabic by Robin Moger

Rita El Khayat

Messalina Unbound

She can never have enough hard-ons,
various as the raindrops
that collect to flood her lair.
Now she spies the next she will wolf down
this evening
nestled on her happenstance bed.

Here is a sweet little one;
he'll make up for any missing members,
will keep her panting
when she takes possession:
huntress with the mostest,
her prey is pinned between her legs.

The same day, another,
his gaze somewhat distracted,
promises her the world in the palm of her hand,
only *after* they've dined.
Appreciating her own belly's soft curve,
already she feels his pressing down.

Afraid to follow him
to the sacrificial trough
where he might kill her
if he cannot fuck her,
she dissolves at the sweetness of his tongue;

he likes to take women first by taste ...

Now love weaves a sensuous veil
around our dizzy lovers;
no choice but to follow this man
to his bed, where he rests like the moon,
its disc upon the ground.

The wine keeps pace with
songs beating out love.
When he goes back to the work at hand,
a cock he holds in fingertips
the perfect object
of supreme pleasures, she arches, taut.

Back with the regular lover of fallow days,
she can spend long daydreams reliving fusion and effusion
with men of the street,
unnamed, fine or plain, men.
She'd take them all:
another day, another lover;

no two pleasures the same.
Soundings and findings
under cloths drawn tight by tumescence,
each a sex to die for,
she wants them all, she needs them, the long, the short, the
    extraordinary.

Messalina is a mere creature of fable:
she likes them blond, Black, Asiatic and smooth-haired with
    slow fingers;
she likes the Italians who sing with date-sweet tongues,
the Jews and Muslims their cocks unsheathed,

the heavy labourers with muscles all a-ripple.

This lady of the night,
this fleet-footed doe of the day
ears pricked for all men:
so long as he comes well hung
and ready, with a single thrust
to lift her up to heaven.

She loves more than love, more than sex,
she takes all men, first-timers too,
and, legs wide as the sky, receives
the glory of raw honey
slowly spilled to her belly's depths
and she is shaken, shocked, an electric storm of the senses,
    complete.

Translated from French by Sophie Lewis

Nathalie Handal

Les Fenêtres – Three Drafts

Draft One

Say *hello. What's your name?*
Place a thought in his mouth.
Whisper you want him – immediately.
Say, *baby you smell like no other.*
And as he enters, leave.

Draft Two

Look at him. But don't greet him.
Leave your coffee breath as is.
Don't speak.
Lower your eyes. You're not
interested. Then stand up,
motion – *follow me.* And as he enters,
enter too. But don't let him know.

Draft Three

Stand naked with heels on.
Ask him to kiss your belly button.
To turn his breathing the other way,
and decide which way to enter.

Leïla Slimani

Adèle (An Excerpt)

Adèle is sitting in the dark in an apartment building on Rue du Cardinal Lemoine. She is on a step midway between the first and second floors. She has not seen anyone. She is waiting.

He shouldn't be long now.

She is scared. Someone might enter, someone she doesn't know, someone who wants to hurt her. She forces herself not to look at her watch. She does not take her mobile from her pocket. Nothing ever happens fast enough. She leans back, puts her handbag under her head and lifts up her knee-length beige slip. It's a light slip – too light for the season – but it hovers through the air when you spin around, like a little girl's skirt. Adèle strokes her thigh with her fingernails. She slides her hand up slowly, pushes aside her knickers and puts her hand there. Firmly. She can feel her lips swelling, the blood rushing under the pulp of her fingers. She closes her fist tight around her vulva. Scratches herself violently, from her anus to her clitoris. She turns her face to the wall, spreads her legs and wets her fingers. Once, a man spat on her pussy. She liked that.

The index and middle fingers. That's all she needs. A hot, lively movement, like a dance. A regular caress, completely natural and utterly degrading. It's not working. She stops then tries again. She swings her head like a horse trying to shake the flies out of its nostrils. Only an animal can be good at such things. Maybe if she cries out, if she starts moaning, she'll find it easier to feel the spasm coming, the liberation, the pain, the anger. She whispers little *ahs*. But a moan shouldn't come from your mouth, it should come from deep in your belly. No, you'd have to be a beast to abandon yourself like that. You'd have to have no dignity, Adèle thinks, just as the building's front door opens. Someone has called the lift. She doesn't move. Shame he doesn't take the stairs.

Xavier emerges from the lift and takes a key fob from his pocket. Adèle has taken off her shoes. As he opens the door, she puts her hands on his waist. He jumps and cries out.

'Oh, it's you! You scared me. That's a weird way to say hello, isn't it?'

She shrugs and walks into the bachelor flat.

Xavier talks a lot. Adèle wishes he would hurry up and open the bottle of wine that he's been holding for the last fifteen minutes. Finally she gets up and hands him the corkscrew.

This is her favourite moment.

The moment before the first kiss, nudity, intimate caresses. That moment of anticipation when everything is still possible, and she is the mistress of the magic. She greedily drinks a mouthful of wine. A drop trickles over her lips and down her chin and drips on the collar of her white dress before she can stop it. It's a detail of the story and she's the one who wrote it. Xavier is jittery and shy. He is not impatient; she is grateful to him for sitting at a distance from her, on that uncomfortable chair. Adèle is on the sofa, her legs folded beneath her. She stares at Xavier with her swamp eyes, viscous and impenetrable.

He moves his mouth toward her, and an electric wave runs through her belly. It hits her pussy and explodes it, fleshy and moist, like a peeled fruit. The man's mouth tastes of wine and cigarillos. Of forests and the Russian countryside. She wants him, and this desire, to her, feels almost like a miracle. She wants it all: him, and his wife, and this affair, and these lies, and the texts they will send, and the secrets and the tears and even the inevitable goodbye. He slips her dress off. His surgeon's hands, long and bony, barely brush her skin. His gestures are assured, agile, delicious. He seems detached and then suddenly furious, uncontrollable. A strong sense of theatre; Adèle is thrilled. He is so close now that her head starts to spin. She is breathing too hard to think. She is limp, empty, at his mercy.

He accompanies her to the taxi rank, presses his lips hard against her neck. Adèle dives into the cab, her flesh still drenched with love, hair tangled. Soaked with odours, caresses and saliva, her skin has a new complexion. Every pore denounces her. Her gaze is liquid. She looks like a cat, nonchalant and mischievous. She tenses her vagina, and a shiver runs through her whole body, as if the pleasure is not yet totally consumed, as if her body still harbours memories so vivid that she could, at any moment, summon them and make herself come.

Translated from French by Sam Taylor

Najwa Barakat

Oh Salaam! (An Excerpt)

Salaam came out of the bathroom followed by a cloud of soap and perfume. She was looking much better now. Well, a little better anyway.

Luqman went with her into the kitchen. She made breakfast. Cream, yoghurt, za'ater, fried eggs and cheeses. Fresh mint leaves, tomatoes and cucumbers. Warm bread, as though fresh from the bakery oven.

He sat across the table from her. As she was cutting the food and seasoning it with salt and spices, she said a little flirtatiously, 'What got you up so early like this? Or after being out all night as usual, did you get fed up and remember Salaam?'

Luqman smiled. Now the sweat was beading on her temples and her cracked lips. After a bit, the spots would appear under her busy armpits. A sweaty woman. That was more than he could endure. Salaam for the winter. Marina was a cool breeze for the summer.

'I didn't sleep yesterday,' Salaam went on.

'Why not?'

'After midnight and after two sleeping pills, the Albino's mother woke me up. She had come down with some kind of fever or delirium. She began stomping on the floor of the room right above my head, calling, "Salaam! Come quickly, Salaam!" I got up like a mad-woman and raced up the stairs four at a time. I thought someone had broken in, to rob or kill her. But I found her all alone in her nightgown. I gave her a sedative and told her, "Calm down, Lurice!" Which she did. I waited until I was sure she was okay, and she fell asleep near dawn. That's when I came down to sleep.. Why are you lighting a cigarette? You haven't eaten anything yet!'

Luqman took a deep drag on the cigarette, leaned his chair back, and puffed out smoke rings. He ought to lead her away from this chattering she loved and was so good at, to induce her gradually to ask about his affairs. He'd plant a bomb for her, and he'd nail it. He intended to see Marina that evening. But seeing Marina required cash, and Salaam had the cash.

Salaam made coffee, still running at the mouth: 'Poor Lurice! She said she saw the Albino in her dream. He was staring at her wide-eyed, and when she asked him what was the matter, he didn't answer. He didn't utter a sound. In the end, he came over to her and started smoothing her hair and caressing her face until both his hands were around her neck, and he began squeezing so hard she felt she was choking.'

Salaam's dress was sticking to her butt. The hem, which had been tied up, went further to reveal little purplish blue veins in the crease of her knees. She stood in front of the sink, cleaning off the plates and rinsing them. The lines of her underwear were visible. They pressed into her butt cheeks in the attempt to hold them in, giving the appearance of four distinct sections. Salaam actually had two butts: one inside her underwear and one outside.

Salaam was cleaning the dishes, and her butt was talking vigorously. Luqman was sweating. His partner stood straight up to reply to Salaam's butt.

What's wrong with you that you get excited and stand up without permission? Take a good look, Partner, and make no mistake: what you see in this kitchen is only Salaam!

So what? Put one of the thick plastic bags over her head to hide her face. Then you can imagine she is some other woman.

Is that how you express your deep gratitude? Fine, and then what, Partner?

Shove her against the sink, lift up her skirt, tear her panties in half and –

Take it easy, Partner? If you did her just once, Salaam would never again leave you in peace. She'd suck your blood until you dried out and withered, and all life left you for good. Or would that make you happy? Is that what you want?

I know it's all too much and you're fed up, but doesn't patience have its limits? I've been in torment since dawn and whose fault is it but yours?

And how is it my fault, Partner, that the blond broadcaster was a vile slut and a lowlife whore? Come on! Forget Salaam and her butt. Even if I gave you what you wanted, you'd be disappointed. Listen, if you stay worked up –

'Luqman, I won't be long.. I'll take Lurice a tray of food. Then I'll come right back,' Salaam said as she went out.

Luqman grabbed his partner, and the two of them went into the bathroom.

Translated from Arabic by Luke Leafgreen

Umm al-Ward al-Ajlaniyya

A Strong Claw

Might there be a young man in whose organ
The water of youth is kept in its vigour?
Walking with a strong claw close to his knee,
Curved, but not due to flawed creation.

Translated from Arabic by Wessam Elmeligi

Ad-Dihdaha al-Faqimiyya

Drooping

A soft drooping glans,
With a head too close and incomplete.
A louse with soft stubble,
Tight with a stinger sliding out,
I inserted that in Al-Farazdaq's anus.

Translated from Arabic by Wessam Elmeligi

Bint Magdaliya

The Trembling Woman

'Of the fever called living that burned in my brain'
Edgar Allen Poe, 'For Annie'

The night I gave birth to Annie, April rain fell like a whisper.

The night she died a few years later, I howled as June rain fell in a roaring torrent. Each drop the soldier of a rampaging army after my heart. My tears fell in a hailstorm, diamonds made of water.

I cry forever. I cry for the feel of her hair. For the tilt of her head. For her delicate little steps. I cry for the passion I lived with her and wonder about her sacrifice. My belly melts under her weight, her reliance, her trust in me. Wound her entrails around my entrails. Bound forever together, bound from the inside out. Her spear of a gaze whenever I walked from her, the eyes hypnotic and bottomless deep; *You and I are one; I know things you don't know... I know time.*

Our souls ablaze together. Madness. A twirling electric storm when she moved, her magnetic field manifest for all to gasp at, disbelieving. Apollo's piercing shaft, the first illumination of the morning. In stillness she was rooted and crowned by the glory of the Infinite, compelling me to join her, to be quiet with her, to deepen our understanding, to merge and meld until our outlines became blurred, because being bound was not enough.

She had revelled in the elements like an animal. Communed with the first daffodils, with motorways of ants, with the long grass of summer fields, hurled herself face first into fresh snow.

We both pretended to forget. The spasms, the vomiting, waking up soaked in liquid that smelt of pine solution. The ravenous, questioning hunger, wobbly and half blind, and neither talked about what had just happened, because there was not enough time.

For the whole of Annie's life I slept with a sword under the pillow. A martial and erotic charge to my despair. *Tyar Bar Tyar.* Like the warrior saint at rest, I was Ready Upon Ready.

And still she died. Despite all the votive offerings, the activation of miracle mantras, despite the consecration of anything that touched her. The destiny that no sacrifice, no altar could alter.

In the meantime, had there been men in their life? A crumbling, dusty thread of images, a hazy backdrop to the unfolding tragedy, to the rot gleefully teeming with life. A pink sunset outlines bare winter trees. The colonising parakeets of a London park accompany her home.

No man was abominable enough. Nothing could match this suffering. The mother needed to shake. She needed the abandon and the frenzy. She needed to shake as the girl shook and to collapse onto her knees half blind. She needed to be cut and pierced and shaved and drugged and restrained and to be prized like that. She needed someone to fuck with her head, to obliterate her with their desire, to impale her with a glance.

All she found was a series of mediocre sadists.

Hit me
Hit you?
Yes
With what?
I don't know. Be inventive?
You disgust me
They were domesticated and wanted to put their mouth on

her cunt. They had internalised juridically agreed modes of fucking. At some point, varying according to the mediocre sadist's self-awareness, their suppressed viciousness would reveal itself. When they did hit her, limply and with a cowardice that made her resent them more, or theatrically as if for an audience, they looked for ways to sanitise the blow. Inevitably she became bored and feigned melting, feigned a well-rehearsed melting to get her off the hook.

Sometimes she gasped loudly, ambiguously, and this made them feel that they had been transgressive, had gotten away with something.

How she despised their hammering, their thick, oily sweat, their hyperboles…

I could lose myself in you.

My flower…

The professor tall and wiry and pressed, not unkind, and not humourless, but without time for either kindness or jokes.

Thank you for referring to me this….

This paradox.

Thank you for referring to me this delightful…

This delightful enigma. This impossible challenge?

With your permission, I would like to write this up as a case study to… It will be completely anonymous of course…

My love for her, it was lofty and devotional. There is nothing wrong with me. I am sick with love. Release me.

There is not much I can do when the patient does not cooperate.

The mother had been called upon to love without hope, without echo, to love in a torture garden, to love like an Olympian.

Much medication was dispensed: anti-inflammatories, anti-spasmodics, anti-emetics, anti-epileptics, sedatives. Anti-convulsants, antibiotics, antiseptics. And the antidotes, the antioxidants.

As the Jupiterian expansiveness of her spirit, so the unrestrained activity of her cells. With every ailment, a novel array of symptoms. She listed them to the specialists with some hesitation, worried that they may flinch when faced with such feebleness, recoil.

Into another country now. Love, where are you? What was your purpose and karma?

Hadn't she boasted of her bias for bruises and blood? Hadn't she searched for a He who would know how to tie her up and twist her without rope? Who would not flinch at lashing her with a belt or call her sick? Who would shiver with pleasure if the buckle hit her somewhere truly unpleasant, if it caught her on the elbow or whacked her sternum?

The Professor wanted to understand, to be in the picture.

And the Light Man?
I commune with him.
You commune with him. Do you do anything else?
Do we fuck!
Did he have any proof?
Proof?
That he is a Demon. Did he hold out anything, show you anything that could have been interpreted as supernatural?
Not as such. But, if you observe from a distance, you notice that the walk is lopsided. Almost as though he had very recently started to walk upright. And if you were implicated, then you would also notice that he crosses distances indiscernibly.
If you were implicated?
Yes, if you had become implicated, if he was taking you in.
Tell me about the evening of being ravished by the Depths.

She laughed and shrugged it off because the ravishment now, in this scientific surrounding, sounded melodramatic.

Oh that! That was just a good, old fashioned, kneetrembler …

The evening when Echo lost her voice and followed Him into the woods…

In search of a cure, she visited an island of volcanic crags, slopes and terraces, of caves and grottoes, of subterranean gases that rose to the surface synchronically, of hot sulphur springs and mineral mud stores.

Her landlady in her sea garden in her straw hat tells her to go out because it is a beautiful place to visit. But I am out she thinks. I am so, so, far out already. Obliging, she eats a pizza one afternoon on the empty terrace of an empty pizzeria in a near empty plaza, absent-mindedly looks at her phone, indifferent to evidence of a hacked email account. With each bite, chew and swallow she wants to gag. She recalls the daily recording of bowel movements dispatched to the hospital as the Poop Scoop, the sound of retching on the baby monitor, the feel of the girl draped across her, light and warm as a cashmere blanket.

A priest she meets on the island tells her that the healing was in the cave things and muddy waters inland and that, conversely, only a seaman could take her there, because here on the island they were the sons of Mermen and knew the waters that ran beneath the grounds well. They knew the submerged canyon beneath the island and the source of the underground vapours that heated the sand.

The priest had come into relief as silently as a moth on a moss speckled gravestone, had become visible only when he started speaking.

As above, so below, my dear. Roots and branches, geometry and stars.
And the cave things?
Cave things and muddy waters; he confirmed.
The seamen… They know the grounds well or the

groundswell?

Both my dear, both. They know the source and spirit of the amniotic spring. They know the sea of limitless life. When you find him follow him in silence, as Echo and Narcissus, into the forest.

The priest left her to the riddles, dozing on a rickety sun lounger at the mouth of a gorge, directly beneath a damp, cool corridor of cliffs and silhouettes. When she opened her eyes again someone was standing over her. Wolf-like and despite his smile, tense. Gold chains dangle from a thick, tanned neck, long shorts hang on his hips. His lips are silverish and his teeth spiky. He takes off his sunglasses and offers a hand to help her up.

His eyes are turquoise and orange. The sky is turquoise and orange. There the similarity ends. The man is of the deep, dead earth. The sea behind him a vast, dull frame. Eyes to burn and bury you.

She scrambles off the sun lounger clumsily and slips, missing his proffered hand and falling on hers instead, her face skimming the glistening clay floor.

The man smiled kindly and bent down to rescue her from further embarrassment;

I'm Dionysus. Delighted to meet you, and that you fell at my feet today.

Dionysus wiped some clay from her face, still smiling. It was *entre chien et loup,* and the man made clear that he himself was crepuscular, his split, that there were two of him.

Which one is Dionysus? You, or him?

They turned their back to the sea and headed inland past the vineyards and set off on a steep a mountain trail. Remembering the Moth Priest's advice, she did not speak. Eventually they reached a forest, dripping with dew and pollen and fruits and flowers. In a clearing, on a plateau, was a habitation carved out of a single large boulder, his house. A large 'D' was engraved on top of the entrance.

It is written in the codices of the etheric libraries that the cervix and the heart are linked by an energetic pathway and that if a man knew how to reach your heart via your cervix by mapping that bridge, you would be together for seven lifetimes... Adepts know when to lower the drawbridge and when and for whom to make ready the portal. Dilettantes do not. Because even though the concept of jurisdiction, and domination, and emotional bondage, are all a by-product of the imagination, seven lifetimes is not.

The entrance to the labyrinth is alluring and she is compelled to enter, to spiral to the centre, where the Master Daedalus was waiting. With each adornment she takes another step in, with each twinkling trinket, a turn. She tinkles when she arrives, pink powder on her eyes and cheeks both to evoke and hide any excitement. The windows are wide but have no air to spare. The wind wails outside, wails its wisdom, begging to be let in.

The evening when blood poured from his forehead in a perfect St George's Cross and everything was splattered with candle wax. The evening when a pungent nectar soaked the bed. The evening of shrieks, and murmured commands, and moans, and grunts and complicity and terror and giggles and pleas and release.

The evening when he promised her that the pleasure would be worth paying for, dying for and that therefore even though it was a game, it was also extremely real. It was a game in that her consent was required, and it was real in that it might not end well. *This is the condition of the world, revealing itself to you* he had said. *Isn't that what you came for?*

She is still at the door and he signals for her to stop. He will make her cross the threshold by slipping his index and middle fingers into her opening and yanking her hips towards him. She stumbles and falls onto him, buries her face in his neck to hide and signal her agitation. He wraps his other hand around her hair and tugs, tilting her head back. *Open your eyes, look at me.*

Open your mouth. Wider. He spits into her mouth and when she starts, he strikes her face with an open hand, and pushes his fingers deeper into her. He slaps her again. And again. *Don't move.* With each slap she feels her resistance subside, her pain receding, her body soften. She tightens the grip on the fingers inside her. The orange in his teal eyes pulsates with another life. His breathing is neither a rasp nor a purr.

He tightens his grip on her hair and pulls her head all the way back, roughly, exposing the thin skin of her neck, the commotion of her pulse. *I'm closer to you than your jugular vein* he hisses. *I am going to degrade and exalt you. I'm going to strangle you until you don't mind dying, just before you come for me, and become mine.*

The words she's kept interred in the depths of the cold hollow furnace of her belly suddenly find form, and travel up her central channel, escaping out of her mouth. *Make me come,* she echoes.

Shurooq Amin

Resurrection

Resurrected – not like the phoenix –
but like Plath's 'Lady Lazarus',
re-fleshed and re-risen
out of ashes
to eat men
alive:
prowl into
his heart
and snag
an artery,
howl with
the full moon,
shear that guttural lisp,
cleft your mammatus-cloud
breasts, offer him one gossamer
milk-leaking pendant
floating away
from the
source,
lure
his lust
with diaphanous
globules of aromatic
promise, light-stipple a kiss,
ease him into the jewelled
foliage of flames,

let the
cool
arc
of blue
strands
enlaced
onto your
face ensnare,
lineaments sifting,
cupping your countenance,
let the tart chaste taste
of you entice,
let him
find
luxuriant
contentment
in the knowledge
that you are
his,
and yes,
emblazon
WOMAN
on his
penis.

Joyce Mansour

Noise in the Next Room

A grain of sand
Wings fluttering
A stool
A citadel
O love's mad cavalry

I'm so mad with my mawkish envy
Hair tight in tight curls
Mammals dulled

Write a letter
A rolled-up towel
A room full of counters
A corridor toward the infamous
O cursed ignorance of love

How alone with my maddening friend
Vengeance tarred with suggestions
And greedy pleasantries

The driver's whip
An upright candle
A wave of black flags
   A buried parent
   O love's extravagant egoism
How old evil spirits

Cabalistic signs
And first-class compartments
How useless
In bed

Translated from French by Serge Gavronsky

Umm al-Ward al-Ajlaniyya

If You Want to Know

If you want to know how the old man fared with me, this is
    what went on.
He lolled me the whole night through, and when dawn flashed
    his private lips thundered rainlessly and his key wilted in my
    lock.

Translated from Arabic by Abdullah al-Udhari

Rasha Abbas

Simon the Matador

Why would we even want to discuss what happened during the final performance of that Valencia Circus thing – a circus utterly devoid of children? Alright, so there were a few early incidents involving adolescent performers. And yes, that did cause such extensive issues with the police that the circus did almost have to shut down. The organisers were forced to stop having minors perform in their shows, despite the complaints from the huge swathe of their clientele who had been thrilled by the sight of those young bucks up close, with their slender grass-fed bodies, garlands of flowers in their soft curly hair. But that's not the point of our story.

The unseen preparations for the magician's tricks – the hidden extra space built to conceal the assistant inside the box, or the place from which the doves actually fly out, when they seem to be emerging from the hat – these are the most exciting things of all, even for us, and by 'us' I mean the most sophisticated of audiences: the audience of the adult-oriented Valencia Circus. It's of no real significance to us that the clown in this circus presents his section of the show wearing a metal penis ring fringed with blue feathers, or that the magician performs his tricks naked apart from a black cloak tied at the throat and a leather gimp mask that only reveals his kohl-lined eyes. We're not here to watch either of these two, in reality do you think we're desperate? These scenes are really no more exciting than spending an evening at a reading by a poet whose verses are carved into slices of fresh meat that he eats when he's done reading, or whatever else goes on these days.

In reality, after that last performance of the show everyone simply stated that they didn't recall how everything that happened had begun, and most of them meant what they said. Perhaps we didn't notice the intention of the agitated magician, because he was masked? Or perhaps it was because we were too absorbed in trying to figure out how his trick worked, to spot the hidden device before he got started. Where would he hide the assistant's body while he sawed right through the middle of the box, we were wondering? Or at least this was the statement we gave to the police. Everyone uttered those exact same words, as if we had all colluded in their composition. No one wanted to admit that we never usually paid much attention to the magician's bit of the show anyway, as it tended to be the same every time and it didn't particularly grab us, especially when we had just that minute finished watching the tiger taming section. That got everyone so worked up. It had actually emboldened some of those present to get started on the orgy, right as the magician was inserting the first of two sharp planks into the box, followed by the second, thereby cutting the assistant's body into three equal sections.

The ancient circus's management was keen to run the performances with finesse, to learn from previous mistakes so that no one's experience would be marred by any discomfort or give rise to any feelings of guilt or shame – they wanted to keep the fun clean. What a wonderful service. It was obligatory for attendees to wear a mask concealing the upper part of the face. For me, this final show was my golden opportunity to get what I had been striving for, for so long. Thus, the events of that night, in their entirety, were especially charged for me personally. I had put a huge amount of effort into seizing the chance to sit in one particular seat: next to Simon the Matador. I do of course realise how vulgar a nickname this is for a man with tyrannical sex appeal, and it certainly wasn't me who bestowed that name on him in the first place, but it had stuck until it ended up sounding normal and kind of nice, classic kitsch, like a tattoo of a dagger plunged into a red heart. Simon works as an editor at a new publishing house that claims to be experimental and the quality of his work is almost equal to how sexy he is; very symmetrical black eyes, black hair, dark gleaming skin and a wide jaw. A beautiful thing. I was practically forbidding myself from staring at his lips each time I glanced at them, attempting to shelter behind an invisible shield so as to ward off the flaming vibrations he was emitting into the air around him. The way he dressed turned me on even more: he behaved as if he wasn't obliged to prove how handsome he was. He seldom changed the black cotton hoodie he wore, accessorised with a single silver ring on his finger. Although Simon the Matador and I didn't know each other I actually always thought I had a chance with him. But I hated to think how many mutual acquaintances we had, and that he could potentially chat to someone I knew about what might happen between us. I didn't want everyone who addressed the phrase 'I hope this email finds you well' to him imagining what I looked like getting choked with Simon the Matador's belt. Even with all these reservations, every step I took was driven by my incessant brooding on Simon (whose narcissistic personality I didn't like, nor his tongue permanently cocked back ready to launch into flirting with whoever caught his eye). It was a haunting topic especially given the way the air was always buzzing with stories revolving around Simon. His latest episodes, his strange sexual proclivities, the latest home he'd wrecked, what his ex-girlfriend had said. The entire city knew every last detail of his private life. Whenever I was hanging out with people and talk turned to Simon my mood would be ruined; if I'd been smoking hash, the burden of my damned desire for him would weigh more heavily on me than ever. I'd have to leave. I'd go home and get under a cold shower in the hope of silencing that rude voice on a loop in my head endlessly clamouring for Simon the Matador, so that I might to be able to sleep or work afterwards. On rare occasions, the image of Simon the Matador would fade gently and effortlessly from my mind, and this would be when the Teacher would come back into my life. In contrast to him, the Teacher, who was a professor in the university – once again, I know how vulgar and trite the nickname is – was nearly twenty years older than me, calm and conservative, with one lover unchanged for decades and to whom he was clearly devoted. It didn't seem like he was particularly interested in what I felt for him, although I was pretty sure that he somehow found my follies entertaining. In those days the Teacher was busy with something or other, and had disappeared for ages, so there was room for the story of Simon the Matador to rip though me once again.

I had walked with the Teacher two months before to Max Lieberman's house, which had become a museum. We'd wandered around the museum a little then we sat on its balcony, which had been made into a little cafe. I hungrily observed the Teacher as he removed his wet raincoat and his wet black hat. He was talking about those Lieberman paintings that were still missing, since back in the day the Nazis had seized the house and turned it into a military hospital. In an attempt to impress him I told him that the places where the paintings had hung, which had deliberately been left empty by the museum management and marked with squares painted in different colours, were an excellent example of the presence of absence, and that these empty squares might be as important as the lost paintings. The Teacher knew perfectly well that all of this nonsense was just a decoy, a pretext to begin talking once again about him and about myself, and so he attempted, in his embarrassment, to change the subject. I didn't give him the chance, but neither did I disappoint him, as I went on to explain that I didn't feel at all frustrated by everything I hadn't got, no matter how much I had wanted him. And I wasn't lying. I genuinely was almost satisfied at that time with the Teacher's sparse presence in my life.

Things had continued in this vein until a few days before the Valencia Circus incident, when I went to visit my friend at the experimental theatre she runs, which just so happens to host the Valencia's shows. I didn't have much patience with the hundreds of tangents she kept going off on and my mind was mainly on other things while she rambled on. But then suddenly the visit turned very interesting indeed; she told me the next Valencia Circus show was almost sold out, despite the secrecy and exclusivity of the invitations. I wouldn't have felt any great excitement about this news if in her enthusiasm at the numbers she hadn't gesticulated with the reservation sheet, making Simon the Matador's name catch my eye on the list. I needed to think quickly. There was no way I was going to reveal what I was after to her, a nymphomaniac who would certainly grow very interested in Simon the Matador if I let my desire for him show, so I pointed to the seat number next to Simon's on the list, which bore the name of a woman I had never heard of. I said that I was interested in sitting next to this woman because I was keen to meet her in connection with a project I wanted to work on. She smiled mockingly as if she had not bought the lie, and for that she really can't be blamed.

In the auditorium on the night in question a digital image of a virtual tomb for an imaginary poet was being shown on a giant screen behind the stage. On the stage the magician stood still, saw in hand. This was one of the traditions of the circus, hosting visual artworks as backdrops to their shows. By this point I had succeeded in starting a conversation with Simon the Matador (who was sitting beside me) on the pretext of the artwork and the imaginary poet's life story. But after that things began to get embarrassing, as Simon the Matador obviously thought he needed to come across as poetic and refined in order to impress me, and then from there try to lure me into talking about sexual topics. At this, I completely lost the desire to be with him in any way. I was very disappointed, as he now seemed utterly vile to me; the memory of the Teacher came bearing down on me once again. I felt that I must take a defensive position and repel Simon the Matador by being unfriendly. But he had swiveled his torso towards me by now, and his hand had begun caressing my thigh. When he drew me roughly towards him, I was embarrassed, thinking about how I would look to the Teacher if he were here right now, concealed behind one of those masks. I tried to force myself to go with the flow, on the off chance I suddenly got turned on, but Simon the Matador's lips felt so damp, and the movement of his tongue in my mouth seemed clumsy, as if he didn't know what he was doing. After a little while he let go of me. He'd obviously given up, both on his own attempts and on my ability to respond to them in any way. Many of the audience members around us had left their seats and gone to do what they'd come here for, and I felt extremely frustrated by what had just happened, and irritated by everything – by my tacky obsession with the Teacher who had not shown me any interest in his whole life, and by Simon who had just destroyed all of my previous fantasies. I got up from my place and tried to make my way out, leaning on the seats backs to wade through the people scattered across the floor and draped over the seats at the height of an ongoing sex fest in which I played no part and had no stake. I suppose I did hear the magician's assistant scream loudly, just before I reached the exit, but it never occurred to me that she might be anything other than one of the many orgasmic female audience members. The sound of the commentary recounting part of the imagined poet's life over the images on the screen was still going.

Before I left the building I looked back over my shoulder for the last time. Screams filled the whole place now, and I saw the magician on stage holding half of his assistant's torso as he turned her pallid face towards the audience. At the time I was unable to conceive that this was not all part of the show, this and another assistant fainting, and the monkey jumping towards the pile of severed legs under the box, and the tiger that smoked – so beloved of the Valencia crowd – running across the stage towards the pool of blood, and of course Simon the Matador trailing behind me, embarrassed for no other reason than not knowing what he was meant to do once I'd left.

Translated from Arabic by Alice Guthrie

Arim Jariyat Zalbahda an-Nakhas

Narrow and Hot

The poet al-Kharki recounts that once, while al-Kharki was
   drunk, he saw Arim in the street and recited,

Would you like a phallus like mine?
And my phallus is like me.
It stands erect in front of me and stretches back behind me.
And I pound with it like a mule's phallus.

Arim chastised him with the following poem,

How about what is so narrow and hot
It would be exhausting for you inside?
If you saw it, it would stress you to death.

He said, 'God knows, you shamed me,' and walked away.

Translated from Arabic by Wessam Elmeligi

Safiyya al-Baghdadiyya

I Am the Wonder

I am the wonder of the world, the ravisher of hearts and minds.
Once you've seen my stunning looks, you're a fallen man.

Translated from Arabic by Abdullah al-Udhari

Adania Shibli

Without Rhyme

They had just made love when he said Lovemaker. She waited a moment, enough to regain a little confidence, then said Lovemaker? Not lover? and in a strong, clear voice he replied, eyeing her dim figure on the sofa: If you like.

He was still holding the tissue he had used to wipe himself a minute before. Then he repeated: Lovemaker, and she repeated after him: Lovemaker, and he smiled and she smiled after him.

It was approaching two-thirty in the afternoon. Their first lunchbreaker, he realised: Our first lunchbreaker. She laughed. Not that she had any desire to laugh, but his presence made her feel so weak that she was close to tears at any moment. She considered leaving, though she had only arrived at two.

He went on cheerfully: Icebreaker, Pacemaker, Saltshaker. But she could only think of the sofa, which did not end in 'ker'. There he sat, silently inviting her to say a word with the same rhyme, but all that floated back to him was a faint hum which had begun again to issue from the walls and furniture of the house. He had heard the sound before while sitting on this sofa, smoking an old cigarette and waiting for her. After a pause he turned to her and said Lawmaker, Notetaker, Codebreaker as she stayed quiet, silently searching for a word to offer him. At last she turned to him and, a little hesitant, said: I can't find one, then dipped her worried eyes, letting them rest on the collar of the shirt she loved. He had worn it especially for her. It had white squares edged in black, which seemed, after a moment's intense focus, as if they were about to leap off the fabric towards her, square by square. To escape them she turned her gaze further down, to his hands. She was convinced that for him this was only a sexual matter and had previously considered introducing him to another woman to replace her, especially since their encounters had begun to drain her anxious soul. But she was afraid of annoying him if she did, and so she went on in silence, stubbornly studying the one finger of his that was not hidden by the tissue like the others. Then he concluded: Baker, Faker, Quaker, and yawned.

She was tired too. She had had only four hours' sleep the night before, having woken at seven with a fierce longing to see him, five hours before they were due to meet. Five hours that might have been four and a half, for he had invited her over at one-thirty, two and she had decided it would be two.

She reached her hand towards his fingers, still clasped around the tissue. Finger, she thought, if only the g would shift to k, then she moved her hand away and he went after it. A bit tiresome, this girl, he thought. He had started to wait for her at noon, and had smoked that old cigarette because he wanted to open the new pack in her presence, but then, when it was one-thirty and the bell had not rung, and when it was one-thirty-five, he sensed that she would not come. Perhaps she had changed her mind and decided against it, when lunch was almost ready.

Then a feeling of tranquility came over her for the first time in days. She looked up to his face and found that he had fallen asleep where he lay on the sofa. So that was why.

Why did she not get up and leave now, pull herself out of this pit where she had sunk. But she remained pinned to the sofa, fixed on his sleeping face, held by the fear that his eyes would suddenly open and meet her gaze and he would think she was in love with him. Her eyes darted back to his finger once more.

He started from sleep. Into each other's eyes they stared and remained like that for some time, neither bothering to look away, until he said: Matchmaker. She embraced him, laughing, and he laughed too. Then she asked: Do you want to sleep?

Do you?

I'll let you sleep.

She stood up and announced she was leaving, then moved towards the chair where she had left her coat, the torn gift wrapping on the floor, when she remembered the shop assistant who had spent twenty minutes dashing from one corner to another trying to wrap the gift. A scandal, how she had wrapped it, as if this gift were destined for some great romance. She, all the while, was angry at herself: rather than torment the assistant, she should have told her the truth.

She put on her coat, not yet her scarf, and returned to where he sat watching her. She came very close to him, bent one of her knees and pressed it between his legs on the sofa, then she wrapped her hands around his neck. Earlier, she had said that she wished she could own a small piece of his body, the strip between his neck and shoulder. The first reason she could think of for saying such a thing was foolish presumption. On second thought, though, it may just have been a pure desire to lay her head very close to his neck. But there was no doubt that this desire too was foolish, purely so. Then, with her hands around his neck, turning over all this at the edge of madness, a thought leapt to her mind to strangle him. To hold her hands to his neck and then he would be dead. Now that would be a scandal. To kill a person, that was not an easy task. He was still watching her. He asked: Did you decide you would leave when you were still at home? She did not fully understand his question but felt she had to say yes, to reassure him that she was leaving. Then she turned her neck the other way, to the ashtray, which contained a single cigarette butt and a little ash.

Caretaker, Glassmaker, he said, but this no longer made them laugh.

Still she had not left. She wanted to leave naturally, and that disgusting naturally did not come. If only she could leave and not see his face again, just like that, without anger or annoyance, and without the obligation even to say goodbye, just slip out of the room naturally. Instead her eyes were fixed to the ground, as if searching for her shoe, when she was on the point of sobbing like a child. Why could she not walk away, careless of him, naturally?

Well? he asked. What did you decide? And she replied: Is it true ... that you want ... Then he shouted at the ceiling in anger: Ah! Now she wants to start a discussion!

She went back to where she had left her scarf and bag, and as she picked them up, quickly but carefully, he said Codebreaker. She looked at him and said with some contempt: You said that one already. She turned her back and moved towards the door. He came after her. There were two metres between them when she put her hand on the key whose jangle dissolved into his question: Are you upset?

She turned and rushed into his arms. Laid her head on his shoulder close to his neck. She could have wept right there, but just in time she said: Not at all. Just tired. I'm very sleepy. Her answer put him at ease, and she returned to the door, crossed the threshold at last, and took to the steps in a hurry.

Behind her, at every turn in the stair he thanked her for something. For the gift. Her visit. The lovely time they had spent together, etc. And she did not miss a single You're welcome, one for every Thank you he let out.

Earlier, she had thought that once she was out in open air her tears would flow, but all that emerged was a lump in the throat and a burning in the eyes. Then, as she walked down the familiar narrow street, along the rows of olive trees, over the gravel scattered on the pavements, at last a word with the same rhyme came to her mind. Heartbreaker.

Translated from Arabic by Yasmine Seale

lisa luxx

Arachnophobia

first there was the fire   how it webs across
empty space   bending & stretching collecting
wood   you sitting with a cider can   calling me
goddess of flames   I'm too drunk   build it
too big & we have to rustle & shuffle our litter
back a little bit   then came the embrace

it's been 358 days   & I'm still in that embrace how we became
something like a spider   an eight-legged ugly thing   weaver
of the web   our limbs scattering   we spider   who appears
from nowhere   beloveds always arrive to us by surprise
we hideous   maker of marvellous satin strings of light

4 seasons later   let me delete a layer   a no reason not to kiss
your neck   bury my mouth so deep within yours I can ask
your heart questions myself   tongues hunger   dig out ink
from the wooden box of each others grin   *kiss me again*
(could never forget how your hair felt against your back   how
I could nuzzle in   nor the nouns I called you when we were
stoned kids   spells)   as we spider   I press you in earth
hands warm against your warm   only black hears   bound in
damp silence   cascade breath   years of waiting within flesh
now *come in*   wash longing   hips search wish   this   is
it   when the rain comes   we spider   flourish & huck
our wanting against flesh wet   against wet against skin tap
suck   rain come harder let it rush the fire is the dancing ghost

189

of fallen wood   our web woven from nothing   fills empty
space   unique   once broken can never be re-made   yet here
we are   we spider

> but   when   the   rain   came   that   day
> we didn't spider   we said *mate*   pulled
> back our arms   I threw wet leaves on
> the flames   found a spider up my sleeve
> shook it out   & we went separate ways
> first there was fire   second   there
> was   the   breath   that kept it   ablaze

Umm al-Ala bint Yusuf

If Love and Song

If love and song were not spoilt by wine, I'd spend my time drinking glass after glass and get what I longed for.

Translated from Arabic by Abdullah al-Udhari

Jariyat Humam ibn Murra

For a Bald Head

O Humam ibn Murra, my heart yearns
For that which men have.
O Humam ibn Murra, my heart yearns
For a bald head near sprouting hair.
O Humam ibn Murra, my heart yearns
For a hard branch to fill my source of urine.

Translated from Arabic by Wessam Elmeligi

Ulayya bint al-Mahdi

Rayb

The heart for Rayb is yearnful,
O Lord, how is that shameful? (As-Suli 1: 20)

Translated from Arabic by Wessam Elmeligi

Sabrina Mahfouz

TALI: one day when I worked at the bakery

you were a buff guy queuing to buy a cheese and onion pasty,
I knew because your eyes became canals when you saw them
in the oven, your perfect head to the side, mountainous.

I stood with my blue gloves on, nails poking out
wishing for a second or maybe ten
that I could be invisible, watch you pay someone else

for the pet-yellow pasty you couldn't wait to eat.
So I wouldn't have to wonder if you knew me
from somewhere that wasn't here, in the bakery.

I stuck calling cards of me wearing fishnets in phone boxes once,
trying to be more professional.
My black and white pic has been up in Debenhams, shoplifter.

I imagine being your girlfriend, how summery that would be.
You'd pick me up in your Golf and we'd go cinema, share
    popcorn.

I imagine being you, looking at me, your new girlfriend,
Wondering what you did to get such a good girl, so sweet.

I imagine being your daughter, waiting for the sound of your
    key
the little jumps my feet would make to extol your heart.

I imagine being your mother, proud of the job I'd done
hoping beyond hope that you never brought home a girl like

that's £1.25 I said and you paid, no change needed.
Our fingers touched once, I almost saw we were married
but you threw me a smile that said I know you and I thought
do you?

Suad Amiry

As Yummy as Kibbeh

As the car tootled along the straight and narrow road, Teta's mood became almost as serene and as open as the Jezreel Valley itself. But as she listened to the noise of the mechanically run engine, Teta missed the two robust horses that once, on her wedding day in 1896, had dragged the two-seated carriage where she, her groom, her mother and her two sisters had sat. Rather than spending the night in one of the Caravan Serais that lay along the road between 'Arrabeh and Damascus, Jiddo and his Jaha opted to make the long trip in one stretch.

Before they'd set off, the groom had said with excitement, 'I can't wait to get home.' All the men in the wedding party had teased him.

'I wonder why!' joked Said, the bridegroom's closest cousin, as he laughed out loud. The other men laughed along with him. The women shied away. Teta pretended not to have heard. She did not understand what his cousin and friends were referring to or joking about then: she sure does now. She blushed then, and she would blush again now, recalling the intimacy of her wedding night.

Having been shy and timid all her life, it was no different on the night of her wedding.

In the company of her groom, Jiddo, Jaha stepped into their matrimonial room. She quietly sighed. Though she was rather relieved that the wedding celebrations, which lasted three long days, had finally come to an end, her heart felt heavy. Her anxiety was amplified as the terrifying moment she had been worried about had finally arrived. She stiffened. No matter how much her mum had explained to her what normally, and naturally, happens between a husband and a wife, she was still afraid. With a sense of estrangement, she looked around the matrimonial room. It felt as if it were not hers, as if she had not seen it many times since she'd arrived at her in-laws a week ago. Only yesterday, she had thought her room the most beautiful room in the splendid Baroudi Mansion, which was itself indeed far more elaborate and magnificent than all the Abdulhadi mansions put together. She stood close to the water fountain in order to cool off. She re-examined the king-size matrimonial bed placed in the middle of the room. She gazed at the painted wooden panelled walls and got trapped in their geometrical designs. She then raised her head up and stared at the wooden ceiling. Realising there was no way out of this, she forced her shaking legs to carry her to her matrimonial bed, and carefully placed herself on its very edge. She almost fell off it. Her groom, who had been standing right behind her, was aware how lost, tense and scared she had been since she had left her home in 'Arrabeh, and especially so tonight.

She anxiously waited for the groom to take the first step and lead her through it or get it over with. She made as though to surrender. She looked at him nervously. He gave her a big smile in return, while considering the best move to release the tension out of her stiff body and bring down the walls she had built around her. He calmly walked in her direction and gave her another big smile, then jokingly said:

'Nothing to worry about or be sacred of. Let's play doctor, like my sister's kids, and roll on top of one another. I am sure you also played doctor when you were a child, didn't you?' A shy smile broke out on her face as he continued: 'Yes, you're gonna love it, enjoy it, and ask for more. It is going to be as yummy as kibbeh with yogurt. The kind you'd never eaten before, but once you tasted it you continued to ask for more!' She could not help but laugh, as she tried to understand the relationship between her wedding night and the additional servings of kibbeh in cooked yogurt. Being the light-hearted and kind man he was, and two decades her senior, he was capable of handling her. It was going to be hard work, time consuming, but it would eventually work out, he assured himself. Considering his huge appetite for sex and his desire to have as many children as God was willing to give him, he did not want to think of any other possibility.

With her wedding dress still on, she sat motionless on the edge of the high brass bed, waiting for her groom to act. He stood right next to her, his thin long legs touching her chubby knees. He delicately and softly took her chin in his fingers and moved her stiff head up towards him. Her shy eyes moved up to look at his face. She shivered as he came closer, softly caressing her face. She felt his gentle kisses, which were slowly but surely moving towards her small mouth, fall delicately on her cold face. As she froze, he sat down beside her, and gently manoeuvred her body so they were sitting in front of one another on the bed. He gave her another round of kisses. While kissing her, he engulfed her in his two strong arms, one arm supporting her neck, while the other he wrapped around her waist. His lips circled her tightly closed lips, then to the back of her ear, and down her neck. She sat still trying to work out what to expect next, as none of this had been described to her by her mother when she had told her, 'He will mount you and rub his body against yours. Once his breathing gets heavy you open your legs and he will penetrate you. He will do some more pounding; I have counted them they will be about twenty or thirty maximum before he comes. And that's it my daughter. With God's help you shall get pregnant soon.' Her mother had continued, 'And yes, it may hurt the first time, and you may also bleed a little, it is no big deal. You will get used to it with time although it gets more boring and tiring by the day.'

She was not looking forward to this. Once again, his tongue wetted her full lips, slipping down the other side of her short neck and behind her ear. He kept at it until he felt a shiver go through her body, and a moan escaped her tightly closed lips. He shifted position; he sat closely behind her and pressed his body against hers. He embraced her tightly towards him with his two long arms until she softened. He slowly slipped his left hand under her dress and crawled under her tight bra to finally get hold of her breast. It filled his palm. With his soft hands he first caressed it then squeezed it. She moaned. That encouraged him to grab the right breast and enjoy a circular rub. He could feel her protruding nipples, and she could by now feel his protruding parts. They enjoyed each other's heavy breathing. By then it was she who voluntarily turned her stimulated body to meet his. He saw her arousal in her parted lips and droopy eyes. He delicately grabbed her by the shoulders and pushed her back against the bed and was on top of her before she hit the mattress. She could feel his protruding parts hard against her body but did not know what to do with them. Hugging her tightly, he rubbed his warm body against hers. He heatedly grabbed her face and gave her a long kiss on the mouth pushing his tongue between her lips. As his tongue moved in and out of her mouth and around her lips, she ran out of breath, and she had to move her head away from him to take a long breath. More kisses landed on her neck as she felt his hand on her chest in an attempt to unbutton her dress. Incredibly, she was stripped of all in no time. As he swiftly stood up to unbutton his shirt and remove his white trousers, she glimpsed the size of his erect penis and got scared. She closed her eyes, covered her face with the white sheet, and wondered how painful it was going to be. His soft, white, tall body was back on top of her, but now that they were both naked, it felt different. Once they were naked, she remembered that things happened very quickly. She timidly lay on her back as he moved in and out of her. 'It is going to hurt you a bit, so if it is too painful, just let me know and I will stop. But it should also be exciting and enjoyable. Tell me when to stop.' But since it was a special kind of pain, an enjoyable pain, she gave in, surrendered, and let it be.

He was pounding over her for hours to come, for days to come and for years to come. Her first wedding night turned out to be like every other night. And as life went on, she waited for him to finish so as to get some sleep so she could have what it takes to get through the heavy chores and mounting responsibilities of the ever-growing Baroudi family.

An Excerpt from My Damascus

Dahna bint Mas-hal

Lay off

Lay off, you can't turn me on with cuddle, a kiss or scent.
Only a thrust rocks out my strains until the ring on my toe falls
  in my sleeve and my blues fly away.

Translated from Arabic by Abdullah al-Udhari

Ulayya bint al-Mahdi

Salma

I wish Salma would see me
Or would be told about me,
So she could free a captive
Suffering with a tired heart.
O houses of gorgeous women,
Beautiful and attractive,
The rain was generous to you
With clouds wet and sweet.

Translated from Arabic by Wessam Elmeligi

Dahiya al-Hilaliyya

Yemeni lover

I hope as my soul lives in hope,
To spend my night with a Yemeni lover.

Translated from Arabic by Wessam Elmeligi

Hoda Barakat

The Stone of Laughter (An Excerpt)

When his father's younger brother moved his household
from the village to come and live at Sitt Isabel's, Khalil's sense
of isolation lifted somewhat, and he felt more comfortable
spending time in other people's company. Perhaps it was the
inevitable bustle of a large family that buoyed him up, keeping
him just above the currents that seemed to submerge his own
room. He opened the curtains. He went out more, coming and
going energetically. He moved between his uncle's household
and his own room below.

That's the way he saw it, mostly. There were moments
when the purity of his intentions seemed suspect as he tried to
account for the changes coming over him, but he just ascribed
it to Zahra and didn't think any further. This family coming
to the city had had a long journey from their remote village,
and they had arrived in a state of utter exhaustion, depleted by
the torments and dangers to which they had been exposed on
the way. They had trudged along beneath the strafing of Israeli
airplanes, and had been forced to sleep unsheltered and to walk
long distances on rough byways skirting the many roadblocks
marking the main routes to the capital. Arriving in the city
did not alleviate their worry. They knew that the city streets
were anything but safe: fiendish alien shadows seemed to haunt
the city night. But at least the city turned out to be a bit less
complicated than they had feared. When they showed up, Khalil
promptly showed them into Sitt Isabel's flat. He moved a lot
of things into Naji's room, piling them up haphazardly, and he

asked them not to use it.

As they inspected the flat minutely, warily, poking into corners or staring at the ceiling as though they were looking for items or bodies that would have no reason to be there, Khalil felt good, even happy. He had a sense of hope that perhaps the evil spirit haunting this flat might be chased away again. With such a number of people moving in, surely the place could once again become a home? Looking something like what it had been before.

Zahra skidded down the stairs in her plastic flip-flops and would stop at his door. Knocking diffidently, she would invite him to come and eat. He always accepted. He would take his seat across from his uncle, and they all consumed the food laid out on the large tray with the same eager appetite every time. But Zahra did not sit down with them. She hovered nearby, scampering into the kitchen the minute anyone asked for anything. Often she got it wrong, coming back with something no one needed. Her father invariably shook his head in feigned regret, before he mocked her loudly. Her mother would call her over to eat, but she would snap back in fury, 'I don't want anything.' Khalil couldn't help fixing on the incongruity – as he saw it – between the bulky solidity of her legs and the fragile hollowness of her waistline. Her eyes held some appeal, but that was not enough to transform her broad face with its rather bloated features into the visage of a pretty girl. Only the sweep from her buttocks to her neck seemed well-proportioned. He found it arousing, even, as his eyes travelled to her small, sharply protruding breasts.

It gave Khalil a true sense of contentment to sense that Zahra had fallen for him. He thought constantly about this attachment; how she threw herself into tidying up and cleaning the place whenever he was about. And how animated she was! Never standing still. Then, she would suddenly lose her appetite. Her gestures became awkward, her movements clumsy. Whenever he looked at her or spoke to her, she would begin rubbing at her right eye. Khalil absolutely loved it that Zahra was in love with him. He even had the sense that her passion had somehow originated somewhere inside of himself. Or, it seemed as if the two of them, he and Zahra, together, were in love with this person called Khalil. He was always daydreaming about what this desire was evidently doing to Zahra. How, when he wasn't around, she would fall into a state of lethargy and incapacity, unable to do anything more than emit loud sighs. How she would train her ears to hear the sound of his particular footfall outside the door. How she must cradle the glass he had emptied, or his coffee cup, before setting it down in the kitchen sink. How she would lay in bed, wide awake, imagining him, conjuring a moment when he would offhandedly touch her face, or by coincidence brush against her shoulder, and then she would fantasise that he would confess his love, telling her he was losing his mind over her, that he couldn't sleep. How her hands must rove over her body, across her hot skin, her hands that had now become Khalil's hands.

In the flat, the air seemed to overflow with Zahra's cassettes, playing singers Khalil knew he had heard on the FM radio without being able to recall their names. But it depressed him to find that the chaotic activity of his uncle's family, what he had seen as the vivacity he had sensed when they arrived, the way they occupied this space, did not manage to wrench what had been an empty, lifeless flat into the semblance of a home – that is, into anything resembling the life-force of Sitt Isabel's home. Now, the objects that took up space here were notable only for their immediate and obvious utility, as though one could not be in this flat for long unless performing some urgent and necessary business, like eating or sleeping or going to the loo or cleaning oneself up. As though this were a workplace rather than a place where one could be still, or relax, or think about things. A place where one lived. The flat had more the air of a post office, items always in transit, nothing in sight that wasn't strictly practical. Even cleaning the place was about being quick, efficient, and mechanical, an operation that was never thorough. The second light bulb – in the fixture on the dining room ceiling – flickered out, but no one replaced it, since apparently the sole light in the sitting room was enough to see by. Some furnishings from the kitchen or a bedroom moved, as if of their own accord, into the sitting room because it was 'more useful' to have them there. This was no longer a home because its internal rhythm had been reset, speeded up. Opportunistic time, not a tempo that was settled into itself, quiet, announcing its own permanence. That those staying here felt so transient didn't seem reason enough to chop up and destroy the flat's time in this way. It saddened Khalil, but it also left him feeling confident that Zahra's feelings were not his responsibility. Without a doubt it was an infatuation that would pass, a temporary love from a temporary girl. The fleetingness of it made it all the more enjoyable. He could savour this passion of hers and imagine himself acting on it, precisely because soon, it would be gone.

The space that Sitt Isabel's home and his uncle's family occupied, as it filled Khalil's head, seemed a space disfigured by artificiality and evasion. The necessary intimacy in which this large family lived, with its cooking and its little anecdotes about relatives, its memories of its own long-gone dignified past, Zahra's infatuation, and Khalil's infatuation with her infatuation, the gratification he got from his feverish imaginings, the way he had emerged from his apparent isolation, that chasm of loneliness, his fixation on the flat and the fleeting rhythm that did not bring back its original spirit – all of it collapsed into a meaningless object of ridicule when his eyes fell on Yusuf.

The moment he saw Yusuf.

Yusuf, younger than Zahra, was rarely in the flat for any length of time, because what he loved was being in the city. He went out all the time, even if these outings didn't amount to much more than going to the end of their street to huddle in a corner of the games arcade there. Yusuf was oblivious to everything but his new experiences and his ventures with boys his own age; Yusuf was breaking Khalil's heart. Really breaking it, like someone carrying a precious, heavy glass vessel who flings it hard to the ground and shatters it. Khalil felt some natural resistance in his body, like an antibody that formed simply by the sight of Yusuf – a vision that surely would have sent the ancient Yusuf of the scriptures to his death.

Every time Khalil saw Yusuf, it was his heart, or his stomach that spoke, not his mind. *Omigod, omigod, omigod* – and then he would feel faint and dizzy. It had been especially hard when the family first arrived.

Yusuf was tall and very thin. He was thin in a way that suggested not weakness, or fragility, or any lack of energy, but rather hardness and concealed strength. His complexion was a soft russet, the brown of earthenware that has just come out of the kiln; a subdued, burnished brown that had an ancient quality to it, like the skin you imagined the slaves of the pharaohs had, or like the wood of the very early icons featured in illustrated art books. His fingers seemed never to have touched a firm substance; they glistened softly as if just emerging from a dried-fruit syrup. His face, when Khalil let his eyes linger on it a little, left a raw, swollen feeling in his throat that reminded him of eating unripe quince. Khalil saw, or felt, the water coursing from Yusuf's eyes, but all it left in his throat was the painfully tickling dryness caused by a maddened bee. Yusuf's honey was poisoned honey, and his body was bruised fruit, blue pulp, beckoning and irresistible as the deep-blue emptiness of a chasm. On the edge, one perished with desire, longing to throw oneself against distant rocks, their killer-sharp edges softened by the faraway mists on the other side.

Yusuf was so handsome he made the Renaissance sculptors' work look gauche and crude – the bulgy marble-white forms they produced, veiny, like the bodies of happy well-fed cattle. Images and forms more akin to beautiful, mute animals that left nothing to the imagination as they put everything into that external form, leaving no interior mysteries to elude the eyes of scrupulous observers. He was more handsome than the human forms without soul found in the photographs in fitness magazines of heroic he-men lifting weights. In contrast, the image of the icon saint, outlined so precisely in liquid gold, or a pharaonic-era mummy's mask with its needle-thin colourful contours, that Yusuf possessed, presented only as much of their face as they want to give: they offered a door through which you can pass to reach that other face, the one you need: the beauty of that other face, one wholly particular to you. These are faces that demand a longer gaze, demand that your eyes spend time there, to accustom themselves, before the face will open to you and reveal itself.

Like the mummy and the icon, Yusuf's face wore this mask. You would not learn easily or quickly how beautiful Yusuf was. Because first, you had to appreciate his coldness, how hard he was, how distant and impossible to approach. Indeed, he was at his hardest and most resistant when he wasn't really there. Like a distant bombardment that would have already ended by the time the sound of it reached you; the wounded and the dead would already be wounded and dead by then, while you continued to cower, shuddering and jolting this way and that like a confused donkey caught in the crossfire. Like an ass – that was how Khalil saw himself in Yusuf's presence, a little donkey separated from his mother, far away from his familiar pasture and the other donkeys, alone and scared and hungering, clumsy and crude; where at the corner of his wide, empty black eye a droning fly lays its egg.

Khalil hated seeing Yusuf. And he loved seeing Yusuf. A lot. Whenever Zahra invited him to eat with them, he felt freed of the responsibility for taking any initiative himself. He would climb the stairs, his knees trembling with the agony of knowing that Yusuf might be there or might not be there. The city was in a state of calm now, more or less; the shelling in the streets had lessened – those bombing raids that Khalil couldn't help but long for, the way one craves a quick and immediate death, because it would stop Yusuf from going out, and would fix him in one location for a stretch of time that was never long enough, and that was always too long to be bearable.

Some evenings, though, or during the night, he could hear the sounds of shelling starting up. He stayed in his room, unless and until his uncle called him, or Zahra perhaps, to come and join them, where they were protecting themselves by crowding into the space on the landing beneath the stairs. In the beginning, he would sit among them uneasily, stiffly, as though he were sitting on the impossibly narrow filament of *the straight path*. But soon his anxiety waned into a state of passive dullness. The shelling seemed to make Zahra happy, but Khalil could not summon any pleasure at seeing her joy. Her intense feelings could not draw him – not once Yusuf was around. Yusuf never settled quietly into the tiny space which was all there was to occupy. He always seemed very agitated, was constantly fidgeting, would move suddenly as though he intended to make a run for the street. He would ask a question or two about what was going on out there, and Khalil could only respond with a string of terse mutters. It was meant to tell Yusuf that he couldn't expect a real explanation at the moment, because any answer to these questions would be long and complicated. No matter how hard Khalil tried to avoid looking Yusuf in the eye, Yusuf's eyes reached him, like drifting seeds from a tree, like those microscopic thorns that cacti release with every gust of wind. When he could feel Yusuf squeezing his chest, Khalil would place his cold palm against the knot in his stomach and press, harder and harder, until the knot inside dissolved into pure pain. And then, body and soul, Khalil would long for the shelling to end – if there was any possibility that this would not go on forever.

Returning to his room, Khalil would turn resolutely to the little preoccupations he had learned to immerse himself in whenever the shelling stopped. He cleaned his room and washed his sheets and clothing. He carried out these tasks with more bustle and show than before, yet the results gave him less satisfaction. In the end, all he had to show for it was a sense of despair about not being able to attain the state of well-being that these cleaning spells had given him before. He was conscious that his ploy of turning his thoughts to Zahra's passion for him had gradually lost its effectiveness, and finally he had to acknowledge that he was completely entangled in this love of his for Yusuf. That his wasting body was attached to Yusuf's body by a tube through which a terrible, demonic substance poured, filling him, swirling and boiling through his insides like volcanic lava. He sat bewildered for hours on end, his head empty. Sometimes he thought about leaving his room and going somewhere far away, but he couldn't think of a place to go. He would tell himself that he must go out and find some hard work to do, so that he could come back completely exhausted and fall asleep. Then he would think about turning down their invitations to come and eat, or to spend the evening in their flat. He would make excuses that they would know meant he was avoiding Zahra's attachment – for surely they had discovered it by now – out of a keen sense of moral duty. But then sometimes Yusuf, with his restless energy, would come by Khalil's room. He never stayed long. He was awkward and uncomfortable because his image of Khalil was that this man was a man of culture, a city sophisticate. He would announce that his quick visit was over by saying that he was going upstairs and would Khalil like to come up and watch TV. Khalil would follow him upstairs. But then one of Yusuf's mates would summon him and a few minutes later, he would be gone, making his apologies. And there sat Khalil, floundering in the swells of hot liquid surging through him. The feeling inside of him, as if a miserable, soaking-wet tomcat sat there scratching to get out, would turn into a concentrated hatred of Zahra, whose reddened cheeks betrayed how intensely happy she was to have him there. He couldn't help feeling intensely aware of her body odour, disgusted by her armpits. He would think to himself that legs as thick as this, hands as red and rough as this, skin like that of an animal – these weren't the marks of a creature with a soul. Now she looked to him like an old, rotting fish, its drooping eyes thickly coated, still thrashing in the water but only so that it could release more of a stink. On an evening like this Khalil would stare long and hard at Zahra, because now all that was left to him was a kind of self-torture.

When he went downstairs, he stood there, in the middle of his room, his body as slight as ever but feeling utterly heavy and useless. He would twist his head, and work his mouth into a grimace, trying to suppress the dry sobs filling the room. Supporting himself against the back of the chair or the wall, he said to himself over and over, *My God, I am dying. Dying of love.*

Translated from Arabic by Marilyn Booth

Yasmine Seale

After Ibn Arabi (poem 27)

You were home for a night

& my heart still glitters,
hungry to spin you

sagas from a trip so dull
I wept to pass the time.

& so much of it: dark
made no difference,

sleep never came. We
drove without marking

the days. Raw, hours
from light, the camels

ran without breaking,
flung me your way

as if they hungered
too & never hoped

to have you, made
light work of rock,

tenderly crushed
sand & never cried

for rest when tender
turned to sore. I,

wanting relief,
misunderstand.

After Ibn Arabi (poem 14)

east/west wherever
the sky superheats
electrifies
eyes
drawn not to surface
lines but forking
light

the wind poured reports
their garlands of talk
in my ear that it aches
to love that it bites
to lose that it clouds
to think that it thirsts
to want that it wets
to eye that it heats
to hope that your love
in your lungs by the air
you move is rocked

I spoke back
he lit this fire
I never asked
for embers
for a heart
kill it & keep
the ash or let it
glow & clear
the lovers

Colette Fellous

Mahdia

My name is Aïna. This dream often comes to me.

I am hidden in a house made of glass that looks out over the beach. I am naked in the centre of the room and I'm dancing. The piano slips into my memory, the waves are breaking as high as my hips. I step into the bay of the window. I let my hand slide across the sky, and suddenly someone is here, close by, right behind me. His lips touch my nape, I recognise his smell, it's the scent of the land. The piano fades out and the man's breath begins to keep time with our movements. To the left, above the mosaic bench, a bronze mirror magnifies us. I rise onto my toes. The man is following me so slowly, my head drops back, time itself splits and we stay, we stay like that, standing, looking out to the sea. A foot comes up, my neck once more, stomach, fingers, exclamation, luck, and laughter, far away. Then the night comes to close our bodies back together as if closing a book. The wind snakes between my thighs, a huge wave crashes through the window filled with sky and I awake.

Every time I watch this scene until I'm in tears. I dry my eyes with the back of my hand, the sheets are crumpled, I let the pounding in my head go on a moment longer, then slip out for a bowl of milk studded with drops of orange-flower water.

My name is Aïna and I'm not from here.

I mean that now I have to forget all that has happened in my country. I must change my name, my geography; I must erase the profile of my town, drive the fear away. From now on I shall live in my dream.

Besides, nothing is keeping me here.

I just want to relive that spinning, the shuddering of the sky and the branches, the wild leap of each second.

I call it my dream to be careful, so no one will go asking questions, but that's not the truth. You can't tell stories here anymore, I've had to learn a new grammar, to come up with divagations, new tricks of language, and other indicators too, new similes. So I could survive, I mean. For it to truly exist, a town must have vanished already, it must already have been destroyed and its ruins buried. Exactly like a love scene.

Wind working into my eyes, dust over fear, mouth half-open. And the story of my town is the story of this vanishing. So it is here, in this ruined palace, that they took refuge. In this country that no longer exists, at this beach that gradually faded off the map. There is always something a little beyond them; they don't know what word to give it. Something that belongs to the very fabric of the country, perhaps; who can say. A thing they sometimes want to drive out of their bodies, so frightened are they, but it traps them, holds them back, enthrals them and only then gives them that immense strength to move one within the other, to burn, to lose themselves. Only then can their eyes both turn away and grow cool, softness of a breast against lips, a drop of blood hardly landed holds the gaze and vanishes as quickly under the syllables of a word, languor of a neck arching out, inflaming skin, and sex, giddiness resting in two almost shy smiles.

Under the vault, up there to the right, are two swallows' nests and, on the floor, three Koranic tablets, a dusting of sand obscuring the letters inscribed on them in red ink. There are fingerprints too on the whitewashed wall to the left, but we won't pause there, we don't wish to understand. On the yellow wooden shelves, beside a candlestick and an old matchbox, sits the terracotta head of a Roman emperor. His eyes are haggard, his smile a grimace, his forehead eaten away by brine. Just above the bed, the little sculpture of a dancer poses, holding the flounce of her dress. There they remain, face to face, stomach to stomach, memory up against memory, at the heart of this country in turmoil.

The man is wearing a red- and black-checked cotton shirt; the woman is still in her woven leather sandals. He has not told her his name, nor what brought him to this town. They meet each time in the rotunda, at the same hour of the afternoon.

Suddenly she laughs. It's strange, she looks and looks but she never can describe his face. What she loves is to forget him, to lose him, then to discover him afresh. Similarly, she has never tried to look through the other rooms in this palace left to crumble, as if its people had fled in a hurry, leaving behind their things and the moisture of their breath. What she would keep is the shape of the window and the sky within it, always only a fingertip away. The white headstones of the little seaside cemetery, the mosaic bench, the rosettes in the floor, the bronze-framed mirror set in the wall. And the humidity that erodes everything, even memories. The colour of his shoulders, the flux of veins that pulse beneath the skin of his sex, the taste of his mouth, the taste of his tears when he climaxes and she throws herself into him again. She holds him back and pushes him away, loses then clasps him close, and then further, both breathless, she loves sinking back into forgetting, forgetting the town, and time. Through the branches of the nettle tree, blending in amid the heartbeat at their bellies, there are the unbroken outlines of the two red-ochre terraces, the one looking out to sea, the other over the garden. Me too, I want to lose you, the man says, again.

When they first came across the little palace, they didn't know it was derelict. In fact they thought it was being restored. Beyond the garden, stonemasons could be heard yattering, drilling into walls, laying slabs around the well; it even came to sound like a musical accompaniment. No one had yet seen them step through that blue door studded with black nails. Besides, they never took the same route to it. She would come through the old city and he preferred to make his way via the port. He enjoyed this moment, this window in time, I mean. The way between his house and the little palace. The intoxication of no longer knowing who he truly belonged to: to his family and country or to the stranger who always waited for him in the same place? Did she truly exist? Why did she keep her eyes closed – and her head tossed back? Was she forbidden to him? He didn't know any more, he was walking faster and faster, as if suddenly afraid someone might break into his thoughts. That happened so often here.

Now we can see him walking in through the great outer gate in the ramparts, where every morning the old women sell embroidered waistcoats for weddings. It always was the city of weddings. They hang them high in the dark vaulted ceiling of the gateway. Above the spices, the gold- and silver-striped silks, the heaps of lighters, batteries, phones, jeans, old film magazines, socks, and also tuna tins, incense sticks, dried rose petals and American cigarettes for buying in ones. Here you can see the morning's true colours. But at this hour in the afternoon, there's nothing left but the heat and the swallows' calling, a few crumpled papers, two or three empty crates and the hint of a smell he couldn't put his finger on. He looks up at the birds just as a powerful voice ricochets from the mosque's loudspeaker. He closes his eyes, automatically touches a finger to his fine gold chain, and his face looks very like those men by Masaccio that you can see in Florence, if you go that way one day.

It is here, near the plane trees, that they first spoke. She was looking through a box of old postcards. A basket on her arm and her long white piqué dress made her look like a foreigner. He hadn't seen her before, not at the market or the café, nor on the beaches. Was she really foreign? He couldn't decide, she seemed so like him, when he glanced at her. He had come that morning to buy his newspaper and a packet of batteries from the blind man and, when he emerged, almost a sleepwalker, he had come up close and pressed a postcard into her hand: 'This one's for you. It's the oasis at Gabès – though it's not there anymore. I used to dive off that outcrop every day when I was a kid. See, I would swim in that green splash, but there's nothing there now. It's all run dry. It's for you, because the woman in the stamp looks like you.' Then things moved very quickly. Of that first encounter, she remembers only the delicate gold chain that shone on his chest and the words he had made her repeat – very softly. In the shade of their bodies, she had pronounced them, without understanding. Like a magical formula or more like a vow she had agreed to sign unwittingly. There was a kind of gleaming path the length of her thighs, that cut through the depths of the darkness and ran up to the edge of her lips – so thirsty, suddenly, such certainty, and in a great rip tide of words, clothes, laughter and elation, they found themselves face to face, stomach to stomach, memory up against memory. Both had forgotten to mention their names. And later it seems that she alone had whispered hers to him.

One day they had stayed very late, mesmerised by this room in the little palace. From outside came the sounds of a celebration starting up – not a wedding, for once. Children were racing around, calling for people to come quickly: men were going into trances, nobody should miss this! Drumming, clapping, the beating of *bendirs*, laughter through the trees, hoarse male voices, the scents of orange trees and incense, and of the red earth. They couldn't leave the room now. They stayed there until nightfall, prisoners of their gestures. No longer looking at each other, instead they followed the melodies with their bodies. But what was it that, so abruptly, in the midst of the bustle and noise of the celebration, under the low vault of that whitewashed room, on the first floor of the crumbling palace, suddenly made her vanish? She tossed her head back and that was the end. The drumming outside flooded in and through the scene, and the little dancer with her tambourine, poised on the shelf above the bed, closed her eyes just then, the moment of the vanishing.

My name is Aïna and I don't come from here.

I can bear witness if necessary. The celebration and my dress, the turbans and my belly, the clothes on the low table and the burning of his sex. The flowers and the sky. I wouldn't move again. I had tossed my head back, the men's voices were now rising into the darkness. My name had gone. You might think I had vanished. Only a faint triangle of light would linger on my dress and prove that the world is still out there. Then night came to fold our bodies back together, as if closing a book, and I welcomed it in, and wept.

Translated from French by Sophie Lewis

Inan Jariyat an-Natafi

My Friend

In response to al-Hasan ibn Wahb visiting Inan and reciting the
following:

> My friend, a lover has no heart,
> There is no sin in the eyes of those who see.
> You who are in love, how ugly love can be,
> If lover and beloved are apart.

Inan altered the poem using the same meter and rhyme and
sang it using the same melody,

> My friend, lovers have no penises,
> And the loved one will have no ecstasy.
> You who are in love, how ugly love can be,
> If a lover's phallus has weaknesses.

Translated from Arabic by Wessam Elmeligi

Tulba bin Qais

Breaking Wind

Hisham is a liar and was not truthful,
Hisham slipped at the slippery place.
His breaking wind left no love,
Like a mare turning away,
Repulsed by a tiring mule.
Ibn Hisham, you tall one,
Of undisputed lineage,
The sly one lied and was not truthful.

Translated from Arabic by Wessam Elmeligi

Arib al-Mamuniyya

To You

To you treachery is a virtue, you have many faces and ten
    tongues.
I'm surprised my heart still clings to you in spite of what you
    put me through.

Translated from Arabic by Abdullah al-Udhari

Ahdaf Soueif

In the Eye of the Sun (An Excerpt)

She thinks of Saif and that first evening at the Omar Khayyam, when he had taken her into the rock maze and kissed her till her lip bled - she had thought they would come together again in Beirut: *really* come together. That that first eighty-three-day separation would break the deadlock between them. That everything that had been buried and hidden would break out in the joy and the relief of their being together again, and again it had all gone wrong. And now a new pattern has been set. That was what it had felt like this time in Damascus: that every three months they would meet and settle into a new deadlock. She tries to pinpoint the things he does not like, the things about her that put him off. She makes a list of them: she can get rid of them – or at least keep them away from him. He does not like:

- Her tendency towards abstract discussion, e.g. 'How do you know *absolutely for sure* there is no reincarnation?'
- Her enthusiasms, e.g. for sit-ins, demonstrations, dancing etc.
- When she takes too long to tell a story.
- When she points out things to him: 'Oh gosh! Look at that moon!'
- Her not liking judgements, e.g. 'But if you look at it from *his* point of view–'
- Her wish to *do* things. He finds it juvenile.

But what about in bed? What *about* in bed? Well, in Cairo, with the pain and the miscarriage and the sneezing, he had decided she had stopped wanting him. But he can't have thought that in Beirut. He can't have been in any doubt at all that first night that she wanted him. And she had been absolutely determined that, however much it hurt, she would not complain. It would not hurt for ever. It would get better and then it would stop hurting and be just wonderful. That's what everybody and all the books said. And the miscarriage had taken care of the hymen and all that. And she had wanted him – so very much. And she had thought if they made love, if they came together – really – if they could be in love again as they had been before, then everything else would adjust itself, would fall into place. On the road to Ba'albek on that first visit she had thought, why am I doing this? Why am I picking arguments with him? I know he doesn't like arguments or scenes or crying or making a fuss. I know he can go away inside himself and wait till it's over – and then some. He's taken days off work, he's got this car, he's glad to see me, so why am I doing this to him? And she had forced herself to quieten down. And she had resolved not to do the things he didn't like and to try to be the way he wanted her to be. It was no use thinking, But he *used* to ask me to talk to him, I *believed* he wanted to know what I thought about things and would tell me what he thought too, I *believed* he wanted us to do lots of things – to explore everything – together. No use at all. The only thing to be done now is to adapt, to be the person he wants her to be: the person he probably believes she is – apart from the odd aberration. And if she does that, and gives him what he wants, maybe he'll love her again. She had seen all that on the road to Ba'albek. But what about last night, she had then thought: she hadn't done anything – yet. And she knows he had been about to make love to her. It had been something about her that put him off. Something about the way she was *then*. What was it? It wasn't that she didn't want him. Maybe he thought she wanted him too much? Maybe he was repelled by that? No. He'd liked her to want him – in the Omar Khayyam and on those Sunday afternoons in Heliopolis. Maybe she was too passive, lying there waiting for something to happen? But that couldn't be it. She'd always been fairly passive. That was how he'd liked it. That was how he'd *made* it. He would be completely amazed – aghast – if she started climbing all over him. Maybe it was – maybe she was too serious about it? Maybe he thought that was phoney? Or maybe he thought she was making too much of a deal out of things? And maybe indeed she was. And then a few days later, when they'd had lunch at the Tamraz's, and she'd had some white wine and braved his displeasure by taking a few puffs of the joints that were going round, and they'd gone back to their room for a siesta and the sun was coming in through the blinds and every move hadn't seemed portentous and fraught with a thousand perilous possibilities, she'd walked up to him and sat next to him on the bed and rubbed his shoulders and nibbled at his ears and kissed him, and felt a sweet hazy desire welling up inside her, and she'd knelt in front of him and rubbed her face against his strong thighs and felt him hard and hot against her lips and her cheeks, and then he'd pulled her head back and looked at her and said, 'You have to be doped up to the eyeballs to do this?' He'd said it with contempt – it wasn't too strong a word. He *had*. He had said it with contempt, and he had put her away. So, what then? After the anger had died down, as anger always does, what then? She has no more cards to play, no more moves to make. Leave him? 'Your Honour, my husband won't perform his conjugal –' Absurd. She might as well talk of leaving her father, or her country. She might as well talk of leaving herself. And when she woke up feeling terrible he was so sweet to her, and nursed her through her hangover and her sickness, and fed her room-service consommé and melba toast and massaged her temples till her headache had gone away, and put her to bed early and held her hand until she slept.

And this time in Damascus she had managed it. Fairly well.

There had been the ulcer and a couple of tricky moments but on the whole she had been good and they had been chummy and happy and – friends. Oh, if only he were here, this place would not be so unbearable. She would give him what he wanted. She would give him peace and quiet and she would be serene and cool and easy to be with. If only he were here.

Every day she waits for night-time. She goes to bed at half past eight because that is the earliest time she can imagine going to bed and because that means the day is officially over and she doesn't have to do anything more about it. About anything.

Nathalie Handal

Love and Strange Horses – *Elegia Erótica*

A horse. A stranger. An anthem. An impossible thereafter.
A lonely rift. A grove of trees. A touch. A cry. A murmur.
In what hours do lovers arrive?
In what hour did mine arrive?
How deep must he be touched to enter?
How deep must he enter to touch?
My lips. Body. Flesh. The curve of my neck.
Come on my flag. On my name. On the tip of my voice.
Horse. Stranger. Anthem.
This love is behind us. In front of us.
This is the bed. Sheet. Table. This is the room, empty.
Or is this now, an elegy to strange horses,
an erotica slipping into a body of questions.

Joyce Mansour

Desire Light as a Shuttle

Why cry on the bald skull of ennui
Odious or other
Aesthetic
Rational
A French ennui
How well I know how to sew false lashes on my eyelids
The mocha stone chases away hate in a waning gaze
I know how to copy the shadow closing doors
When love
Smacks its lips standing in the hall
Rereading your letters, I remember our walks
Summer's promises late on Place Dauphine
Yawns under the bells
It's already five o'clock
Gone the kits wise sidewalks imprudent dust
Confused the ground folded like a handkerchief
Caught a lascivious gaze
Wool gathers on coat hooks
Night gurgles motionless
A handsome mess on my table
Why cry above a tub full of blood
Why forage in between the thighs
Of ancient Venice
   I'm ready to cover you
   With my rosy tongue of a soft copse
Ready to prune my skin

Steal from shopkeepers
Jump over the ditch without panties or blinkers
To fall again humid in between your shoddy arms
Why float put on make-up have fun
Why answer
Why flee
The thought of your glacial sleep
Follows me wherever I go
When will I see you again
Without shedding tears
On myself

Translated from French by Serge Gavronsky

Nathalie Handal

Love and Strange Horses – Intima'

.— ·

One hundred breaths split the air
as I lean
on the only pine tree I find.
It's early or late, it's breezy or hot.
The fields are dry. Summer is near.
The horses are everywhere,
strangely galloping a dream,
but I can't remember
how to call them,
so I stand back, watch them pass.

.— ١

The first time I rode a horse
my body found the music of fire,
crackling the wind. An unbearable pleasure
that also left me with a burn on the side of my leg.
A sign, the horsekeeper told me, *of longing.*
A need to return—to belong.
After all, departure is like
pushing the weight of our heart
against the village
whose name has kept us awake.

٢ —.

Rafael came from somewhere in Eurasia.
I passed my hands through his mane—
saw a history of conquests and battles,
a field of hay, a mount of truth,
heard a silent ring,
his eyes asking me to go with him,
to confess something sacred,
to name something lustful.
Nothing of where he came from,
or who I was, disturbed us.

٣ —.

I knew he was different by the way he ran—
without pause,
without grace,
without distraction,
without ease.
He was told how to move in the world
and resented it.
He knew he would never own anything.

٤ —.

He came towards me.
It was a quiet afternoon.
I stood unmoving.
And we listened to untitled music
circling the earth like an anthem
free of its nation.

.— ٥

He was unfamiliar to me,
approaching as if he possessed the land.
Every morning he stopped five feet
from the river.
He waited for the light
to touch the leaves,
waited for me to look away
before he disappeared.
One day he stopped coming,
I assumed he had finished burying all he needed to
five feet away from the water.

.— ٦

*Darkness has no shape except
the one you give it,* he told me.
And handed me
an apple, an orange, a lily,
and a basket of grapes.
I said, *Are these the shape of darkness
or a distraction the heart needs?*

.— ٧

One day, as the horses passed by,
one left a strangeness inside me.

.— ٨

The stranger he became
the stronger his memory grew inside me.
That's the thing about love,

it likes to leave its mark
while counting birds in reverse.
It's about belonging, it whispers, *intima.*
I suppose we need evidence of desire –
to have broken a heart in this dangerous world;
evidence that we belonged somewhere once.

Hanan al-Shaykh

Cupid Complaining to Venus

I woke up this morning thinking I was a tin can stuck away on a shelf, wanting to be picked up by a pair of hands and opened so that some of the air trapped inside could escape. It wasn't the spring urging me to open up even though it has always stirred animals and birds to cover thousands of miles for the sake of sex. No, it was my night-dress.

Why do I keep wearing it when I know I'll be disappointed as usual in the morning after sex? Now I only have to picture it to get that feeling.

I pull it off and fling it away and put on a dress suitable for cleaning the house and scrubbing bathrooms. Perhaps this will bring me back to reality. But I still feel like a fruit stone discarded on the sidewalk: a mango, my luscious flesh sucked from its fibres by a voracious tongue. I pick the nightdress up off the floor and stand holding it. I should be grateful it's this ivory colour, not rose pink. Rose pink would be too much.

I know that colour of pink which promises uninterrupted passion, but it's a colour you don't see anymore: maybe the people who mix fabric dyes have never seen pomegranate seeds, and you can be sure that nobody examines the colour of a woman's nipple anymore except the doctor.

But there must be women like me looking for it, and if they find it unfortunately it's in nightdresses that have seen better days in second-hand-clothes shops, and bras and corsets that depend on more than plastic bones to give them shape: they were made for women like my mother's friend whose breasts used to be the object of regular attacks by me and my brother. I mean we would sit on her knees as close as possible to the two big mountains and she would fend us off, laughing until her whole body shook, including the two mountains, and we were happy when they touched us. She told my mother of the salesgirl who stuck her head in the cup of a bra she'd been looking at and said, 'This one's the right size for you.'

I forgot to say that this colour has a smell like a powder puff, the smell of roses. And I also forgot to describe its silky feel as it slips through your fingers like quicksilver.

I look at myself in the mirror, so disappointed and sour, and vow that this will be the last time I wake up in this state.

I didn't think about liberating my body until I was on a summer holiday with my friend Muna. Sex began cropping up in our conversations all the time and dominated our thoughts as we sat in our white summer cottons under the gentle sun, arranging our long hair, or appeared in the restaurant in all our finery after a long day's preparation of our bodies: stretching them out under a layer of hot wax that picked up even the downy little face hairs so the surface of the skin was smooth as pearls, surrendering them to the masseuse's hands, soaking them in frangipani milk, giving them a siesta, dressing them in underwear so soft it almost slipped off the skin, then sitting them down to wait and enjoy more conversations about sex and fidget with lust. Even so, they showed no interest in flirting with the other guests in the hotel, quite the opposite: they couldn't wait to be alone with the men they pictured waiting in bed for them, naked and scarcely able to contain their impatience. Meanwhile, we dawdled, fuelling our desires and tantalising these creatures of our bodies' fantasies. But this intimate atmosphere changed at once when Muna began describing how she felt when she was with someone who understood what her body wanted: how she became like an unweaned baby content to lie back and suck on its pacifier, day-dreaming about the flood of warmth and nourishment to come.

'But that kind of desire isn't always there,' she added. If she hadn't said that, my throat would have exploded with the pulse that was beating there and preventing me from speaking. 'It's not always like that. I've had some disappointments too. There was one man who brought his big heavy hand down on my breast like a flyswatter and tweaked my nipples as if he was picking dust off a curtain. And I remember another who couldn't work out where the well was in spite of the wetness all around. He whispered to me, demanding to know if I was normal, did I have a hole? And he hung on to my hair the whole time, as if he was scared he'd lose his balance and fall off! And of course, there was the one who began to groan and sigh and gasp for breath and had his eyes shut. I thought he was having a heart attack, I didn't realise it was just passion, so I sent for the doctor!'

We laughed together, her laughter submerging mine because she saw them as she talked, and then her laughter silenced me. Suddenly there was the pulse beating in my throat again and it squirted out creatures that tried to throttle me as I listened to her saying how she used to rage like a fire, keeping the men off her with her hands, her tongue; scolding, mocking, angry as she laid down her terms for sex. And I was still behaving like a donkey, going down a road against my will, and on top of that, reassuring whoever was riding me that this was the ideal way, the way I'd always dreamed of, sometimes going to the lengths of hiding the hooves that had been bloodied by the sharp stones on the bumpy road.

When I owned up to this, Muna was shocked to the core. She had always known me as the mistress of manipulation and deceit, a woman who took a thirsty man to water and led him back thirstier still, plucked words from a mute's mouth, pulled out an eyelash even if there were no lashes there. Had I still managed to fall into the trap of my own cunning? Here I was complaining to her, like little Cupid to tall, sublime Venus, that I'd been stung by a nest of bees on my face and hands and chest, because my face was turned to the wall and I was lying on my front with one arm underneath me and the other hanging down desolately in space. All this just so that the joiner could try and make a hold for the screw to go into.

Muna stroked my hair and twisted my curls around her fingers, just as Venus must have done to Cupid, and tried to soothe away my sadness and irritation with wise words that were addressed to the depths of my soul rather than being designed to instruct me on what my tongue could do.

'But why do I have to teach him how to kiss me? How to make love to me? Why doesn't he –?'

'Shhh. Listen.' She wouldn't let me talk at all, being rational just like Venus, and I was following her advice as if I had no choice. Her eyes were fixed on me following me wherever I went. She controlled me as if invisible strings were attached to every part of my body and I only moved when she jerked them.

My lover and I watched the video Muna had picked out for me. I wasn't relaxing and enjoying it as I was meant to. Instead I was searching for clues like a detective, wanting to grab hold of the tongue as it moved up and down, in complete control. I watched intently, wishing that one shot would last longer, or another could have been in close-up. When my lover turned his attention to the dish of sliced carrots, I felt the strings working my feet, my head, my whole body and I wanted to make him turn back to the television for fear the golden opportunity would be missed. I saw that he was shaking his head in disgust. 'Did you see how wide they were opening their mouths? Thank God I'm not that guy eating the woman's tongue. It's revolting! It distorts the shape of her lips, makes her look grotesque.'

This was only the first stone to come rolling down the mountainside. Others followed: 'That's way over the top!' and 'Why can't they be satisfied with portraying sex as it is?'

When I repeated this last remark to Muna, she stopped pulling my strings and acted on her own behalf. She gave a little shiver and clapped her hands. 'If only he could see me making love! He'd take it back and understand that what he saw on the video was one hundred percent realistic!'

She wouldn't let me despair and gave me some more movies, assuring me that he was the man I'd been looking for, because smell was the elixir of sex and I was always excited by his smell; even the thought of it drove me crazy. She told me how she'd paid a huge sum to have her lover's scent manufactured artificially and distilled into a little bottle, so that she could sniff it and load herself up with it when she wanted things to flow with another man.

I watched the new videos with my lover; they had scenes depicting the five senses, as if the lovers' creators had given them life and immediately withdrawn his breath from them, leaving them in this raw state to take in smells, to be numbed, to plunge deep into the images before them and take on their colours and absorb their tastes until they came the tastes themselves. The woman lay down and spread her thighs like aeroplane wings; her's was the aircraft's belly, her breasts its propellers, her pussy the engine. She soared away without leaving the ground.

I followed her movements breathlessly, wishing that I too could fly without leaving the ground.

'How beautiful it was!' I said.

'Did you notice? Just like we do it sometimes,' he said.

'Wasn't it a new way?' I pretended innocence.

'That! It's the most classic of all!' he asserted like a scientist in a laboratory.

I swallowed and bit my bottom lip and wondered if this means I was losing my nerve. Then the words come involuntarily. 'No. We've never done it like that,' I said firmly.

'Your memory seems a bit rusty.'

'No. I haven't forgotten. I don't remember opening my legs like that.'

'What? Are you really saying that you've never opened your legs!'

'I mean I've never opened my legs the way the woman in the video did.'

'Opening the legs is opening the legs. No two ways about it.'

'You're wrong. There is a difference. Those legs opened like a pair of scissors.'

'You're ungrateful! That's all there is to it. Ungrateful!' He said irritably.

'Did you hear me saying anything except that I've never opened my legs like it showed on the video?'

'You're ungrateful. So ungrateful. Shall I remind you how you moaned? Shall I remind you how much you enjoyed it?'

'I just said I didn't open my legs like the actress.'

Now he was shouting. 'You don't know when you're well off. Naturally you've forgotten that I'm always ready. You're the one who's tired or not feeling well.'

Now I was shouting too. 'I don't open my legs like her. That's all I am saying.'

'And I'm telling you that you must have forgotten. That you don't know how lucky you are. Ask your imagination. Perhaps it would have been better if I'd made love to that. It might remember how strong I was. How exuberant.'

'But … all I wanted –'

'Tell me which of your friends had a man like me, with my strength …'

Later, when my lover, whom I love, wanted me to have a glass of wine with him, I refused. I told him there was a magnetic force in my blood, pulling my energies down between my legs, while wine went to my head, and I wanted all the ecstasy for the black lace at the centre, the focus of all feelings, crude and sublime. The moment I found myself underneath the man whom I love and who loves me, I spread my legs just like a crab. If crabs kept their legs together, they wouldn't be able to move around and find food; to put it bluntly, they'd die.

But my lover bundled me up and returned me to the foetal

position. I was squeezing my eyelashes tight shut – he'd once said they were like fans – so that I couldn't see what my heart was feeling. I couldn't believe that one of my ears – which he'd said were as sweet and tempting as cotton candy – could be pressed so hard against the pillow, while the other strained to hear a single passionate word. When my arm went numb under the weight of my body, I tried in vain to extricate it with the other arm. To counter my disillusion, I tried to convince myself that I should be satisfied with feeling the way I did about my thighs. Letting my mind wander, I pictured them as two smooth slopes that the traveller had to climb in order to find the Venus flytrap, the welcoming flower that would give him squeezing, sucking kisses and spread its nectar around about him.

My thoughts must have given me the energy to turn toward my lover, not to complain this time, but to offer him my face or, to be more exact, my nose, the one out of all the body's orifices through which the spirit enters and leaves. This was to remind him that when we slept together it was like a continuation of our whispered conversations, our shared smell, the looks we gave each other. The whole of him had to enter me, not just a part of him, enter me holding the thread of water that would irrigate every corner of me, all that is me: my heart, which wants and desires him, and my mind likewise; two bodies in one soul or two souls in one body. So, I stretched before him like a cat, but as always, he shut my legs again with an unconscious gesture, as if he were folding a deck chair, and rolled me up like a ball of wool, pinning me in with my arms. I was squeezing my eyelids shut again to block out what was happening between my legs. I noticed he had summoned all his strength, and he was racing along like a man on horseback, every sinew and bone and drop of blood in his body hell-bent on winning the race.

I took my head in my hands and drew my limbs in tightly like a mummy. Later I unwrapped myself and went to the local arts centre, where I was to give a reading. I felt myself relaxing as I settled myself comfortably to read a short story.

There was a woman in a village in the country who used to leave her mud-brick house every morning wearing a black headcover fixed with a coloured rope and a translucent face veil which left only her eyes free. As she stepped out, she was well aware that the sight of veiled women sets hearts ablaze, because the imagination cannot rest until it has seen the whole face. She made her way through the fields and trees, carrying an earthenware water jar on her hip, which looked like a man resting comfortably in the hollow of her waist. As soon as she got to the river, she put the jar down at the water's edge, raised her veil, and splashed water over her neck and face, then under the arms of her dress. She filled the water jar and went back but this time she took the route through the village. She balanced the jar on her head and began swinging her hips from side to side and sticking out her breasts and moving them to the right and to the left. Buttocks, breast. Buttocks, breast. Until the men's eyes were fastened on her and their signs followed her, as she walked firmly on, saying to herself, 'Even if you make me wear a veil and hide my face from the world, you can't hide my body.'

Soon afterward this woman married a man whose imagination wouldn't rest until he had seen the face which complimented the eyes and lashes and beautifully arched brows. This was why, when they had a daughter who was the spitting image of her mother, her father wouldn't let her hide her face behind a veil.

I stopped reading and let my eyes wander over the audience. I knew my black, low-cut dress, dark eyes and skin and Rita Hayworth hair, long rippling waves the colour of aubergines, attracted their attention more than my reading. Once I felt they were listening, I recrossed my legs, pursed my lips, made the warmth ooze from my voice and finished reading my story.

This girl refused to help her mother with the housework. When she was reprimanded, she exploded in anger: 'What right have you to call me lazy? If you knew what happens to me when I do housework, you'd bless my disobedience. Every time I go up and downstairs my breasts roll from side to side and my hips sway and I get aroused. Every time I rest against the sink to wash the dishes the hardness of the concrete arouses me. When I knead the dough my bottom shakes and makes my pussy vibrate. When I bend down to scrub the floor, the sweat collects between my thighs and makes me excited. When I hollow out the zucchini with the vegetable corer it makes me think of fucking.'

In no time at all her excuses were making the rounds of young and old and making people toss and turn in bed. Then a young man came knocking on the door in the middle of the night, asking to marry her, and the next day they were married, and she bore him a daughter as beautiful as the full moon. The girl grew up and followed the same path as her mother and grandmother, beset with feelings and desires. But she made a big mistake when she found herself with her lover, and wanted to spread her thighs like a leaf opening as the light touches it.

I stopped reading to have a sip of water, confident that among the audience I had found someone who would take my face in his hands and let me lie the way I wanted to. I saw him even though my eyes had not left the page. But his eyes grazed my skin, and started heating up my blood.

Translated from Arabic by Catherine Cobham

Fadl al-Sha'irah

The Night's Full Moon

Wine like a mesmerising moon
In a cup like a bright planet.
Stirred by a young buck
Like the night's full moon
On a fresh and long shaft.

Translated from Arabic by Wessam Elmeligi

Naomi Shihab Nye

Two Countries

Skin remembers how long the years grow
when skin is not touched, a grey tunnel
of singleness, feather lost from the tail
of a bird, swirling onto a step,
swept away by someone who never saw
it was a feather. Skin ate, walked,
slept by itself, knew how to raise a
see-you-later hand. But skin felt
it was never seen, never known as
a land on the map, nose like a city,
hip like a city, gleaming dome of the mosque
and the hundred corridors of cinnamon and rope.

Skin had hope, that's what skin does.
Heals over the scarred place, makes a road.
Love means you breathe in two countries.
And skin remembers – silk, spiny grass,
deep in the pocket that is skin's secret own.
Even now, when skin is not alone,
it remembers being alone and thanks something larger
that there are travellers, that people go places
larger than themselves.

Wallada bint al-Mustakfi

Come

Come and see me at nightfall, the night will keep our secret.
When I'm with you I wish the sun and moon never turn up and
  the stars stay put.

Translated from Arabic by Abdullah al-Udhari

Silvia El Helo

Cure

may whatever
happens
happen
i'll still come
& kiss you
on your
blindspot.

Zaynab Fawwaz

Happy Endings

Then the Emir Aziz bid his sister Fariaa to the task, entrusting
her with the benevolent care of her paternal cousin Shakib
and reminding her that she must not leave his needs to the
household's female servants. She agreed, for he was her elder
brother and she must obey him, but she felt deeply unwilling.
She had not set eyes on her cousin before, and so it distressed
her that her brother would task her with such an obligation. She
went to her mother to complain.

'My dear', said her mother, 'he's your cousin. He is known
to be a shining example of kindness and refined conduct, and
so you must not feel any doubts or suspicions about him. It is
your duty to care for him and ensure his comfort exactly as you
would your own brothers'.'

Fariaa bowed to her mother's pronouncement. She went
into the room Shakib had been given. She found him lying in
bed, beset by a painful fever, heavy and sluggish and half asleep.
She sat down and waited for him to come around. She was
pondering her mother's words, especially that description of his
praiseworthy qualities. Her confusion grew as she gazed at his
fine features. For he was splendidly handsome.

Emerging slowly from his groggy state, Shakib found her
there beside his bed. She must be his cousin Fariaa, he thought;
for surely it would be out of the question for any women not
of the family to come into this room unveiled. And there was
nothing about this lovely maiden's appearance that suggested
she was one of the palace's servants. Whoever she was, God had

singled her out for heavenly adornment, giving her features of beauty and perfection, bestowing on her a lightness of spirit and a gentle demeanour, over and above the ornaments and precious gems she wore.

When she saw him sit up in bed she came closer, hoping her action would signal that she was asking him to make his needs known to her, and would be honoured to fulfil them. She was too shy and embarrassed to utter a word. He raised his eyes to her. 'You have left me feeling grateful indeed,' he said, 'as I can see your kind solicitude towards me, O noble lady. Especially since you were here and waiting for me to wake up, when any of those who serve this household could have done so instead.'

'I am at your service, sir,' she replied. 'None of the servants would feel the sort of concern that I feel, because for me you are just like my brothers, Aziz and Khalid. Ask me for whatever it is you wish to have, I am subject to your requests.'

At her response, Shakib felt his chest swell with contentment. He sensed a strong attraction to this young woman tugging at his heart. Conscious of a tender compassion in her glances, he could not repress the thoughts rushing through his head. She had gotten up and gone to fetch some salve. She changed his bandages and brought him a cup of broth. He took a few sips, which was all he could manage. She seated herself again near the bed and began speaking, letting him hear her delicate turns of phrase, expressions as luminous as pearls, locutions of perfect eloquence, all the while casting his way the arrows of her bewitching glances. Those arrows found their target so surely that he felt all the fever-weakness in him vanish and his old accustomed forces returning. He found her conversation so very pleasant. He began asking her questions, wanting to elicit what she knew, especially about the geography of the immediate area. She responded to his every question with all the mental quickness she possessed; her speech was fluid and elegant. And thus did she possess his heart. His affections encased all his senses like a tent, and swathed his heart. Her speech intoxicated him, as did her lissom form. He thanked God that this wound he had been afflicted with had given him, in his life, another life.

He turned to gaze at her. 'Fariaa, bring me ink and paper so I can write to my uncle. I must tell him that I am delayed here for several days, which I hope will allow my wound to heal.' She got to her feet – after tossing him a glance that could not but reveal the emotions of love rifling her soul – and quicker than anything, she brought him what he requested.

Translated from Arabic by Marilyn Booth

Nabt Jariyat Makhfarana al-Mukhannath

Musk

Nabt, your beauty overshadows the joy of the moon.

She said,
Your beauty almost took away my sight.
Your scent is like musk, fanned with a garden breeze
Late at night.

May I have the good fortune of having a relationship with you,
Or not? If I must content myself with only seeing you, I might.

Translated from Arabic by Wessam Elmeligi

Naomi Shihab Nye

San Antonio

Tonight I lingered over your name,
the delicate assembly of vowels
a voice inside my head.
You were sleeping when I arrived.
I stood by your bed
and watched the sheets rise gently.
I knew what slant of light
would make you turn over.
It was then I felt
the highways slide out of my hands.
I remembered the old men
in the west side cafe,
dealing dominoes like magical charms.
It was then I knew,
like a woman looking backward,
I could not leave you,
or find anyone I loved more.

Yousra Samir Imran

Catch No Feelings

It takes six hours and fifty-five minutes to drive from Riyadh to Doha. I know this because it's the journey Bandar makes every two months to see me. It would be easier to fly, but it's cheaper to drive. Many people think that all Saudi men are rich, but the reality is that most of them are middle class, some working class. We split the cost of the hotel room between us – he pays 500 riyals and I pay 500 riyals. It has to be a five-star hotel – they're the only hotels that will turn a blind eye to an unmarried couple. I don't want to risk a three-star or four-star hotel ever again – the one time Bandar booked a four-star hotel room under his name, I got caught by security sneaking into his room.

Just five minutes after I slipped quietly into his room a heavy knock had landed on the door. I almost jumped out of my skin. 'Hide in the closet, quick!' Bandar whispered. My heart was beating so wildly I could hear it in my ears. 'I saw her sneak into your room,' a deep male voice tinged with an African accent said from the direction of the door. I thought I was going to pass out right there inside the closet. 'We're brothers and I wouldn't want you to get in trouble. Do you want to help a brother out?' Bandar had to give the Kenyan security guard a bribe of 200 riyals to stop him from calling the police.

It was the summer of 2012 and Twitter was in its heyday. The summers in the Gulf were long, brutal and stifling. While my friends were vacationing in glamorous cities like Paris, Vienna and London, I was stuck in the sauna that is Doha in August. Work, gym, home, that was my life. I spent hours each night tweeting back and forth with my Twitter friends. My favourite Twitter friends were the Saudis. These were the years before concerts, cinemas or women driving, and the *Hay'ah*, the moral police, still ruled the streets. Saudis on Twitter made jokes about their dreary existence, careful not to tweet anything that even subtly hinted they were anti-government.

I came across Bandar's profile via a retweet.

زوّج لك وحده تسمع دافت بانك

Marry someone who listens to Daft Punk

The tweet was nothing profound. It was his avatar that had me hooked. I went into his profile and clicked on it. Slim face, eyes wide set, black moustache and goatee that weren't connected, a dimple in each cheek. Red and white checkered *shemaagh*, the ends casually thrown over his shoulders. My type. My stomach somersaulted when I received the notification that said he had followed me back. We began to DM, then quickly moved our conversation to WhatsApp. We knew exactly what we wanted, and exactly what it was we were doing. I was single and bored, approaching 30 and had still not had a single decent marriage proposal. He was also single, approaching 30 and finding it too risky to hook up with a girl in Riyadh, which was how we reached an understanding. He'd come for one weekend every two months and I'd lie to my parents and say that I was sleeping over at my best friend's house. The frequency was perfect: any shorter than two months and I might have raised suspicions and had my request denied by my father, and any longer and the sexual frustration would become too much. We wanted to be exclusive bed buddies, but not boyfriend and girlfriend. A long-distance relationship would have been too hard. We rarely called each other – we needed to minimise the risk of emotional attachment.

This would be his third visit. I owned no short and sexy

dresses, no delicate lacy underwear. Such items of clothing if discovered among my personal belongings would have given the game away to my family. I tried not to think of what would happen if I was ever found out, it gave me too much anxiety. I slipped my black *abaya* made of the finest Saudi crepe over my head and tied my black chiffon *shayla* snugly around my face, tucking the fabric in at my right ear. The dark blue skinny jeans and black sleeveless top that I was wearing under my *abaya* was as risqué as it could get. I'd save the red lipstick and the *dehn oud* for when I got to the hotel. No need to cause any doubt about where it was that I was going.

My mobile phone vibrated. *I'm waiting for you,* Bandar texted in English. He had studied at university in America and his English was perfect. *I'll be twenty minutes,* I texted back. Doha was small, and it was easy to get from one side of the city to the other in less than half an hour.

My hands were sweaty with anticipation as I gripped my steering wheel. I turned up the AC in my car. I wasn't going to meet Bandar all sweaty and smelly. I had to smell good – it was my trademark. 'You smell so good it's *haram*,' Bandar had said drunk with desire the last time I was with him, his nose softly nuzzling my bare neck. 'It *is haram*,' I laughed.

Stepped out of my car at the hotel's main entrance, I gave the valet guy my car keys. Made a beeline for the ladies' toilets, applied the red lipstick, touched up my black eyeliner, a perfect flick on the outer corner of each eyelid, and then I spritzed myself all over with *dehn oud*. Took the end of my *shayla* and made a *ghishwa*, placing the fabric sideways over my face so that my face was hidden from plain view. Sauntered out of the toilets confidently, carrying my overnight bag over the crook of my left arm, and pressed the lift button to take me up to Bandar's room.

A Qatari man wearing a white *thoub* and *ghutra* stepped into the lift just as the doors were about to close. I could see him looking at me slyly from the side of his eye. *'Sab'ah, waahid, sifr, khamsa sab'aat,'* – seven, one, zero, five sevens, he said smirking, reciting the digits of his mobile number. I pretended not to hear. *'Keyfich,'* – it's up to you. Fortunately he exited the lift several floors before me.

Room 503, room 503. I searched for signs with arrows leading to Bandar's room, scanning the corridors with my eyes. If there was anyone in the corridors I would have to go back into the elevator and return several minutes later. A woman walking along a corridor of hotel rooms on her own wearing an *abaya* and *ghishwa* was cause for suspicion in the Gulf.

Room 503.

I texted Bandar. *I'm here, open the door.*

My heart was tachycardiac with excitement, and the mixture of nervousness and elation on his face when he opened the door proved he felt the same.

White crocheted *gahfiya* on his short black hair, *thoub* buttons unfastened. Only he could make this *khaleeji* schoolboy get-up look so enticing. Once the room was safely locked behind me, I dropped my face veil. He gathered my face up into his hands, and pressed his lips against mine. As he devoured my mouth I loosened my *shayla* and allowed it to drop onto the floor. We edged backwards in a slow tango until I was lying on the crisp white linen of the king-size bed, and he climbed on top of me. I could feel his hardness through his *thoub*.

We weren't fans of foreplay and wasted no time, tearing off each other's clothes. Our garments lay tangled on the maroon carpet in a similar fashion to our entwined bodies. The AC was set at 16 degrees Celsius, the lowest temperature it could go, yet beads of sweat still ran across his forehead and his back. On anyone else it would have been a turn-off, but when it came to Bandar nothing was a turn-off.

Sixty or so nights of telling each other over WhatsApp what we were going to do to each other meant that the first round was super-charged and culminated within minutes. But the second and third rounds were longer, calmer, less panicked. I savoured every meeting of our lips, appreciated every stroke of his fingers and relished every thrust.

Between each round Bandar would light up a cigarette and crack open a bottle of Corona, alternating between a puff of his cigarette and sip of his beer. When we ordered food to the room, I had to lock myself away in the bathroom until his three knocks on the bathroom door signalled that it was safe for me to come out.

'Two months is too far away, can't you find a job in Doha?' I asked him as we lay side by side after Round 4. We didn't cuddle or spoon – we avoided affection, fearful of the oxytocin. Used condoms were carefully wrapped in tissues and placed inside a plastic bag on the bedside stand.

'It would never work if I was in Doha,' Bandar replied, propping up his head onto his right arm.

'Why not?'

'Because then you'd want a relationship.'

'Would it be so bad? I mean, we have this arrangement because you are there and I am here, and we agreed that a long-distance relationship would be unfair to the both of us.'

'Are you catching feelings?'

'No one's catching any feelings.'

This time when Bandar returned to Riyadh there was no text from him after six hours and fifty-five minutes to let me know he had arrived home safely.

'Did you get home okay?' I messaged on WhatsApp.

One grey tick.

His profile picture had disappeared.

Umm al-Ward al-Ajlaniyya

My Tiger Cub

Are you obeying me, my tiger cub, once,
Then in betrayal disobeying me when the sun breaks,
Making it a world with only a shade to live in,
Its well is dry, and its lands are without pasture?

Translated from Arabic by Wessam Elmeligi

Zeina B. Ghandour

You Cunt

I am not your consort;
I am not your muse;
I am not waiting in the wings;
I am not the support act or the sideshow;
I have not come to nurture, love or partner you; not to birth or
    earth you.
I am not my gaze my voice my scent my pulse.
You seem to be fixated on my milk and blood.

I am not the temptress leading you astray,
Destructress of your divine destiny.

I will not rise above or lie below;
I am neither super nor subhuman;
I am not your shadow or your saviour;
I am not your Work – your growth opportunity? Oh, the
    audacity!

Not your sacred harlot, temple whore, courtesan to the Gods.

Not your patient mother, wise witch or sweet vacant maiden
    waiting for laden with your seed.
I am not a metaphor or a literary device;
I am not your Yin or your Moon.
No, I am not your Shakti.
I am not Allat, Kali, Isis, Tara, Ishtar etc.

Not a goddess for your altar or a wife for your pedestal.
Your platitudes are endless!

I am not your refuge or your darkness.
I don't complete or finish you.

Listen. I am nothing to you.
I am you unaware.
I am the pause between each breath.
I am the endless, resonant void and depth.
I am the soul of this earth.
I am the sentience of the stars and the beat of the Yoniverse.

Shurooq Amin

Rosewater in the Boudoir

Bulbul warbles
   tinder notes
on a windowsill

unopened
   voice
catches fire

cleaves through
   heat–heavy air
like tin foil
   slicing moist-hot
cotton balls

voluminous
   with
waterlogged
   love

exuding
   amber essence
burnt in a
   mubkhar

waiting for
   you

here
    as your
wife waits
    for you
there.

Rita El Khayat

The Affair

Then I found myself in bed again, with no idea how or why I'd followed him there. A good thing, because otherwise I was probably going to be bored. I was probably going to feel a familiar nausea, and disgust, because he really isn't all that amusing. Even in bed – which, let's admit it, is the real goal.

Then, suddenly, amid this low-key contentment, drama broke out.

He had been ploughing away for a while when he commanded, imperiously, that I get on top. And me, well, even though I'd progressed through every stage of love, of the body, the bedroom, liberation with him, I found it difficult at times to simply obey his orders. I answered sharply, with a final 'No', and 'I don't want to.'

… Which bothered him more than you can imagine. Usually that's when we start hitting each other. He slaps me, I hit him back, hard, building in force, conviction. Sometimes I start screaming. That time, we reached new heights. Without backing down he threatened to leave. I didn't believe him. He did. He got up, got dressed in unbelievable speed and slammed the door behind him. I was a wreck. His repressed violence always devastated me. On top of that he'd openly threatened to leave for home.

I had to give in, after reflecting how sick I was of screwing everything up in my love life. I took off looking for him. I can still hear, as a condition of his turning around and coming back: 'And you'll do everything I tell you?'

Naturally, I did everything he said, and a lot more besides. He came back as fast as he'd left. Maybe that's all he wanted, the slightest sign from me, to change his mind? He undressed, got on top of me, forced me to take him in, stretched out on me, and, while pounding away furiously, said: 'In bed, I give the orders – understood?'

Something imperious, previously unknown and violently physical, sexual, made me almost die. I came to a second peak after trying every love move I knew. This was the beginning of the taming of this man, and, for every step that he conceded, he contested what had been yielded – for months, refusing to see me, for example, granting me absolutely nothing, not even a little time on the phone. This adjustment to that incisive, masculine stipulation – I am the master – caused me to admit, definitively but not without difficulty, that even if he wasn't superior to me, still I had consecrated him as such – something he clearly loved, and which was indispensable.

How can a woman derive pleasure from a man's insisting on his dominance? Aren't the most recalcitrant women also the most feminine? And what kind of woman am I, shivering under a man who's capable of showing his pre-eminence with such ferocity?

But there you have it, that's how it is between him and me.

A particular phenomenon, more serious, and inexplicable, had arisen – and it bound me even more tightly to him – I no longer felt a moment of needy rebellion after intercourse. I could be panting right up to that moment, and, once the caresses were over, I felt only one need – to create some distance. What is not possible, on the other hand, is a fusion, a vanishing of the self into this union, thus replacing duality, the duality of the bodies, souls, sufferings – so much suffering, between those of man and those of woman, a whole universe, an abyss …

After this lovemaking, we got out of bed. Something was missing, something that might have brought a smile after delirium, after death, after thunder and rain, after the China Sea and love's own ocean. No, that was just one more session. And you'd have to use more painful terms – after coupling, or worse, after bedding.

We needed to get something to eat. And, calm as could be, he suggested going for seafood, since we were at the sea's edge. Triumph for me! We were going public. No more of that obsession of hiding from everyone. Still, it was careless and crazy both for him and for me, considering all the social zones involved. Breaking the law felt great. This was one of the first times we risked ourselves out in the open. Like two very young people who just want to be together.

He sabotaged all my wardrobe choices. Even though I usually went around with everything you'd need to outfit a whole music-hall scene. I got dressed agelessly, androgynously, in espadrilles. He was fine with the plonk they served us as if it were a fine vintage. I brought up, like a good soul, one of his favourite subjects, long-settled memories and rather stale ideas, and once again I savoured his ease with life and living. In the end, he's very accommodating and kind, if only it weren't for that fearful ability to suddenly disappear.

He ate bread, lots of it, without offering any opinion on all the things we were offered. He might have been a likable travelling companion, easy and intelligently open to the world. When we came back, it was back to bed, and we made love again.

There has only been one moment in my whole life when I am really alive: it's having him in me, and my being completely surrendered and consenting, and his being over me, as concerned for himself as for me. I called him Sire in those moments and he called me My Lady. He often demanded that I play the part of slave. I did this over and over, with no relief and also no faith in the role, without believing it in the slightest. The fact is that I made sacrifices to his banality; that was the price to pay in order to be with him. He needed to think he was more important than I, in pursuit of ends I can't imagine.

The specific quality of this affair – which made me lose control over the flow of time and events – is in essence passionate. Sprigs and whole armfuls of joy that I gathered up in my flesh, in a rainbow flowering of every joy I could have dared to try, or to hold back, ever since I've been of an age to desire anything. That is, for all eternity. And the ultimate distinction is that this conflagration could only have happened when our two beings came in contact – it's that my pain is truly great if he's not part of this cosmic movement along with me, a moment that soars beyond the impossible, a flash of light that mocks death and all the vanities. This twosome pursuing a chaos of the senses – that's what has left me washed up, alone, on shores where this kind of paroxysmal frolicking is unknown. I caught a touch of his sexual obsession, and that has left me weak before other men. When this wickedness took hold of me, there existed only one possible remedy – more of him, and him alone. I can die calmly or in convulsions, it makes no difference. The slightest rain could sate the drought that reigns when he's stopped touching me. And yet, I was completely unsatisfied because he was so incapable of giving; he was weak, he didn't have the gift. He compensated for his weakness by the will for strength – which I confused with strength of character. These feelings and this passion badly borne and badly shared could never last in the profound absence of real pleasure.

A woman, a real woman, can't really give in to what seems like love if the man doesn't really fulfil her, in her intimate, innermost being, in her belly.

Translated from French by Peter Thompson

Mariam Bazeed

the most expensive mushroom

My girlfriend she says
you smell like jasmine
holding my lips apart,
face propped up between my legs
breathing me in
                                        like

I am some Provence postcard
purple lavender running
all along my snatch.

My girlfriend she says
you taste like truffles
her tongue on my tongue
lips on my lips
stealing breath straight
from my lungs.

and I do my best
to be the most expensive
                                mushroom
I know how to be.

My girlfriend she says
you are so beautiful
grabbing of me fistfuls

in her fists
to put in her pocket for later.

My girlfriend she fucks me
so it hurts

          and I don't even have to ask.

My girlfriend she sees me with eyes
blinded by a magic
I did not know I possessed.

      I think, probably I have it out on some loan
whose terms I've forgotten
whose paperwork I've lost
whose principle and interest rates
I couldn't tell you anything about.

          Best, maybe, not to find out.

My girlfriend she eats me
like I am a Ramadan feast
on the 27th night.   a Table of the Merciful,
laden: lamb, saffron rice, every raisin plump. kibbe, sumac and
Spanish pignolia blessed in the gaps between her teeth.
          And tamarind,
like fasting in the summer,
sticky, moving slow, sour-sweet.

My girlfriend she eats me
then spits me out
prune pits   apricot bits   crunching seeds of fig
from the river of khoshaaf
running
between my legs.

Maybe you think my girlfriend
says   fucks   sees   eats
like a pretty metaphor
or like a scene in one of those butter-coloured movies
all panting,
muted bronze glowing sex –
nary ever a condom in sight.

No.

She fucks me
like that dog you saw one time
or like that monkey in the zoo
a different one time
baring its canines
unabashed in glee.

                    and I find strands of her
          long bronze hair in the crack of my ass later on.

What I mean to say is,
there is no poetry in it –
only her hunger
which I will one day
chew up
swallow
digest

deserve.

this poem is inspired by Ella Boureau,
whose eyes are open
& who's taught me to see

Nuzhun al-Gharnatiyya

Bless Those Wonderful Nights

Bless those wonderful nights, and best of all Saturdays.
If you had been there you'd have seen us locked together under
   the chaperone's sleepful eyes like the sun in the arms of the
   moon or a panting gazelle in the clasp of a lion.

Translated from Arabic by Abdullah al-Udhari

Mouna Ouafik

Unknown Soldier

I stick my middle finger up his full arse;
Bite my back teeth into what's between his thighs.
My 400-metre runner: owes to me
His excellent performances
In sprints.

Translated from Arabic by Robin Moger

Salma al-Badawiyya (The Bedouin)

My Complaint

Ibn Mayyah, to you my complaint would be.
An owner after you now owns me.
In my body you roamed sovereign and free,
Having what you desired wantonly.
But now in a locked palace I reside,
Where I only see a vile one
With no stride.

Translated from Arabic by Wessam Elmeligi

Noor Mohanna

Tangled Roots

They tell you things about the desert: that it is hot, that it is cold. That day and night are not brothers, but cousins far removed. They tell you of the breeze at dusk, of scorpions that sting, of stars that sparkle just above your nose and suns that shine forever. But I know things they haven't told you about the desert, stories you've never heard before. Stories like mine.

The day I set out on my journey was like any other day on that stark wilderness. The heat was blistering. The wind whipped my *ghutra* over my mouth as I shoved my belongings into the woolen saddlebag and climbed onto Sultan, a stallion my father had bred. He called it the most glorious beast in all of Arabia. 'Just like us, boy,' he said, watching me as I sat upon Sultan. 'A thoroughbred one, I made sure of it. I watched his father mount the mother over and over again until it was done. She was wilful too. You need him to be wilful, or else you'll be riding a corpse and my son can't ride a corpse,' he said, glaring at me as he handed me the reins.

'I will never ride a corpse,' I replied. The vibrant red of those reins was bright against my brown hand. My skin, dark due to the cruel sun, refused to be altogether black. We were always refusing something here – even the variant extremes of flesh colour. Everything was always a battle. This was what my kind did. We stormed this land that no one else wanted, this wretched pit, this vomit of God, and made its golden expanse our pride lands, our home. Don't ask me why. It happened before my father's father and I was born into it. This place is all I know.

The horse carried the barest of necessities: a waterskin and my latest kill, a *houbara*. Birds weren't the easiest prey here. The desert made them fast and wary. It had taken me months to catch my first one. Mastering these difficult hunts was a small yet important part of my boyhood. Every dune told a story of Bedouin boys lost or at play, of bare feet running over the slippery slopes, of spiny-tailed lizards fleeing from those children, of snakes that leapt from their holes in the sand and hissed at being disturbed. Snakes may be a nightmare to others, but my friends and I laughed over them.

But now I no longer leapt over snakes; I stabbed their heads back into their holes. Nor did I jump in glee for a *houbara*. Instead, I stuffed it into my saddlebag and guided my horse into a trot. Men will tell boys of all the things they should know, all the things they ought to be. My father spoke to me of horseflesh and tribes and dead men. He didn't, however, talk about the loss of joy you feel after your first kill. Nor did he say how much the desert sucks out of you.

A fish man (what we called our seafaring brothers) once told me I looked like a falcon ready to launch into flight. He also said that men of the water and beyond use their eyes to seek further horizons for glory, while men of the desert seek only to survive our blank motherland. At that time, I hadn't seen my face in weeks. I washed it and wiped it clean. I barely recognised my own reflection in the shallow banks of what little water Sultan and I had come upon. Now, I tossed away the image the fish man had once used to describe me. Perhaps he had thought it was a compliment, but all I had heard was a description of *hunger*, an inner wanting yet to be found. Falcons were owned, like dogs – and I despised that connection.

As a Bedouin traveller, you move on and on, like the rest of your nomadic world. We rarely stayed in the same place twice. It was an endless journey to rejoin our brothers, to seek water and grazing land. Arabia was a prolonged debate between empires.

But we did not care for kings or white men. We were what we were; the world could go on arguing. And so, Sultan and I moved onward until dusk descended. I dismounted then and could feel Sultan heaving out his breath. No doubt he was grateful for the respite. The desert is never a friend to wanderers. I checked the ground well before I laid my thin blanket down. It didn't take long before I had a small fire going, my cloak heavy around me, a shield against the cold air.

I didn't hear anything at first. Only the desert's silence. Then there was a vibration, a definite presence. The sound of footsteps was all around me. I leapt to my feet and rushed for my sword, anticipating wolves, a lion, or a marauder. I did not expect a woman.

Yes. Beyond the fire sat a woman, wearing a black cloak that covered her body. Her face glowed with the light of the sleepy embers, as if a fire imbued her skin. She stared at me. I recognised that gaze. I knew what her look meant.

Hunger.

I unsheathed my sword slowly as she watched me. 'Who are you?' I asked. She did not answer, and I noticed how unafraid she was. A woman alone in the presence of an armed man would have shrieked and run for the hills. This one did not. Instead, she gazed at my weapon, then lifted her dark eyes to mine and smiled. The bright white of her teeth, as pale as her opaline skin, surprised me. She looked as though she had come from beyond the natural world – or any world, for that matter.

Still, she did not speak. Instead, she stood up leisurely, as if the action was meant to steal my breath away, which it did.

What I had thought was a black cloak around her was actually her hair. It fell in long sinewy strands down her back and front, streaking her body like black silk against white marble. She was naked underneath. Her hair flowed unnaturally to the ground and through the sand as if it were roots of an invisible tree.

'Have you no modesty, woman!' I said, my throat dry. I turned my face away despite my quickening heart. Her beauty had a savagery that tore at my very being. She was as luminous as the full moon, and just as shameless.

But she was not affected by my outburst. Instead, she tilted her head and walked around the fire toward me. Her breasts nodded as she stepped closer, and her waist shaped her like a pear. Her hips swayed; every curve swayed as she moved, enough that I could glimpse her small black triangle of feminine hair.

My hands lunged for my saddle. It was an instinct, a pull. I couldn't explain it now if I wanted to. I simply needed to move, put as much distance as I could between myself and that creature. I had just mounted Sultan when I felt her weight fall behind me. I did not feel her grab on to the horse. She was simply there suddenly, holding me, gripping my waist in her small pale hands. I could taste the heat from her breath as we both panted. She laid her cheek against the back of my shoulder. I glanced back and noticed how her hair still flowed behind us to the ground like roots.

'This isn't right,' I said, sitting very still.

'Forget God and man, and just be,' she murmured into the nape of my neck, addressing my unspoken fear. As a Bedouin, you are taught that faith and tribe must come first. But that night, I hanged it all. I gave it all over when her hand slipped inside my *thoub*. She ran her palm over my torso and down my belly until she finally cupped my erection.

It was a strange sort of joy: raw and earthy, the very base of happiness. The woman knew what she was doing; her hand was no novice. My experience with my first bride had not been pleasurable. It had been a pillage, a fast taking that had ended with her in tears. She wept pitifully and later ran back to her father, calling me a brute while the men of my tribe called me a man. I was troubled afterward, struggling to own that sort of hurt I had forced my woman to endure. I had lunged into manhood and away from the boyhood I had known of playing in the sand, of running over dunes and evading snakes and lizards. After the first wife, every new one I took would leave my tent in tears as soon as we had finished. My brothers and cousins called it a testament to my valiant member. They called me a man because of the loudness of each woman's weeping. But no one ever tells you of women and men and what makes us. More often than not, I had found more pleasure with my own hand. At least no one cried then.

Here, the woman in the desert touched me easily. Her hot fingers kneaded my leathery skin. She didn't tremble. Rather, she touched me as if she wanted it – as if she would tear off my robes and take me within her with the same eagerness. My breath rippled out of me as a sigh. She began stroking me faster and faster, and I felt moisture slide past the fabric of my pants. It made her hand slick and more agile. She kissed my cheek as I pressed my head back against her shoulder, a chaste action compared to her bold grip on my groin.

Perhaps it was my years of 'pillage' that persuaded me to move next. I held on to her wrist, climbed down, and pulled her with me. She pressed her body against mine and kissed me like no other woman had kissed me before. Her tongue slid inside my mouth, and her hands dipped into every corner of my rigid body. I led her to the sand beside the fire I had built. I took her, and she made the sounds I had longed to hear a woman make: short, breathless cries, simple yet incoherent noises. They were sounds I had wanted to hear every night. I wanted to kiss that sound, to lick it all up and swallow it down. I wanted that woman of the desert. Every thrust into her sizzling core was proof of my pure, raw want. My fists clutched her hair and her hands clawed at my back. I wanted to bleed for her. I wanted every pain she would inflict on me. It felt like nothing existed beyond our wild breath, nothing but the heat of my body and hers; nothing but her skin, her hair, her eyes. This was paradise on earth, this joy in finding my other self.

When I was finished, my seed was a dark stain on the ground. My hands no longer clutched her hair, but rather the evasive sand. I felt no flesh, no warmth. Nothing but a single strand of hair remained. I studied it more closely in the firelight. It was a dead tree root, a long winding thing that curled upon the dune and away from me.

Hafsa bint al–Hajj Arrakuniyya

Ask the Lightening

Ask the lightening when it roarrips the nightcalm if it's seen my
    man as it makes me think of him.
By Allah, it shakes my heart and turns my eyes into a raining sky.

Translated from Arabic by Abdullah al-Udhari

Shamsa al-Mawsiliyya

She Sways

She sways in a saffron dress bathed in camphor, ambergris and sandalwood like a narcissus in the garden, a rose in the sun or an image in the temple.

She's gracefully slim, and if time tells her, 'Rise,' her hips will say, 'Slow down no need to rush.'

Translated from Arabic by Abdullah al-Udhari

Umm Addahak al-Muharibiyya

The Contentment

The contentment of love is hugging, kissing and bellylapping, then hairpulling and bodyrocking that flood the eyes.

Translated from Arabic by Abdullah al-Udhari

Glossary

Abaya – a loose-fitting full-length robe worn by women.

Bendir – a type of frame drum used in North Africa.

Dehn oud – literally meaning 'the oil of oud', this is a concentrated perfume made from oud.

Faneed al-makana – little rock-hard multi-coloured sugar candy beads on an elastic or string.

Farish – a mattress

Gahfiya – a white skull cap men wear under their *ghutra* or *shemaagh* to stop the headdress from slipping off the hair.

Ghishwa – an ad-hoc face veil worn by women in the Gulf made by draping one end of a headscarf sideways over the face.

Ghutra – the white headdress worn by men in the Gulf.

Gueddid – Moroccan dried meat similar to jerky, made from ribs and tripe.

Haram – forbidden

Houbara – a type of bustard (bird) native to North Africa and southwestern Asia.

Houri – a beautiful young woman, also the virgin companions believed by some to reside in paradise.

Intima' – 'belonging' in Arabic

Jabaan kul obaan – children's brightly coloured candy sold outside schools and in fair grounds.

Keyfich – meaning 'it's up to you' or 'as you like' in the Gulf dialect.

Khaleeji – a Gulf male, also used as an adjective to describe something as being 'Gulf'.

Kilim – a tapestry-woven carpet or rug.

Mahleb – an aromatic spice.

Marabout – a Muslim holy man or hermit, especially in North Africa; *also* a shrine marking the burial place of a Muslim holy man or hermit.

Mawsim – an annual Sufi festival celebrating a *marabout* or saint, usually at a shrine. People can travel a long way to attend, seeking healing as pilgrims; but the *mawsim* is also a social gathering, and involves music.

Sarir – a bed

Shayla – a long rectangular headscarf worn by women in the Gulf.

Shemaagh – a red and white checkered headdress worn by men in the Gulf, in particular Saudi Arabia and Qatar.

Tagunja (also known as *taghnja* or *talghenja*) – an Amazigh rainmaking ritual, predating Islam, still a familiar folkloric reference in contemporary Moroccan popular culture, where it is often renacted in schools, for example. The ritual is performed by women and girls and revolves around the union of the rain god, Anzar, with his earthly bride.

Thoub – considered the male national dress in the Gulf, this is a long-sleeved shirt dress that reaches the ankles.

Zakat – a kind of payment made under Islamic law.

Further Reading

Anthologies of women's writing from the classical periods
The Poetry of Arab Women from the Pre-Islamic Age to Andalusia,
edited and translated by Wessam Elmeligi (Routledge, 2019)
Classical Poems by Arab Women: A Bilingual Anthology, edited and
translated by Abdullah al-Udhari (Saqi Books, 2017)

Women's writing in context
Beyond Elegy: Classical Arab Women's Poetry in Context by Marlé
Hammond (Oxford University Press, 2010)
Loss Sings by James Montgomery (Cahier Series No. 32, March
2020)

Classical Arabic literature
Classical Arabic Literature: A Library of Arabic Literature Anthology
selected and translated by Geert Jan van Gelder (Library of
Arabic Literature, NYU Press, 2013)
*Nights and Horses and the Desert: The Penguin Anthology of Classical
Arabic Literature* edited and translated by Robert Irwin
(Penguin Books, 2000)

Abbasid poets and the courts of Baghdad
*The Wine Song in Classical Arabic Poetry: Abu Nawas and the
Literary Tradition* by Philip F. Kennedy (Oxford: Clarendon
Press, 1997)
*Female Sexuality in the Early Medieval World: Gender and Sex in
Arabic Literature (Early and Medieval Islamic World)* by Pernilla
Myrne (Bloomsbury, 2019)
The Sultan's Sex Potions: Arab Aphrodisiacs in the Middle Ages, Nasir

al-Din al-Tusi, A Critical Edition, translated and introduced by
Daniel L. Newman (Saqi Books, 2014)

*The Rude, The Bad and the Bawdy: Essays in Honour of Professor
Geert Jan van Gelder* edited by Adam Talib, Marlé Hammond
and Arie Schippers (Gibb Memorial Trust, 2014)

*Consorts of the Caliphs by Ibn al-Sa'i: Women and The Court of
Baghdad* edited by Shawkat M. Toorawa, translated by the
editors of the Library of Arabic Literature, introduced by
Julia Bray, foreword by Marina Warner (Library of Arabic
Literature, NYU Press, 2015)

On the Arabian Nights

Stranger Magic: Charmed States & The Arabian Nights by Marina
Warner (Chatto and Windus, 2011)

Islam and Sexuality

Sexuality in Islam by Abdelwahab Bouhdiba, translated by Alan
Sheridan (Saqi Books, 2004)

Beyond the Veil: Male-Female Dynamics in a Muslim Society by
Fatema Mernissi (Saqi Books, 2011)

Sex and Society in Islam by B.F. Musallam (Cambridge Studies in
Islamic Civilization, 1983)

Sexuality in the Arab World

Sex and the Citadel by Shereen El Feki (Chatto & Windus, 2013)

Sex and Lies by Leïla Slimani, translated by Sophie Lewis (Faber,
2020)

On Love and Sexuality in the Arab novel

Love and Sexuality in Modern Arabic Literature edited by Roger
Allen, Hilary Kilpatrick and Ed de Moor (Saqi Books, 1995)

*Crossing Borders: Love Between Women in Medieval French and
Arabic Literatures* by Sahar Amer (University of Pennsylvania
Press, 2008)

Poetics of Love in the Arabic Novel: Nation-state, Modernity and

Tradition by Wen-chin Ouyang (Edinburgh University Press, 2012)

On portrayals of Arab Sexuality
Desiring Arabs by Joseph A. Massad (University of Chicago Press, 2007)

Cairo Nightlife during the Interwar Period
Midnight in Cairo: The Female Stars of Egypt's Roaring '20s by Raphael Cormack (Saqi Books, 2021)

Faris Ahmad al-Shidyak, who is in a category of his own
Leg over Leg (four volumes) by Faris Ahmad al-Shidyak, translated by Humphrey Davies (Library of Arabic Literature, NYU Press, 2014)

Acknowledgements

This work would not have been possible without the support of an Arts Council England grant and the enthusiasm and vision of Saqi Books, who published many of the works that motivated this one; Publisher Lynn Gaspard and Editor Elizabeth Briggs at Saqi were both central forces for this project.

Thanks also go to the authors, editors and translators of the works contained in the 'Further Reading' section, whose scholarship was relied upon in the writing of the introduction to this anthology and the framing of its contents. Gratitude also is expressed for the men who throughout history sought to record, preserve and promote the writings of women.

Special thanks also go to the organisers of the *Library of Arabic Literature* and the Arabic *Poetry and Stories in Translation* seminars and workshops held at All Souls, Oxford, SOAS and Birkbeck, London and the *Stories in Transit* Project (Oxford, London, Palermo) that I participated in between 2014–2019, which provided inspiration for this work in a multiplicity of different ways.

I am particularly grateful to Wen-chin Ouyang at SOAS for her translations, judgement and guidance. I am also grateful to Dr Marlé Hammond, also at SOAS and Dr Pernilla Myrne at the University of Gothenburg, for their work, support and time. Thanks also go to my writers, judges, translators and advisors, many of whom went above and beyond the call of duty to assist me with assembling this anthology, namely Hanan al-Shaykh, Marilyn Booth, Alice Guthrie, Sophie Lewis, Cécile Menon, Robin Moger, Yasmine Seale, Emily Selove and Claire Savina. Special thanks also go to Hiba Farid and the Na'ima Masriyya

Project, Robert Irwin, Mona Kareem, Frédéric Lagrange, Raphael Cormack, Daniel Newman, Youssef Rakha as well as The Gibb Memorial Trust and the Arab British Centre.

Biographies

Details of the lives and works of writers from the classical periods is not known at the same level of detail as those of contemporary period, for obvious reasons. For some of these poets, all that is known is the era that they lived in. To provide rough guidance, the pre-Islamic, or Jahaliyya period according to the editor and translator Abdullah al-Udhari, ran from 4000 BCE–622 CE, the Islamic or crossover period as it sometimes referred to, as 622–661, followed by the Umayyad era running from 661–750 CE, the Abbasid Period 750–1258 CE and the Andalus period in Spain, which loosely overlaps with the Fatimid and Mamluk periods in Egypt from 711–1492 CE.

Rasha Abbas is a writer from Syria, based in Berlin. She is the editorial director of 'Hamesh', the cultural supplement issued by Aljumhuryia website. Her short story collections include *Adam Hates the Television* (2008), *The Invention of German Grammar* (Mikrotext), and *The Gist of It*, published by Almutawaset (Arabic). In 2014 she contributed to *Syria Speaks: Art and Culture from the Frontline* edited by Malu Halasa, Zaher Omareen and Nawara Mahfoud (Saqi Books, 2014).

Umm al-Ward al-Ajlaniyya, also known as JUML, lived during the Umayyad period and was known for her erotic poetry.

Salwa Al Neimi is a writer from Damascus, Syria. Since the mid-seventies she has lived in Paris, where she studied Islamic philosophy and theatre at the Sorbonne. She has published five volumes of poetry and a collection of short stories. Her novel, *The Proof of the Honey* (Europa Editions, 2008) became an instant bestseller.

Fadwa Al Taweel is a Kuwaiti crime fiction novelist. She holds a BA in English Literature and has led creative writing workshops in Kuwait, the UAE, and Qatar. A member of the Kuwait Writers' Association, her works include *Hadatha Fi Soho* (Platinum Book, 2017) which sold more than thirty thousand copies. This is the first translation of her work to appear in English.

Shurooq Amin is a mixed-media interdisciplinary artist and poet. She has a PhD in Ekphrasis, the relationship between art and poetry, and has been published and anthologised internationally in two books and 40+ literary journals. As an artist, she has had 14 solo exhibitions and participated in 45+ group exhibitions. Her work has regularly been banned in her native Kuwait.

Suad Amiry is a writer and conservation architect. She is the founder of RIWAQ: Centre of Architectural Conservation in Palestine and has taught Architecture at universities including Columbia and Birzeit. Her non-fiction works include *Sharon and My Mother-in-Law,* which has been translated to twenty languages and received Italy's most renowned literary award, Via Reggio. Amiry's latest novel is *An English Suit and a Jewish Cow* (2020).

Anonymous – author/s of *the 1001 Nights.* A collection of storytellers, translators and writers of Arab and Persian origin. Assumed to be male, possibly erroneously.

Anonymous – author of *You Don't Satisfy.* Nothing is known about the author.

Hafsa bint al–Hajj Arrakuniyya was a noble lady from Granada. She was in love with the vizier and poet Abu Ja'far ibn Sa'id. When she spurned the Caliph's affections, he killed Abu Ja'far. Heartbroken, Hafsa moved to Marrakesh, where she tutored Almohad Sultans Abdulmu'min ibn Ali al-Kumi, Yusuf ibn Abdulmu'min and Ya'qub al-Mansur ibn Yusuf.

I'timad Arrumaikiyya (1041–1095 CE) was an Andalusian slave girl who was bought by a prince and married in Shilb. Her husband later became King of Seville. He was then overthrown by the Almoravid Sultan Yusuf ibn Tashigin and imprisoned in Aghmat. I'timad died a few days before him.

Salma al–Badawiyya (The Bedouin) was a Fatimid poet from the South of Egypt, sometimes referred to as Salma. She was in love with her cousin Ibn Mayyah when the Caliph Mansur al-Amir bi-Ahkham-il-lah saw her during a visit and became infatuated. He built a palace for her in Fustat.

Safiyya al–Baghdadiyya. Nothing is known about this Abbasid poet.

Hoda Barakat (b. 1952) is a Lebanese novelist currently living in France. Her novels include *The Stone of Laughter* (1990), *Disciples of Passion* (1993) and *The Tiller of Waters* (2000). Her work has received the most prestigious of literary awards, in the Arab world, France and internationally, including the Naguib Mahfouz prize in 2000 and the International Man Booker Prize for Arabic fiction in 2019.

Najwa Barakat is a novelist, journalist and prominent voice in the Arab literary world. Born in Beirut, she has written five novels in Arabic and one in French. Her novel *The Bus of Good People* (1996) received the Prize of the Best Literary Creation of the year by the Lebanese Cultural Forum, Paris. Barakat has translated *Camus's Notebooks 1935–1942* (Ivan R. Dee; translation, reprint edition, 2010) into Arabic and founded Mohtaraf, a programme to encourage and train young Arab writers.

Farah Barqawi (b. 1985) is a Palestinian writer, performer, podcaster, editor, translator and a feminist activist. Her work has been published by *Mada Masr*, *Al-Jumhuriya* and *Romman*, amongst others. In 2019, she produced, directed and hosted the 4th season of the Arabic podcast Eib (Shame) with SOWT, tackling contemporary stories and issues related to love and relationships in the Arabic speaking region. She is the co-founder of two feminist projects: Wiki Gender and The Uprising of Women in the Arab World. In 2018, she wrote and performed her solo performance, 'Baba.. come to me'.

Mariam Bazeed [they/them] are a non-binary Egyptian immigrant, writer, performer and cook, living in New York. Bazeed received an MFA in Fiction from Hunter College in 2018 and is currently at work on their second play, *faggy faafi Cairo Boy*; and, with poet Kamelya Omayma Youssef, on *Kilo Batra: In Death More Radiant* (working title). Mariam curates and runs a monthly(ish) world-music salon and open mic in Brooklyn and is a slow student of Arabic music.

Nayla Elamin was born in Bucharest, Romania. Her mother is of Levantine descent and her father is Sudanese. She attributes her love of poetry in part to her parents, who shared poetry with her from an early age. Her mother taught her that pleasure is her birth right and her body is her own territory. Elamin continues to explore poetry in Italian, Romanian, Dutch and rudimentary Arabic and Greek.

Silvia El Helo is an artist and linguist, with Jordanian and

Slovakian roots. She has worked intensively with the Bratislava English Language Theatre Society (BELTS) in Slovakia and appeared in several productions of the alternative theatre ensemble STOKA. She currently lives in London.

Rita (Ghita) El Khayat is a novelist, poet and essayist from Morocco. In 2008 she was a candidate for the Nobel Peace Prize. She is the author of over thirty-six books including *Le Liaison (The Affair)*, which was first published in 1994 under a pseudonym and was described as the first erotic novel by an Arab woman writer. This is the first time her poetry has appeared in English.

Ad-Dihdaha al-Faqimiyya was an Umayyad poet from the al-Faqim clan. The poem contained here was written in response to a lampoon written about her clan by another poet.

Zayynab Fawwaz (d. 1914) was born in Jabal Amil in what is now south Lebanon. She immigrated to Egypt, and began publishing essays in the Cairo and Beirut press in 1892. She published two novels and a play – the first known published play in Arabic by a female author. She is best known for her mammoth biographical dictionary of world women (1893–6).

Colette Fellous is the author of more than twenty novels, including *Aujourd'hui* (Gallimard, 2005) for which she received the Prix Marguerite Duras. *This Tilting World*, her first novel to appear in English was published by Les Fugitives in 2019. A photographer, publisher and former radio producer for France Culture, she lives between France and Tunisia.

Zeina B. Ghandour is a writer and barrister by training and academic. She is the author of two books, *The Honey* (Interlink Publishing Group, 2008) and *A Discourse on Domination in*

Mandate Palestine (Routledge-Cavendish, 2009), as well as academic articles, essays, poems and short stories. Born in Beirut, she moved to the UK as a child, and currently teaches yoga and meditation as a volunteer for charities focusing on mental health.

Nuzhun al-Gharnatiyya (d. 1100 CE) was one of the most accomplished Andalusian poets. She held a literary salon where she recited poetry and gave lectures. It is said that the vizier Abu Bakr ibn Sa'id was infatuated by her and attended all of her salon meetings.

Joumana Haddad is an award-winning Lebanese author, journalist and human rights activist. She was the cultural editor of *An-Nahar* newspaper for numerous years. She has been repeatedly selected as one of the world's 100 most powerful Arab women by *Arabian Business magazine*. Her works, which have been widely translated and published around the world, include *I Killed Scheherazade* (Saqi Books, 2010) and *Superman is an Arab* (The Westbourne Press, 2012). *The Seamstress' Daughter* (Hachette, 2019) is her latest novel.

Umra bint al-Hamaris was an Umayyad poet known for her humorous obscenities. According to her translator Wessam Elmeligi, the poem contained here was said to have been recited to her father, who did not want her to get married, while he was sharpening fence pickets.

Isabella Hammad lives between London and New York. Her first novel, *The Parisian* (Penguin Random House, 2019), won the 2019 Palestine Book Award and has been translated into fifteen languages. She has been awarded the 2020 Sue Kaufman Prize from the American Academy of Arts and Letters, a Betty Trask Award, and was a 2019 National Book Foundation 5 Under 35 Honouree.

Nathalie Handal is a poet and professor at Columbia University. Her works include *Life in a Country Album* (University of Pittsburgh Press, 2019), winner of the Palestine Book Award and finalist for the Foreword Book Award, and *The Republics* (University of Pittsburgh Press, 2015), winner of Virginia Faulkner Award for Excellence in Writing and the Arab American Book Award. She has written eight plays, edited two anthologies, and her writing has also appeared in *Vanity Fair, Guernica Magazine, The Guardian, The New York Times, The Nation, The Irish Times* and *Words Without Borders*.

Laura Hanna is a British-Egyptian writer, performer and theatre maker from London. She has a degree in English Language and Literature and trained at LAMDA. Her published work includes *Egypt, a story (A History of Water in the Middle East,* Methuen Drama, 2019) and 'All the Things I Hear (Sounds of Isolation)' in *Heartache and Hope; Voices of a Pandemic* (Birch Moon Press, 2020).

Dahiya al-Hilaliyya was a Yemeni poet of the pre-Islamic period known for love poetry.

Yousra Samir Imran is an English-Egyptian writer and freelance journalist based in West Yorkshire. She has written for a number of well-known publications including *The New Arab, Cosmopolitan UK* and *Grazia Arabia* and identifies as a Muslim feminist. Her debut novel *Hijab and Red Lipstick* is forthcoming from Hashtag Press.

Qasmuna bint Ismail was an Andalusian poet. The daughter of the influential poet and vizier Isma'il ibn Naghrila, Qusmuna wrote poems in both Arabic and Hebrew. Only three of her poems have survived.

Samia Issa is a Palestinian writer, journalist and TV producer, born and currently living in Beirut. Her novels include *Haleeb al-Teen* (Dar El Adab, 2010), and *Khilsa* (Dar El Adab, 2014). She regularly contributes to publications such as *Al-arabi al-jadeed, The Independent,* and *Orient XXI.* This is the first time her work has appeared in English.

Randa Jarrar is a writer, performer, professor of creative writing, and Executive Director of RAWI, a literary non-profit organisation for Arab American writers. Her works include *A Map of Home* (Penguin Group, reprint edition, 2009), *Love Is an Ex-Country* (Catapult, 2021) and *Him, Me, Muhammad Ali* (Sarabande Books, 2016). Her essays have appeared in *The New York Times Magazine, Salon, Bitch* and *Buzzfeed.* She is a recipient of a Creative Capital Award and an American Book Award. Jarrar's acting credits include *Ramy,* and short films *Got Game* and *Finjan.* She is based in Los Angeles.

khulud khamis is a Slovak-Palestinian feminist writer. The Italian translation of her novel *Haifa Fragments* (Spinifex Press, 2015) was awarded second place in the 2018 Premio Letterario Citta di Siena literary award. Her short stories have appeared in *Verity La, FemAsia Magazine* and *Consequence Magazine.*

Zahra al-Kilabiyya was an Abbasid poet. Allegedly, al-Kilabiyya was in love with Ishaq al-Mawsili, one of the greatest Abbasid singers and composers. In her poems, Zahra calls Ishaq by the female name of Juml, to disguise his identity.

lisa luxx is a poet, essayist, activist and Founder of The Sisterhood Salon, currently living in Beirut. Her work has been published in newspapers, magazines and anthologies including by Hachette, Verve Poetry Press, *i-D, Dazed, The International*

Times, Sukoon and *Wasafiri*, and she has appeared on channels including BBC Radio 4, VICE TV and ITV. She has headlined literary events at Royal Albert Hall, Latitude Festival and Station Beirut. She was winner of the Outspoken Prize for Performance Poetry 2018.

Bint Magdaliya is an Arab-British writer living in the UK. She writes under a pseudonym in recognition that Arab women are carrying the tiresome burden of a patriarchy that intimidates and bullies them in the name of respectability. Her pseudonym is in honour of Mary Magdalene.

Ulayya bint al-Mahdi was the sister of the fifth Abbasid Caliph Harun al-Rashid. Ulayya's mother was a well-known singer and composer from Medina and concubine of Caliph Mahdi. Ulayya's father died when she was young and she was bought up by her brother, who was enthralled by her music and singing.

Sabrina Mahfouz is a writer and performer, raised in London and Cairo. She is a Fellow of the Royal Society of Literature and resident writer at Shakespeare's Globe Theatre. Her most recent theatre show was *A History of Water in the Middle East* (Royal Court). Her edited collections include *The Things I Would Tell You: British Muslim Women Write* (Saqi Books, 2017) and *Smashing It: Working Class Artists on Life, Art and Making It Happen* (The Westbourne Press, 2019). Her non-fiction debut is *These Bodies of Water* (Tinder Press, 2022).

Khadija bint al-Ma'mun was the daughter of the Abbasid Caliph Ma'mun. She was taught poetry and music by her aunt, Ulayya bint al-Mahdi.

Joyce Mansour (1928–1986) was born in England, raised in

Cairo, and moved to France where she quickly became one of the major Surrealist figures around André Breton. Mansour is known for her works of violent eroticism.

Zainab bint Farwa al-Mariyya was an Andalusian poet mentioned by ibn al-Jawzi in his work, *Akhbar al-Nisa (The News of Women)*.

Dahna bint Mas-hal was the wife of the poet Ajjaj during the Umayyad era. Famously, Ajjaj failed to consummate their marriage and Dahna subsequently complained to the courts.

Shamsa al-Mawsiliyya was a highly respected and learned Abbasid poet. She was described at the time as an older woman of great knowledge and wisdom.

Zad-Mihr was a slave girl belonging to the merchant Abu Ali in Jumhur in eleventh century Abbasid Iraq. Her life was recorded and letters reproduced by Abu-l-Mutahhar al-Azadi (5th/11th c.) known only as the author of *Hikayat Abi l'Qasim al Baghdadi al-Tamimi,* a story of a Baghdad party-crasher.

Noor Mohanna (pseudonym) is a Bahraini native. Her work has been published in *The Flaneur* (online) and local magazines *Guide, Daily Tribune* and *Perle*. She is currently finalising her first novella, *The Pearl Thief,* while working on an anthology based on women of the Arab Gulf region.

Malika Moustadraf (1969–2006) was a writer from Morocco. She suffered from chronic kidney failure which hampered her formal education and resulted in her death at the age of thirty-seven. *Housefly* is one of four stories published posthumously by the Moroccan Short Story Research Group and is one of the last things she wrote. More of her work will appear in the forthcoming collection *Blood Feast: The Complete Short Stories of Malika Moustadraf,* translated by Alice Guthrie (The Feminist Press, 2022).

Hiba Moustafa is an Egyptian poet and translator. Her publications include an Arabic translation of Lucille Clifton's 'poem in praise of menstruation' (*Rusted Radishes,* 2019) and 'Spaces' (*Sister-hood,* 2020). Currently, she translates for *My.Kali,* a conceptual webzine that addresses and defies mainstream gender binaries in the Arab world. She holds an MA in English Literature.

Umm Addhak al-Muharibiyya lived during the pre-Islamic era. She was from the Muharib clan and her husband was from the Dabab clan. Their love story is known for its poignant development from marriage to divorce. They remained in love even after their separation. *The Contentment* is described by translator Wessam Elmeligi as being among the earliest erotic love poems by women in Arabic.

Nabt Jariyat Makhfarana al-Mukhannath was a slave girl of al-Mutamid. The poem cited in this anthology was in response to a flirtatious poem being recited to al-Mukhannath by the poet Ahmad ibn Abi Tahir.

Arib al-Ma-muniyya (797–890) was born in Baghdad and thought to be the daughter of the vizier Ja'afar al-Barmaki. She was sold to slavery at the age of ten after the downfall of her family and was trained by her master as a poet, singer and composer, becoming the favourite singer of Caliph Ma'mun (786–833). She also was a fine chess player.

Jariyat Humam ibn Murra was one of the slaves of Humam ibn Murra during the pre-Islamic period. Ibn Murra killed her after hearing her recite the poem contained in this anthology.

Wallada bint al-Mustakfi was an Andalusian poet and daughter of Umayyad Caliph Mustakfi. al-Mustakfi allegedly sewed couplets of poetry onto her clothes in golden thread. Her love affairs were infamous, particularly her relationship with the bisexual Ibn Zaidun.

Qabiha Jariyat al-Mutawakkil was an Abbasid poet and the slave girl of al-Mutawakkil. He freed her when she gave birth to her son al-Mu'taz. Once, after he had been away, Qabiha sent him the poem included in this anthology, along with a concubine, to welcome him back home.

Sahib Jariyat ibn Tarkhan An-Nakhas was an Abbasid poet and slave. In his book *Female Slave Poets*, Ima' al-Shawa'ir, al-Asfahani wrote that the poet Ibn Abi al-Shawa'ir, al-Asfahani was in love with An-Nakhas. Nothing else is known about her.

Arim Jariyat Zalbahda an-Nakhas was from Basra and known for lampoons. The exchange contained in this anthology was her retort to al-Kharki when he was drunk.

Inan Jariyat an-Natafi (d. 871 CE). Together with Ulayya bint al-Mahdi and Fadl, Inan is among the best-known Abbasid female poets and was part of the Majinun group (see Introduction). She was bought from Yamama by a man called Abu Khalid, who mistreated her. One poet, Marwan ibn Hafs, once swore that he would free all his slaves if any of them could beat Inan in a poetry contest. No one did. It is said that she eventually was freed, either by Harun al-Rashid himself, or because her reputation as a poet had overwhelmed Abu Khalid. She sought to free her sisters.

Nedjma is a pseudonym used by the author of *The Almond*. She lives in the Maghreb region.

Samira Negrouche is a doctor, poet and translator from Algiers. Her poetry has been translated into 20+ languages. Her books include *A l'ombre de Grenade* (Lettres Char-nues, 2003), *Six arbres de fortune author de ma baignoire* (Éditions Mazette, 2017) and Quai 2 | 1 and *partition à trois axes* (Éditions Mazette, 2019). 'Between scrawls and sketches' was translated into English by Marilyn Hacker and was published in a bilingual edition titled *The Olive Trees' Jazz & Other Poems* (Pleiades Press, 2020).

Mouna Ouafik is a Moroccan poet, short story writer, columnist and photographer. She has worked as a culture editor for a number of Arab periodicals and newspapers, and together with other journalists in Egypt, founded the International Federation of Electronic Journalism. Ouafik's awards include the BBC Radio Award, the Kuwaiti Arab Magazine Award, and the Jazan Club Prize for Saudi Literature. Her published works include two short story collections and three collections of poetry. This is the first time her work has been published in English.

Tulba bint Qais was an Umayyad poet. Little is known of her life, beyond the detail that she lodged a request for divorce with a certain judge named Ibrahim ibn Hisham al-Makhzumi, claiming that her husband was impotent.

Aisha al-Qurtubiyya is an Andalusian poet from Cordoba, possibly of Algerian origin. A calligrapher and a book collector, she was respected by major public officials of the time. She was independently wealthy and never married.

Saeida Rouass is a novelist from London. She is the author of *Eighteen Days of Spring in Winter* and *Assembly of the Dead*

(Watchword, 2015), and has contributed to anthologies *The Ordinary Chaos of Being; Tales from Many Muslim Worlds* (Penguin Random House SEA, 2019) and *Our Morocco*. Her work has been published in *The Independent, Media Diversified, Newsweek* and *Skin Deep*. She is a 2019 Churchill Fellow for her work exploring gender and white supremacy in the USA.

Salomé is a pseudonym of a published author.

Yasmine Seale is a British-Syrian writer. Her essays, poetry, visual art, and translations from Arabic and French have appeared in many places including *Harper's, TLS, Apollo* and *Poetry Review*. She was the winner of the 2020 Queen Mary Wasafiri New Writing Prize for poetry. Her translation of *Aladdin* (2018) was published by W. W. Norton to critical acclaim, and she is currently working on a new translation of *One Thousand and One Nights* for the same publisher. *Agitated Air: after Ibn Arabi,* a correspondence in poems written with Robin Moger, is forthcoming from Tenement Press.

Fadl al-Sha'irah (d. 871 CE) was born to a free man and a slave mother from al-Yamama, Bahrain. She was sold to a leading court secretary, who gave her to Caliph Mutawakkil in Basra.

Hanan al-Shaykh is a celebrated and award-winning novelist, playwright, journalist and storyteller from Lebanon, now living in London. Her books include *I Sweep the Sun Off Rooftops* (Bloomsbury, 2002), *Women of Sand and Myrrh* (Bloomsbury, 2010), *Two One Thousand and One Nights* (Bloomsbury, 2011) and *The Occasional Virgin* (Pantheon, 2018). Her work has been translated into twenty-one languages. In June 2019, al-Shaykh was made a Fellow of the Royal Society of Literature.

Naomi Shihab Nye is a Palestinian-American writer. She has written and edited 30+ books, including *The Tiny Journalists* (BOA editions Ltd, 2019), *Cast Away* (Greenwillow Books, 2020), *Everything Comes Next* (Greenwillow Books, 2020), *Voices in the Air: Poems for Listeners* (HarperCollins, 2018), and *Tender Spot* (Bloodaxe Books, 2015). She is the Young People's Poet Laureate of the United States through the Poetry Foundation.

Adania Shibli (Palestine, 1974) is a writer and teaches part-time at Birzeit University, Palestine. Her novels that have been translated into English include *Touch* (Clockroot, 2010), *We Are All Equally Far from Love* (Clockroot, 2012) and *Minor Detail* (Fitzcarraldo Edition/UK, New Directions/USA, 2020), which was shortlisted for the National Book Award. She has twice been awarded with the Qattan Young Writer's Award: Palestine.

Leïla Slimani is a Franco-Moroccan writer and journalist. She was awarded the Prix Goncourt 2016. Her novels include *Adèle* (Faber & Faber, 2019) and *Lullaby* (Faber & Faber, 2018), which has been translated into 40 langauges. Slimani has also written two non-fiction books, *Sexe et Mensonges: La Vie Sexuelle au Maroc* (Éditions des Arènes, 2017) and *La Baie de Dakhla: itinérance enchantée entre mer et désert* (Malika Éditions, Casablanca, 2013).

Ahdaf Soueif is a novelist, short story writer and political and cultural commentator. Born in Cairo, her novels include *In the Eye of the Sun* (Bloomsbury, 1992) and *The Map of Love* (Bloomsbury, 1999) which was shortlisted for the Booker Prize for Fiction. She is the Founding Chair of the Palestine Festival of Literature (PalFest).

Umm al-Ala bint Yusuf lived in Wadi al-Hijara (Guadalajara). Nothing else known about this Andalusian poet.

Credits

We are grateful to the following copyright holders who have given us permission to reprint the selections found in this anthology.

Shurooq Amin
Poems *Resurrection, Hymen Secrets; Girl with A Box* and *Another Kind of Love* taken from *Call Me Starseed* by Shurooq Amin (Gatekeeper Press, 2021).

Suad Amiry
Excerpt taken from the novel *My Damascus* by Suad Amiry (Interlink Books, 2021). First published in Italian as *Damasco* (Giangiacomo Feltrinelli Editore Milano, 2016).

Najwa Barakat
Excerpt taken from the novel *Oh, Salaam!* by Najwa Barakat, translated by Luke Leafgreen (Interlink Books, 2015).

Rita (Ghita) El Khayat
Excerpt taken from the novel *The Affair* by Rita El Khayat, translated and edited by Peter Thompson (L'Éditions Harmattan, 2016). *The Affair (La Liaison)* was originally published under the pseudonym Lyne Tywa.

Wessam Elmeligi
Translations of the following poems were published in *The Poetry of Arab Women from the Pre-Islamic Age to Andalusia* by Wessam Elmeligi (Routledge Books, 2019). Reproduced with

permission of the Taylor and Francis Group. *Narrow and Hot* by Arim Jariyat Zalbahda an-Nakhas, *You Who Are Riding* by Zainab bint Farwa al-Mariyya, *That Buck* by Khadija bint al-Ma'mun, *Enjoy this Girl* by Qabiha Jariyat al-Mutawakkil, *Rock and Shake* by Umra bint al-Hamaris, *Your Cool Lips* by Sahib Jariyat ibn Tarkhan An-Nakhas, *Give My Greetings, We Wrote in Symbols, Rayb* and *Salma* by Ulayya bint al-Mahdi, *Drooping* by Ad-Dihdaha al-Faqimiyya, *I Walk My Walk* by Wallada bint al-Mustakfi, *Yemeni Lover* by Dahiya al-Hilaliyya, *My Friend* by Inan Jariyat an-Natafi, *The Night's Full Moon* by Fadl al-Sha'irah, *Musk* by Nabt Jariyat Makhfarana al-Mukhannath and *My Tiger Cub* by Umm al-Ward al-Ajlaniyya.

Colette Felous
Rights in the story *Mahdia* are reserved to the author Colette Felous.

Isabella Hammad
Excerpt taken from the novel *The Parisian* by Isabella Hammad. *The Parisian* was published in the United Kingdom by Penguin Random House and in the United States of America by Grove Atlantic (2019).

Nathalie Handal
Poems *Les Fenêtres – Three Drafts, Love and Strange Horses – Elegía Erótica* and *Love and Strange Horses – Intima'*, taken from the collection *Love and Strange Horses* by Nathalie Handal (University of Pittsburgh, 2010).

Randa Jarrar
Excerpt taken from the novel *A Map of Home* by Randa Jarrar. *A Map of Home* was published in the United Kingdom by Penguin Random House and in the United States of America by Other Press (2008).

Sabrina Mahfouz
Poem *TALI: one day when I worked at the bakery* taken from the collection *How You Might Know Me* by Sabrina Mahfouz (Outspoken Press, 2016).

Joyce Mansour
Poems *Noise in the Next Room* and *Desire Light as a Shuttle* are taken from the collection *Joyce Mansour: Essential Poems and Writings* by Joyce Mansour, translated by Serge Gavronsky (Black Widow Press, 2008).

Malika Moustadraf
Short story *Housefly* by Malika Moustadraf, translated by Alice Guthrie, taken from *Blood Feast: Collected Short Stories* (The Feminist Press, 2022). Reprinted with the permission of The Permissions Company, LLC on behalf of The Feminist Press at the City University of New York, www.feministpress.org. All rights reserved.

Salwa Al Neimi
Excerpt taken from the novel *The Proof of the Honey* by Salwa Al Neimi, translated by Carol Perkins (Europa Editions, 2009).

Nedjma
Excerpt taken from the novel *L'amande* by Nedjma (Plon, un département de Place des éditeurs, 2004), published in English as *The Almond: The Sexual Awakening of a Muslim Woman* by Nedjma and translated by C. Jane Hunter (Grove Press, 2004).

Samira Negrouche
Poem *Between Scrawls and Sketches* taken from the collection *The Olive Trees Jazz & Other Poems* by Samira Negrouche, translated by Marilyn Hacker (Pleiades Press, 2020).

CREDITS

Yasmine Seale
Translations by Yasmine Seale of the following poems were first published on Youssef Rakha's website *The Sultan's Seal: Epigram* by Ulayya bint al-Mahdi, *On Being Proposed to by a Male Poet* by Aisha al-Qurtubiyya, and *The Unnamable Remains* by Qasmuna bint Ismail. Poems *After Ibn Arabi nos. 14* and *27* are taken from *Agitated Air: after Ibn Arabi*, a correspondence in poems by Yasmine Seale and Robin Moger (Tenement Press, 2021). Excerpt *What is its Name?* is taken from *The Tale of the Porter and the Three Women of Baghdad* in *One Thousand and One Nights*, translated by Yasmine Seale (W. W. Norton, forthcoming).

Emily Selove and Geert van Gelder
A selection from *Letters of Zad-Mihr*, translated by Emily Selove and Geert van Gelder, are to be published by Gibb Memorial Trust in 2021 under the title *The Portrait of Abu l-Qasim al-Baghdadi al-Tamimi*. Reproduced with permission of the editors and translators and the Gibb Memorial Trust.

Hanan al-Shaykh
Cupid Complaining to Venus was published in *I Sweep the Sun off Rooftops* by Hanan al-Shaykh, translated by Catherine Cobham (Bloomsbury, 1994). Reproduced by permission of the author c/o Rogers, Coleridge & White Ltd., 20 Powis Mews, London WII IJN.

Naomi Shihab Nye
Poems *San Antonio* and *Two Countries* reprinted by permission of Naomi Shihab Nye, 2021.

Leïla Slimani
Excerpt taken from the novel *Adèle* by Leïla Slimani, translated by Sam Taylor (Faber, 2014).

Ahdaf Soueif

Excerpt taken from the novel *In the Eye of the Sun* by Ahdaf Soueif (Bloomsbury Publishing, 1992). Reproduced with permission of the author and the Wylie Agency.

Abdullah al-Udhari

Translations of the following poems were published in *Classical Poems by Arab Women: A Bilingual Anthology* edited by Abdullah al-Udhari (Saqi Books, 1999). Reproduced with permission of Saqi Books. *Shall I Call?* by Hafsa bint al-Hajj Arrakuniyya, *You Don't Satisfy* by Anonymous, *Love Thrives* and *Lord, It's Not a Crime* by Ulayya bint al-Mahdi, *I Keep My Passion* by Zahra al-Kilabiyya, *If You Want to Know* by Umm al-Ward al-Ajlaniyya, *I Am the Wonder* by Safiyya al-Baghdadiyya, *If Love and Song* by Umm al-Ala Bint Yusuf, *Lay Off* by Dahna bint Mash-hal, *To You* by Arib al-Mamuniyya, *Come* by Wallada bint al-Mustakfi, *She Sways* by Shamsa al-Mawsiliyya and *The Contentment* by Umm Addahak al-Muharibiyya.